THE ORPHAN'S GUILT

ALSO BY ARCHER MAYOR

Bomber's Moon

Bury the Lead

Trace

Presumption of Guilt

The Company She Kept

Proof Positive

Three Can Keep a Secret

Paradise City

Tag Man

Red Herring

The Price of Malice

The Catch

Chat

The Second Mouse

St. Albans Fire

The Surrogate Thief

Gatekeeper

The Sniper's Wife

Tucker Peak

The Marble Mask

Occam's Razor

The Disposable Man

Bellows Falls

The Ragman's Memory

The Dark Root

Fruits of the Poisonous Tree

The Skeleton's Knee

Scent of Evil

Borderlines

Open Season

THE ORPHAN'S GUILT

A Joe Gunther Novel

ARCHER MAYOR

MINOTAUR
BOOKS
NEW YORK

This is a work of fiction. All of the characters, organizations, and events portrayed in this novel are either products of the author's imagination or are used fictitiously.

First published in the United States by Minotaur Books,
an imprint of St. Martin's Publishing Group

 For information, address
St. Martin's Publishing Group, 120 Broadway, New York, NY 10271.

www.minotaurbooks.com

The Library of Congress Cataloging-in-Publication Data is available upon request.

ISBN 978-1-250-22414-9 (hardcover)
ISBN 978-1-250-22415-6 (ebook)

Our books may be purchased in bulk for promotional, educational, or business use. Please contact your local bookseller or the Macmillan Corporate and Premium Sales Department at 1-800-221-7945, extension 5442, or by email at MacmillanSpecialMarkets@macmillan.com.

First Edition: 2020

10 9 8 7 6 5 4 3 2 1

ACKNOWLEDGMENTS

As with all my books, I am in debt with this one. All along each story's progress, I rely on others for their suggestions, guidance, criticisms, and judgment. In some cases, where the plot takes me to places I know little about, that number grows considerably. In others, such as *The Orphan's Guilt*, I am writing closer to home experientially and so require fewer scouts if just as many proctors. I give thanks to them all.

Dan Davis
Steve Shapiro
Elizabeth Mayor
John Martin
Ray Walker
Margot Zalkind Mayor
Castle Freeman, Jr.
Allan Herzig

THE ORPHAN'S GUILT

PROLOGUE

The Deathwatch Beetle

"Perfect."

John Rust spotted the cruiser as he was leaving Putney, parked under a tree down a side street, almost completely shaded from the nearby street lamp. A shark lurking by a rock in gloomy waters.

John had missed sideswiping a parked car moments earlier, overcorrected in response. As soon as he saw the cop, he knew what to expect.

On cue, the inside of his vehicle began pulsing with blue lights from behind, making him feel trapped inside a hyperactive pinball machine. Additionally, all three of his rearview mirrors lit up from the cruiser's takedown strobes, completely blinding him. It wasn't the first time John had been subjected to this light show. Designed to protect the cop and intimidate the suspect, it had been well researched and tested. Resigned to his fate, he pulled over, feeling as deflated as he'd been contentedly anesthetized twenty seconds earlier. John didn't even bother reaching for his paperwork in the glove compartment. He just sat motionless, his hands in his lap, numb once more.

The sharp rap on his front passenger-side window still made him jump when it came, however, along with the fidgety darting about of a powerful flashlight beam—an intrusive, inquisitive Tinker Bell designed to strip him of his secrets.

"Roll down the window, sir," came the order.

John did so, using the control button at his left hand. The cool night air felt good. It was early spring, which in Vermont could mean a serious careening of temperature shifts. But right now, depressed, at loose ends, and convincingly drunk, he wasn't thinking about the weather.

Nor was he thinking much about what was happening.

He was wandering the corridors of his own recent past, suffering the loss that had encouraged him, yet again, to fall off the wagon.

The trooper, Tyler Brennan, six years on the job, had made his stop by the book. The Vermont State Police, and cops in general throughout this supposedly peaceful region, had come under increasing pressure to be more respectful, considerate, sensitive, and caring with their targeted population. At the same time, the very same people, to Tyler's mind, had been ramping up their aggressiveness, use of weapons, and numbers of overdoses.

These were complicated times, Tyler's sergeant had told them at a recent briefing. "No shit," had whispered a colleague, tapping the naloxone dispenser they now carried in their pockets, designed to reverse an opioid OD. And as for the days when a Vermont cop could almost depend on spending his career without pulling his gun on duty, those had been relegated to the past.

So, yes, complicated times—with increasingly little room for error.

Therefore the passenger-side approach. Tyler had taken the new caution to heart. Years ago, most officers pulling over a car walked up to the driver's window and engaged in immediate conversation. Nowadays, they emulated what Tyler had just done. Each tended to circle the rear of their flashing cruiser—therefore not cutting in front of the blazing lights and outlining themselves—to unobtrusively peer through the suspect vehicle's rear right window. This tactic afforded a number of advantages. It distracted the driver, who was squinting into the left outside mirror, expecting to see a shadow approach; it gave the cop a brief contemplation of the interior, including the driver's often hidden right hand; and it supplied an element of surprise when the request to talk was finally issued. It also didn't hurt that it lowered the chance of the officer's being struck by a passing car.

But in Tyler Brennan's experience, it also had a final, paradoxical, effect. Because of its emphasis on lowering the threat threshold, the covert approach actually made Tyler more paranoid, as did an additional habit of placing his bare hand on the suspect's car, in order to leave trace of his DNA and fingerprints behind, in case things went haywire.

In all, by the time he'd knocked on John Rust's right front window, he was ready to draw down on his suspect at the slightest provocation.

But Rust barely moved. Quite the opposite of a trigger-happy possible killer, this guy appeared borderline catatonic.

The revelation spurred Brennan to preface his usual spiel with a note of concern. "Sir, are you all right?"

Rust had jumped in his seat upon the rapping of Tyler's flashlight on the glass, but he now merely blinked, as if stirring from sleep. "Sure," he said vaguely.

"You don't seem that way," Brennan countered, adding, "and so you know, this conversation is being audio- and video-recorded. Have you been drinking alcohol tonight, sir?"

Rust seemed to consider the question. The requirement to announce any bodycams or recorders was routinely done casually, so as not to draw attention to the fact.

"Yup," Rust said slowly, still not moving.

"How much would you say you've consumed?"

After a pause, the answer was, "The usual, I guess."

"Thank you," the cop responded, genuinely grateful, hoping his camera was fully functioning. "Could I see your driver's license, proof of insurance, and registration, please?"

John Rust liked the young cop's face, even under the severe forward tilt of his imposing campaign hat—wide eyes, hint of a smile, an open expression. It almost compelled John to be honest, although he sighed inwardly when he heard himself admitting to being drunk. That wasn't going to improve things any.

He sat waiting in his car as the trooper retired to run his paperwork for priors, a process guaranteed to end poorly. John couldn't even remember how many times he'd been pulled over.

He wasn't upset, however. He no longer felt any reason to be. His life, as he'd known it for forty years, had ended. Whatever happened now would be like cutting a kite loose of its tether—freeing it to float away.

Or plummet.

The ensuing roadside minuet of nystagmus eye test, walk-and-turn and one-leg stand, and finally the forceful breath into the Alco-Sensor occurred sequentially, politely, almost courteously toward the end, as trooper and driver found their rhythm.

Many such interactions are punctuated by anger, impatience, and, especially, sloppiness by the offender. But this one was very different for both men. For a number of reasons—mood, time of night, overall state of being, or, more likely, the simple fact that these two just connected somehow—their ritual of command-and-obey, perform-and-observe, oddly suggestive of two tall, thin birds acting out a ceremonial, nature-driven encounter, became almost pleasant. This wasn't hurt by the fact that Rust performed his dexterity tests quite well, a result usually restricted to either the sober or to seasoned alcoholics, whose tolerances could be alarmingly high. The Alco-Sensor reading had indicated that John was among the latter, but his demeanor throughout remained peaceful and courteous. By the time Tyler Brennan eased his now-handcuffed subject gently into his back seat for the trip to the barracks, a genuine if unacknowledged affection had bloomed between them.

DUIs, DWIs, or sometimes deewees in the jargon, are lengthy affairs, quasi-liturgical in their formality. There are steps to be followed, protocols to enact, tests to endure, and forms to be completed. A decision tree algorithm dictates which path to engage, depending on the investigator's discoveries and the arrestee's cooperation and choices. The whole exercise can take hours and result in a trip to jail, or end at the barracks with a citation and the arranging of some form of transport back home.

Phones, computers, and faxes are variously employed, necessitating a lot of sitting around, waiting. It was during this phase that Brennan entered the room Rust had been assigned, bearing two mugs of coffee. His compulsory guest was sitting with his head cocked, like a dog's listening to some tiny siren call from afar.

Tyler didn't interrupt as he handed over one of the mugs and sat in the room's remaining chair.

"Hear that?" John asked him, a small smile on his otherwise permanently sad face.

Tyler yielded to the building's silence long enough to shake his head and admit, "No. What'm I listening for?"

"That ticking."

Tyler now heard it. "Hot-water pipe," he explained. "I got the same thing at home. When the nights are cold, it can get pretty loud. You must've heard that before, John."

Rust hadn't been very talkative so far, responding to questions quietly and in a surprisingly soothing tone that Brennan had come to appreciate. Now, for the first time, he gazed at the trooper and spoke off topic.

"Yes, I have, and of course you're right. It's just that I heard the same thing earlier today. It got me thinking."

"'Bout what?" Brennan asked, taking a sip of his coffee.

"You ever hear of the deathwatch beetle?" John asked.

"Deathwatch?" Tyler repeated. "Doesn't sound good, whatever it is."

"It's nothing nasty," John assured him. "Ironic, maybe. It's a wood-boring beetle, mostly in England, from what I've read. Kind of a termite, I suppose. It lives in the wood of really old houses, destroying the integrity of the beams from the inside. People don't discover it until they notice a little wood dust here and there. Then, when they tap on the surface, it gives way to huge holes of underlying powder. It's actually quite startling. Very destructive while being almost invisible. I've seen pictures of the damage. Impressive."

"Okay," Tyler replied slowly, wondering what any beetle had to do with noisy pipes—and if Rust's level of inebriation was maybe worse than he'd imagined. But he was amused by this almost abrupt evolution from virtual silence to random eloquence, and was happy to allow it some rein.

John seemed to understand the cop's inner debate and waved a hand reassuringly. "I know. I'm rambling. The deathwatch beetle blows its cover when it's searching out company. It actually thumps its head repeatedly against the wood to attract a mate."

"No foolin'," Tyler said, partly humoring him. "Must be huge."

"It's not. Third of an inch or so. You can't really hear it at all unless things are absolutely still. That's how it got its name. Here's the irony I mentioned: Back in the day, people held vigils for the dead and dying, all through the night. In the silence, they'd hear the beetles hard at work, calling out so they could create life. But the two phenomena got weirdly combined—death became associated with the tapping, to the point where people started saying the poor beetle was calling for death itself, counting down the seconds."

Brennan put down his coffee and stood up, headed for the fax machine in the other room to see if his paperwork had come through yet. "Well, take comfort, John." He jerked a thumb overhead. "*That* is a hot-water pipe."

John smiled again. "Oh, I know. All this goes back to before indoor plumbing. But it does make you wonder—if nature sometimes knows more than we do."

That stopped Brennan at the door, caught up by the notion and recalling something else John had mentioned. "You said this was the second time you heard ticking today."

Rust looked caught out, and furrowed his brow, staring at the floor. "Did I?"

"Yeah." The young cop released the doorknob and watched the older man closely. "When was that?" he pursued.

Rust spoke reluctantly. "I lost somebody today. That's when I heard the tapping. It was more in context then."

"Somebody died?" Tyler asked. In his experience, people talk to excess, usually about themselves, and drunks can be especially talkative. Here he was learning that Rust had just suffered the death of someone close, and yet hadn't said a word until now, and then virtually by accident.

"My brother," Rust said.

Tyler sat back down, his elbows on his knees, leaning forward. "He was ill?"

"It was expected. Still"—he looked up, his expression so troubled Tyler was quite moved, and added—"it came as a surprise. You know?"

Brennan thought of his grandmother last year. A woman in her nineties, whose death had nevertheless left them bereft and longing. "I think I do. I'm sorry, John."

Tyler got up to leave again, but this time, in violation of one of his own practices, he touched Rust in passing, gently pressing his shoulder.

That gesture notwithstanding, Brennan was in no way deflected from his course of action. Another revelation over the past few hours had been that John Rust, as mellow and soft-spoken as he presented, was nevertheless a committed and unrepentant alcoholic. More to the point, this was his fourth DUI recently where he'd registered a BAC of over 0.16—twice the allowable limit.

It wouldn't be the first time Tyler had enjoyed the company of someone his charges put behind bars. It was one of the peculiarities of the profession that bonds often formed between cop and crook, considering all the time they spent in each other's company.

Jail wasn't going to be a feature tonight, though. Rust was going to be cited and released on his own recognizance. He'd been cooperative, pleasant, and coherent. His car had been impounded and he'd be taken home in a cab. Additionally, he'd just suffered a personal loss, and, if standards were followed, he'd be losing his privilege to drive in a few days anyhow, this being his fourth offense. Tyler saw no risk to public safety in letting the poor guy go.

Not immediately, however. As Brennan entered the dispatcher's office, she informed him that a domestic dispute involving a knife had just been reported a few miles away, and all hands were being requested. Rather than wrapping up with Rust—collecting his fingerprints and mug shots before release—Brennan would have to detain him at the barracks for a few more hours, under the dispatcher's watchful eye via camera, until this new emergency had been addressed.

It was a routine-enough occurrence, and one that Tyler doubted his new acquaintance would mind.

Indeed, John Rust used the extra time to slowly grasp his new reality, emerging from the trancelike state Brennan had found him in to something like an epiphanic awakening. Whether it was the alcohol's release of his brain or simply his meditation on the deathwatch beetle, John had glimpsed a possible new direction for his life that he hadn't considered previously.

Following Pete's inevitable if slow-coming death, John had fallen upon habit, and emptied a bottle. But was that what he wanted, acting as he had before, even without Pete at the center of things?

In the countdown that measures one's time alive, that suddenly seemed to John—surrounded as he was by the stark reality of a police station—a poor destiny to embrace.

Especially if the same long-expected death could serve as a springboard for something more rewarding.

By the time Tyler Brennan returned four hours later to complete the booking procedure, he found Rust clear-eyed, engaged, and confident in his movements—the picture of a man with a mission in mind.

Tyler could only wish him well.

CHAPTER ONE

Searching Out the Weak Spot

Sally Kravitz liked Scott Jezek. A runner, a reader, a family man, he was the kind of lawyer who made lawyer jokes ring hollow. He was a small-time operator, owner of a one-man practice in Brattleboro, Vermont, a town that, since the 1970s, had earned an eccentric, politicized, left-wing reputation that allowed unusual types like Jezek to fit right in.

His most winning feature for Sally was his soft spot for the underdog. Having cut his legal teeth for two decades in Boston, Jezek had amassed a small fortune and was yearning for a simpler life, if still within the practice of law. He'd chosen Brattleboro for this, and opened what he referred to as a "boutique firm," where he could pick and choose his clients based on whether he believed in their cause over their ability to pay, often charging just enough to settle his bills and, for the most part, rejecting the very people who could easily afford his high-octane background and credentials.

This made Sally and Scott kindred spirits, since, though wildly different in nature, their backgrounds had sculpted in each a sympathy for the downtrodden. A homegrown Brattleboro girl, Sally had been reared by a father devoted to experiencing and learning from the hardscrabble lives of society's lower rungs. He had moved her around the town like a nomad for years, camping out in other people's apartments and trailers and homes, exchanging labor and gifts for shelter, while absorbing a culture from which most middle-class residents only dreamed of escaping.

But just as Scott Jezek no longer depended on money to function as a lawyer, Dan Kravitz, Sally's father, hadn't lived among the disadvantaged through fate or misfortune. It had been a choice. In fact, he had money. Quite a bit, not that anyone knew it. He'd developed a covert career as an information thief, and a good one, complete with a rigid and moral standard of operations, who broke into high-end homes to bug people's electronic devices and thus follow—and benefit from—their activities, whether legal or not. As a result, once he felt that his daughter had learned what she could on society's ground floor, he'd put her into a prestigious prep school so she could study the flip side.

Now, at last an adult, Sally had chosen a profession that helped her again to peer into how and why people function as they do, as a private investigator.

And like Scott Jezek, she selected many jobs despite a lower income. Differing from most of her colleagues, she tried to avoid domestic work—the euphemism for spousal cheating cases—and weighted her business toward defense mitigation. Lawyers like Scott hired her to discover good things about their clients, for use in tempering the prejudice of prosecutors or judges or both, since their grasp of a defendant's entire personality was often based solely on the charges against them.

That explained Sally's being here now. Scott had phoned earlier that morning to ask if "an unusual DUI" might be of interest.

Sally didn't drink alcohol. At all. Never had. It was one of her personal details that, despite the influences that had formed her, she had created for herself an unreachable behavioral niche, where she remained safe like an eagle high on a cliff.

That being said, she understood addiction and the various forces leading to it. She didn't necessarily disagree that some drunks were self-indulgent boors, too inconsiderate of others to merit much slack. But Sally's own view was more charitable, having found that most addicts were caught up in emotions exceeding their ability to control them.

Jezek's office matched his profile. Housed in an old Victorian mansion, now home to a preponderance of psychology practices—of which Brattleboro had an impressive number—it consisted of a single room flooded with light from a large bay window and appointed with hardwood floors, wood paneling, and a coffered ceiling. Lining the ancient mantelpiece above an inoperative fireplace was a parade of some of Jezek's collection of antique Christmas cards, lined up like a colorful if faded paper train.

The lawyer himself, dressed casually in jeans and an open-necked, button-down shirt, rose from his chair upon her entrance and fairly raced around his desk to greet her.

"Sally," he said, smiling broadly, shaking her hand, and waving her into one of two guest chairs. "You came. I am delighted."

He took the chair catty-corner to hers as she replied, "Sure. You thought I wouldn't?"

"I didn't know if this met your principles. I know you're pretty selective."

"If you took a case," she told him, "it's a fair bet I would too. You're a good gatekeeper."

He laughed before saying, "All right, enough, before we both overdo the compliments."

"What've you got?" she asked.

He reached over to his desk and removed a file, which he opened on his lap. "John Rust. Pulled over by the VSP—Trooper Tyler Brennan—a couple of days ago in Putney for weaving, in what appears to be a righteous stop. Blew way over the legal limit at roadside, did the same on the Datamaster at the barracks, and was released on a citation, even though this is his fourth DUI."

"That's unusual," Sally observed.

"True," Scott agreed, "but it's largely officer discretion, and I guess the two of them hit it off. John's a nice guy, he was heading back to his home in Westminster—was almost there, in fact. Maybe that played a role."

"He is in a world of hurt, though," Sally said. "It's beyond officer discretion from here on out. He's gotta be looking at jail time, and definitely a suspended license. What's his problem, that he keeps circling the same hydrant?"

Scott held up a finger in emphasis. "That is precisely why we're meeting. What doesn't surface in this—" He tapped the file. "—is that John had sole custody of and responsibility for a handicapped younger brother who died on the same day as the DUI. According to John, Peter Rust was diagnosed with some form of hydrocephalus at birth and gradually became a vegetable. When he died at twenty-eight, he weighed sixty pounds."

"And John took care of him all on his own?" Sally asked. "How could he do that? He independently wealthy?"

"Hardly. He works as a freelance web designer. But you're right in implying Peter's need for full-time care. I think John came up with that job in large part so he could stay at home and still make a living. From what I gather, finances have sometimes been tight. Nevertheless, I spoke with Peter's physician on the phone, and he told me he never had a vegetative patient so well cared for. He called John a saint, and stressed that wasn't a word he used often."

"But he drinks," Sally suggested.

Jezek agreed. "He does. He was twelve when Pete was born, eighteen when he took over his care, his father having walked out on his birthday, saying, 'Welcome to adulthood. Good luck. You'll need it,' or something similar. John's mom had already died of an overdose."

Sally was shaking her head in sympathy. "The implication being that John was probably already doing most of the caregiving, even before he turned eighteen."

"A reasonable assumption," Scott agreed. "Can you see why I called you?"

"I can," she said. "Did Rust phone you from the barracks? Take a blood test? Admit to driving under the influence?"

"He did not phone, to answer the first question. I think because he was in shock. He told me later that through it all, he was in a daze, what with Pete's death, and that it was only toward the end that he began thinking he wanted to fight what he'd first seen as inevitable. In the past, whenever he was busted, he had Pete's care to think about. This time, he said, he felt he had nothing to live for."

"But he changed his mind."

Scott looked thoughtful. "Yeah. I'm not sure what that's about, exactly. He wouldn't tell me. He just said it was important that he not be put behind bars for this."

"You have anything you'd like me to start with?" Sally asked him. "Or are you letting me off the leash?"

"Well," the lawyer said, "I know and trust how you work, so you're mostly on your own." He searched the file and extracted a DVD. "This is a substantial recording of John's arrest and processing that I'd appreciate your looking at. That'll most likely answer some other questions, too. From what John told me, it seems the trooper did everything right, but you never know, and I would love to find something to blunt the state's attorney's zeal."

"The SA's already talked to you about this?" Sally asked, surprised.

"Not specifically," Jezek said. "But it's an election year, he's facing opposition for the first time in a while, and he's not the most popular man around. Coming down on drunk driving has become one of his key talking points. I want to be as armed as I can be, going in, and I know for a fact that he and his staff are too swamped to check out the contents of this—" He waved the DVD. "—before we all have to show up for the arraignment."

Sally took the recording from him. "Got it." She rose to leave, adding, "You have a problem with my talking to John, if the need arises?"

Scott escorted her to the door, handing her the file. "None. Be my guest."

Investigations require a lot of sitting—in cars, behind surveillance cameras, in court, writing reports, and, as Sally was doing now, studying DUI-processing footage. This last was perhaps her least favorite. The viewpoint was static—usually from high in a room's corner—as was the subject matter, an arrested subject sitting in a chair as the officer comes and goes over a period of hours.

Felony interrogations demand focus. They consist of two people verbally parrying as one pursues the truth while the other evades admitting it, and they entail a reasonable amount of drama.

DUIs are mostly waiting, however. There's the occasional back-and-forth, the conversation as the officer fills out the relevant multipage form, maybe a fight or a shouting match if the subject is uncooperative. But otherwise, it boils down to one person waiting out the hours until they're either taken to jail or released on a citation.

It therefore made Sally sit up and take notice when Trooper Brennan appeared in the corner of the screen and informed Rust that he had to leave for a domestic, being the only cop in the barracks at this hour, and that Rust would have to sit tight until he returned to finish the booking process.

"I'll be damned," Sally said to herself, and noted the time stamp at the bottom of the image.

Several long hours later, she phoned Scott Jezek.

"What d'ya got?" he asked.

"I think you'll like it," she reported. "My butt grew numb watching that recording you gave me, but it turns out Rust did request a blood test to corroborate the Datamaster findings at the barracks."

"What?" Jezek responded, clearly surprised. "I don't have the results of that. Where did he get it done?"

"He didn't," she said. "You know how, when they're going through the form, they get to the part where it says, 'Since you are being released, if you wish an additional blood test, to be paid for at your expense, you will have to make your own arrangements. Do you intend to obtain an additional test, yes or no?' Well, your client said he would. It's on tape. The trooper even explains that because he's being let go after processing—as against being detained—the responsibility for getting the blood test is on him, and the cop won't supply transportation."

"I'm still not following," Jezek said. "What happened?"

"That's the point," she replied. "Nothing. Next thing you know—after the paperwork but before the mug shot and fingerprinting—the trooper comes in and tells Rust he has to go out on an emergency call and that Rust has to wait for him in a holding cell until he gets back to wrap things up."

"You're pulling my leg," the lawyer said, his excitement audible. "They did detain him?"

"For over four hours. Then the trooper shows up again, they go through the printing and mug shot portion, the trooper offers to drive Rust home since he lives so close by, and that's it."

"No mention of the blood test."

"Not a word. I think they both forgot. Like you said, Rust was distracted, not to mention drunk, and the trooper had other things on his mind, being fresh back from that call, and probably hankering to go home after a long shift. By the way," Sally threw in, "you ought to know that John aced his roadside dexterity tests—the walk-a-single-line, stand-on-one-foot, and the rest. Being an Olympic-level drunk has its advantages—what he had in his system may have been twice the legal limit, but it doesn't look like it had the slightest effect on him physically. That'll help you in court, too, I would guess."

"This is textbook," Jezek said. "If an accused says he wants a blood test but is being released, then you are absolutely right. It's up to him to get the test at a hospital of his choosing, and in a timely manner. But that emergency call means John wasn't released. And the law is crystal clear. If you are being detained, but you asked for that test, you have to be escorted by an officer to a hospital or wherever for the blood draw to occur. God, I love it. So, since they both forgot about it, the trooper's oversight's gonna mean that the Datamaster results'll have to be thrown out. Them's the rules. Jesus. The SA's going to flip out. Nice work, Sally."

"You're welcome," she replied, smiling at his enthusiasm. "You remember that this only kills half the case against him, right? The civil charge will no doubt be tossed, but the criminal charge alongside it still has meat on it."

"Yeah, yeah, yeah," the lawyer said dismissively. "I know that. But it gets weakened. One supports the other, or not, thanks to you."

"Not me," Sally corrected him. "Sadly, we have poor Trooper Brennan to thank, not that he could've done anything else. He had to go on that call, and after he got back, too much time had passed for the blood draw to count, anyway. Talk about a rock and a hard place. I hope to hell they don't jam him up."

Jezek wasn't sympathetic. "If they do," he said, "you can volunteer as a character witness."

"Okay, then," Sally said, sensing the conversation ending. "Well, if that's enough to do the trick, I can send you my bill and we'll part ways, unless you want more."

"I do," he countered. "I've spoken to John since you came to my office, and his resolve to get out from under this has only grown. I'm therefore thinking you could dig in to the whole Peter thing, maybe create a chronology, interview a few people, and find whatever you can that'll cast John in a favorable light."

He paused before continuing, "I'd love to double-tag the SA on this one—combine a technical legal glitch with a legitimate sob story. But not to just score points. I have no problem with holding John's feet to the fire. He's a drunk and he needs to straighten up. I'm just saying he's gotta have help to do that, not punishment, and I don't want election rhetoric chewing him up."

Once more, Sally was hearing why she liked working with this man. "I got it, Scott. You're preaching to the choir."

He laughed at that. "Okay, okay. You got me all wound up. I'll shut up and you go find me a suitably sentimental story."

"Will do."

CHAPTER TWO

Getting to What Lurks Below

Scott Jezek had supplied Sally with the name of Peter Rust's doctor, a position referred to within medicine and law enforcement as a PCP, for primary care physician. She was called Cinnamon Decato-Murray, which to Sally was a perfect fit for Brattleboro's countercultural image, as viewed by most of the rest of Vermont. Using the internet, Sally discovered Decato-Murray's address on the Brattleboro Memorial Hospital campus.

The town's renown as an often-contradictory enclave of old-fashioned and progressive, native-born and flatlander, traditional and avant-garde, was routinely regarded in both complimentary and dismissive terms, from residents and outsiders alike.

There was no mistaking why Sally's father, Dan, had chosen the place for his experimental child-rearing. Enough eccentric practices had been witnessed across town to make someone like Dan at once appreciative and unnoticeable.

Certainly the presence of a doctor with a hyphenated last name preceded by a spice was no standout.

The doctor herself, however, stood out remarkably. She was tall, athletic, short-haired, and with a strong face and sharp, intelligent eyes. Her handshake matched Sally's in firmness, as did her manner, when she gestured to a chair in her office and said, "There."

Sally sat, taking in the usual anatomical posters on the walls, along with an oversized, not very subtle wall clock. "Can you talk to me about Peter Rust?" she asked straight off.

Decato-Murray perched one hip on the corner of her desk, reaching into a pocket of her lab coat for a tube of lip balm, which she applied as she spoke. "John had power of attorney, and called me earlier to say I could, so I guess the answer is yes. What do you want to know?"

"Let's start with the basics," Sally said. "What did he have?"

"In layman's terms?" the PCP replied, pocketing her lip balm. "Irreversible brain damage."

"He was born that way?"

"That's what I was told. I inherited his case from a predecessor who retired to Florida and died, I think. Peter was twenty-eight on his last birthday, so his chart predates any of our computer systems. A lot of data's also been lost on its way to me. Technically, my understanding was that he suffered from fetal ventriculomegaly complicated by later hydrocephalus. Not a happy prospect, but also one I was never really allowed to test."

"Why not?"

Decato-Murray looked rueful as she answered, "In this country, at least so far, we can't force you to undergo a medical procedure. Not usually, anyway. And we certainly can't impose a detailed and expensive investigation into a preexisting condition. We can only suggest that it be considered. I did and John Rust passed on the opportunity."

Sally reacted to the careful phrasing. "You're saying John refused treatment?"

"No," the doctor corrected her. "He opted not to subject his brother to any tests. My diagnosis remained an educated guess."

"Why did he do that? I thought he took good care of Peter."

"He did. That's a different issue. He was fully aware that his brother's condition would never improve. That didn't mean he wasn't going to do everything he could to make him comfortable. In this business, I sometimes have to look past individual eccentricities to assess the medical realities, and I have to say, I have never seen a better-cared-for patient than Peter Rust. What his brother, John, did for him, day-to-day, was nothing short of heroic. So, I have no argument with his wanting to spare Peter the possible discomfort of a bunch of scans and blood draws and the rest."

"You had no doubts when you filled out the death certificate?"

Cinnamon Decato-Murray gave Sally a severe look. "Are you suggesting I missed something?"

"Not at all. It's a straightforward question."

"When I have doubts," the doctor said, rising, "I call the medical examiner. I did not."

Sally took that as a less-than-subtle cue, and also got to her feet. "What about John?" she pressed. "Did you ever get any insight on *why* he was so devoted to Pete?"

The older woman had already opened the door and was holding it there invitingly, apparently resisting the urge to throw Sally out bodily. "I have enough to deal with wondering why some of my patients have welts or fractures. I do not question when their home care has been immaculate."

The interview was over.

"Have fun with the tiger lady?"

Sally looked up from studying her smartphone, on which she'd been searching for a contact number while sitting in the doctor's waiting area, and saw the sweet, familiar, almost ancient face of a nurse she'd known from childhood trips to the pediatrician.

"Elizabeth Pace," Sally said, putting away the phone and wrapping her arms around the white-haired woman. "It is so good to see you."

"You, too, sweetie," the nurse said, reaching out and patting her shoulders.

Pace was possibly better known on this campus than most of the hot-shot physicians. She'd worked here for uncountable decades, in as many different departments and practices as anyone could remember, to the point nowadays that it seemed she could choose her base of operations at whim, if she wished. Her reputation was such that anyone who employed her counted themselves blessed.

"You referring to the weirdly named Cinnamon?" Sally asked her small, spare friend. "How did you know I was here seeing her?"

Elizabeth laughed. "You're kidding, of course. This is not really a hospital," she said, waving her hand in an all-encompassing circle. "It's a bee's nest of information buzzing back and forth, nonstop. I even know you came to ask her about poor Peter Rust, may he rest in peace."

"I'm impressed," Sally said. "No wonder they make such a big deal about confidentiality."

Elizabeth agreed. "Oh yes. It's like the dark net and the regular internet, combined. We know all the secret stuff."

Sally was laughing. "The dark net? You surf the dark net? *Elizabeth*."

The nurse gave her a playful push. "Oh, for God's sake. I'm old. Not brain dead. I like keeping up."

Sally remembered something Pace had mentioned earlier. "Did you know Peter?"

"We all did. We tried to make it a big deal whenever he came by, even if we weren't sure he knew what was going on. And of course, he wasn't always that way. Years ago, he was more aware of his surroundings. We just sort of kept it up since those days."

"Do you know anything of his birth and early childhood?" Sally asked. "My new best friend Cinnamon wasn't too forthcoming."

"She wouldn't know," Elizabeth replied. "She's a relative newcomer. The person you want to talk to is Marcia Ethier. She's so old now, she makes me look like a teenager, but her brain's sharp, and if my own memory serves, she'll have what you're after."

"How's that?"

"She was a midwife her whole career. Probably helped half this town's older citizens into the world. Peter Rust was one of her last, in fact. She's at the Maple Tree nursing home down the street. Tell her I sent you. That might help, not that she'll need coaxing to open up. Confidentiality was never one of her hang-ups, either."

In the sliding scale of nursing homes, Maple Tree was solidly in the middle. It was neither an imitation country club, where the residents seemed hell-bent on ignoring that they'd left the fast lane behind and treated all staffers like idiot domestics, nor a storage facility for penniless oldsters whose care was seen as a monstrous inconvenience to those responsible for keeping them alive.

Indeed, Maple Tree's trademark, despite being a little threadbare and lacking in the latest amenities, was the ongoing warmth between residents and employees. With few exceptions, to Sally's knowledge, everyone there was happy with their circumstances.

She wended her way up to the third floor after consulting a receptionist in the lobby and walked to a room at the end of the hall, exchanging greetings with people along the way. Some were in wheelchairs, others pushing walkers, a few seemed to be navigating more inside their own minds than the outside world.

In large part because of her upbringing, Sally had acquired a universal ease among people. She wasn't accepting of bad behavior, nor immune from favoritism or criticism, but she had virtually no interest in a person's gender, race, cultural background, or disability. For all of Dan's unusual teachings, there he'd been successful.

The door she was seeking was halfway open when she reached it.

Leaking into the corridor were not the usual sounds of a TV set, but the soft strains of Vivaldi.

She rapped hesitantly on the doorframe and poked her head inside.

"Come in," called out a small woman, sitting in an armchair by the window, peering in her direction.

As Sally entered and crossed the neat and homey room carpeted and furnished like some well-loved cabin in the woods—complete with a hundred framed baby pictures crowding the walls—she noticed that the woman had a quilt she was repairing bunched up on her lap.

"Hello," the woman greeted her as she drew near. "Who are you? Are you one of mine?"

Sally happily gestured to the portraits around them. "It looks like I'd be in good company if I were." She reached out to shake hands. "No, ma'am. My name is Sally Kravitz. I'm a friend of Elizabeth Pace's, who recommended I drop by."

"Well, I'm glad you did," the woman said. "I guess I shouldn't have to say that I'm Marcia Ethier, then."

"No, ma'am," Sally replied, sitting on the edge of another armchair facing Ethier's.

"Marcia, please," Ethier corrected her, putting down her sewing project and sitting back to study her guest. She had gnarly, deeply veined hands, and her face was an urban road map of wrinkles. But her eyes were an electric blue, very intense, and all the more remarkable for not needing glasses.

"How did Elizabeth think I could help?"

Sally pointed to the small faces taking them in, as if a stilled audience were attending with a collective bated breath. "It's actually one of these little guys," she said. "I was hoping you could tell me about one of them. I'm afraid it was a long time ago, though, so don't worry if you don't remember."

Ethier smiled, taking up the dare. "Try me. I might surprise you."

"Okay," Sally replied. "Peter Rust."

"Brother of John, child of Karen Taylor," Ethier responded without pause. "Father was a big waste of a man named Daryl Hicks. I didn't understand why the kids had a different name from their mother's, till she told me she just preferred the name Rust. I suspect she didn't like who she came from and had little use for Daryl. It was a peculiar family. Mismatched names are common enough, though, especially nowadays."

"You remember," Sally uttered reflexively, feeling silly as the words floated between them.

But her elderly host wouldn't embarrass her, turning it into a joke. "All those years watching *Jeopardy!* haven't been for nothing."

But then she turned serious, adding, "Folks like them were always a reminder to me of how close to the edge we all live, without even knowing it." She gave a soundless snap of her crooked, sculptural fingers. "In a heartbeat, everything can change."

Sally was touched by sadness, as much by Marcia's tone as her words. In that moment, Ethier struck her as a sage of yore, all-seeing and yet powerless in a life she could only wish to improve.

"I don't know if you heard," Sally said, almost against her will. "Peter died just a few days ago."

Marcia's eyes drifted to some middle distance, off to the side. "Yes," she said. "I suppose that was inevitable. You always hope they'll have long lives, and if not that, then at least happy ones. I'm afraid Peter was never slated for either."

"It must have been heartbreaking," Sally sympathized. "Seeing a little baby come out like that."

The pale blue eyes returned to Sally's face, sharpened to a hard edge. The midwife's voice was cutting as well. "'Like that'?" she echoed.

Sally was briefly horrified, thinking she'd been misunderstood as having made a social judgment. "I didn't mean it like it sounded. I meant to be born with such a challenge."

But Marcia was shaking her head. "I'm not being politically correct, young woman. I'm saying that Peter Rust came out just fine. The challenge was what was facing him, not anything he brought into the world."

"How do you mean?" Sally asked, confused.

"Peter was born perfectly normal. Passed all the tests, and I used to check on all of my babies later. I called them 'warranty visits.' Peter was no victim of bad genes or a biological hiccup. He was made how he was the old-fashioned way."

Sally filled in the blanks, her expression registering her surprise and disgust. "He was beaten?"

"Not that you could prove it."

"Hicks? The dad?"

"I assume so."

"How do you know?"

Ethier paused before answering thoughtfully. "We live in times where more and more people speak as if they know, when in fact, they just have an opinion. Who made Peter the way he was? My opinion is that it was Hicks. Was Peter born with the affliction that shortened his life? I think not, but I suppose you could say that's *only* my opinion. Still, I was a midwife for five decades. I've lost count of how many I helped bring into the world. If any of us can be called an expert about a subject, then I'm an expert on newborns."

She held up a crooked finger in warning before continuing, "Now, I realize that some deformities and handicaps develop over time, and that upon presentation, many a child might look normal, and pass all the tests. Peter was not such a case, and I say that less because of what I saw when his mother delivered, and more because of how he changed between one home visit and the next."

She leaned forward for emphasis. "I know, by all that is holy, that Peter Rust was damaged by another. A blow to the head, being violently shaken, maybe almost suffocated to stop him from crying. Which, I don't know. But I do know babies, and he was a victim of violence, not nature."

Sally absorbed that before asking, "Have you ever told anyone about this?"

The old woman seemed to shrink into herself, enough to prompt Sally to leave her chair, get down on one knee, and cradle one of Ethier's warm, soft hands. "I'm sorry," she said. "I didn't mean to upset you."

"No, no," Marcia replied. "You're quite right. I should have. I was a coward. I was frightened."

"What happened?"

Ethier let out a shuddering sigh. "The father scared me. I came by, as I said, like I used to with so many of my babies, and Karen let me in. She was distraught, as was young John. I could tell I'd stepped into a bad situation, but I kept going, not thinking things through. I told Karen I was there to see Peter. She told me he was asleep, and like an idiot, I just kept blundering on, saying that didn't matter, it didn't bother me, and so on. I walked into the house, into Peter's room, that he shared with his brother, and immediately, even though Karen had been truthful, and Peter *was* asleep, I could tell he'd been damaged. I picked him up, and was about to really examine him, when the father came into the room."

She stopped, her breathing rapid and her hand now moist in Sally's own. Sally looked around, wondering if she shouldn't ring for assistance, unsure of what she'd unwittingly unleashed.

But Marcia seemed to understand, and reassured her in a whisper, "It's all right. I'm fine. I'm sorry. Please don't be concerned. It's hard, after so many years."

Only slightly comforted, Sally asked, "Did he threaten you?"

"Not in so many words. It was like everything else in that family. There was a cloud over all of them, but nothing you could get your hands around. It was the way he looked at me, his body language, and

Karen's, too. She came in and took Peter from me, and said something like, 'I told you not to.' It was as if they were united somehow. Not at all what you'd expect, where the bully husband is dominating and noisy and throwing his weight around. With these people—all of a sudden, in that one moment—I felt my life was in danger."

She began to cry. Sally reached for a box of tissues and placed it on her lap, where Marcia ignored it, letting her tears blotch the fabric of her quilt.

"I lived alone," Marcia explained. "I had no children of my own. I never felt I had time for romance or a family. There were too many babies needing help, too much to do. That was what frightened me the most, you see? After Karen removed Peter, that man took my elbow—not harshly, mind you—and led me to the front door, where he said, 'Not to worry, Marcia. I know exactly how to find you, day or night.' Then he closed the door behind me. I'll never forget that. It changed my life, or at least how I dealt with people forever after. I became watchful, even nervous, and I never again made presumptions like I had when I entered that house."

She took a tissue and blew her nose at last, adding as she daubed her upper lip, "I know it sounds weak and melodramatic. I should have protected that boy."

Sally almost interrupted her. "That's not true, Marcia. What happened to Peter was over. Hicks exploited your vulnerability. Even now, John says Peter was born the way he was. It sounds like he had no clue about Hicks having caused it. I think you're being too hard on yourself."

She comforted Ethier for a while longer before taking her leave. But, in truth, as she retreated through the building to her car outside, she was torn. In fact, Sally didn't believe the comforting words she'd fed the ancient and frightened midwife. Marcia should have reported her suspicions about Hicks. Yes, those were earlier times, when child abuse was just starting to be addressed as the crime it is, but Ethier had been accurate in her self-assessment. In Sally's eyes, Marcia had been a coward.

And now, although Daryl Hicks might never in fact have hit another child, it was looking as if he had hurt Peter. If true, that made Peter's death, even so many years later, a homicide.

CHAPTER THREE

Jezek Prepares the Ground

Joe Gunther was sitting at his desk when Scott Jezek appeared in the open office doorway and asked, "No security?"

Joe, the squad leader of this Vermont Bureau of Investigation team, merely smiled and shrugged. "Normally, yeah. I guess I like the circulating air better than the odds that you're here to shoot me."

The lawyer quickly reassured him. "Whoa. I think you're safe there."

Joe beckoned to him, rising at the same time. "Come on in, Scott. Save me from report writing. Please. Want some coffee?"

Jezek entered, looking around. He'd never been here before, although he and Gunther had met multiple times at the courthouse across the street. It was a one-room office, not much larger than his own, but with four desks, filing cabinets, several metal guest chairs, the usual bric-a-brac that adorns a workplace—including, in this instance, a large and incongruous toy stork hanging over a desk also festooned with stork-illustrated mugs, ball caps, and postcards.

"Sure. Thanks," he said to Joe's offer. The space was at once functional and awkwardly cluttered, screaming out—in his opinion—for larger quarters.

Gunther was already at a half counter in one corner, handling the coffee maker and readying a cup. "Anything in it? I won't drink the stuff without maple syrup and that French vanilla creamer that doesn't qualify for an expiration date."

Jezek crossed over to him, slightly alarmed by the comment. "That sounds disgusting. No, plain'll be fine."

Smiling, Joe handed him the cup. "Chicken," he said. "Rumors notwithstanding, I'm not one of the cops hankering to kill a lawyer."

Scott peered into his drink, no longer sure he wanted it. "Thanks, I think?"

Joe sat on his desk, which not surprisingly was right behind him. Scott felt free to do the same under the stork. He gestured to it overhead. "What's with the bird?"

"Lester Spinney," Joe replied. "He's taller and skinnier than anyone you're ever likely to meet. He gets stork-related toys and stuff all the time. It was his nickname at the academy."

Jezek nodded at the reference. "I've seen him. Never met. There are four of you in here?"

"I know," Joe acknowledged. "Tight fit. We could move, but it would probably mean co-locating with somebody else. None of us wants that."

"You like your autonomy?"

Joe allowed for a gentle smile. "Well, it is sort of how we're structured."

Jezek knew that to be the literal truth. Created years earlier to run parallel to the state police's Bureau of Criminal Investigation, or BCI, the VBI was exclusively assigned to major crimes, whereas BCI covered all plainclothes investigations.

VBI was no maverick operation, but it was small, tightly focused, independent, and with none of the state police's much disparaged bureaucracy. As proof of its appeal to those "inside the tent," the VBI had been swamped upon its creation with applications from an inordinate number of BCI's best investigators.

Gunther had not been one of those. He and most of his squad had segued from the Brattleboro police, where Gunther had attained the status of grand old man within the law enforcement community. He was, either despite or because of his steady, self-effacing manner, a star.

Jezek didn't deal with VBI much, if ever. He represented drunk drivers, so-called deadbeats, or financial incompetents, mostly people who didn't know enough to get out of their own way. They were of little interest to Gunther and his crowd.

But this time was the exception. Jezek had something to pitch he thought merited the best minds in the business, and they—appearances notwithstanding—mostly resided in this small room.

After taking a swallow of his appallingly accessorized drink, Joe put down his mug and cocked his head slightly, watching his unexpected guest. "I'm guessing you didn't drop by for the tour," he suggested.

Scott matched Joe's gesture with his own mug—without sipping from it. "No. I'm hoping I have something that might interest you."

"Sounds like you're selling a car."

"A homicide, actually," Scott countered. "Dating back almost thirty years."

Joe took him in carefully, at once friendly and analytical, like a veteran horse trader gauging fresh stock.

"Do tell," he said.

Willy Kunkle was in a bar, on the last stool at the far end, leaning slightly against the wall, as if yielding to a combination of alcohol and a long day's troubles. His left arm—withered, limp, and on display in a short-sleeved shirt—was propped before him in full view, its pale, lifeless hand an image of loss and depression.

But he wasn't drunk, nor was he down-and-out. He was on the hunt, alert and poised to move quickly. The arm was real enough, however, acquired years ago on the job via a rifle slug to the shoulder. This made him the only working cop he knew of still fully employed despite being disabled.

That was due exclusively to Joe Gunther, for whom he'd worked most of his career. Willy was the first to admit he wasn't a low-maintenance kind of guy. He was a type A poster child, saddled with PTSD and a past of violence-prone alcohol dependence. To boot, he'd been a combat sniper in his youth, with a kill rate and a reputation only a felon might envy. Gunther had been the one superior in Willy's professional life to see beyond the distractions and recognize an inner core of integrity, compassion, commitment, and drive.

It wasn't a view even Willy agreed with, whose outer show of brusque assertiveness disguised a corrosive self-deprecation. To this day, he remained astonished by Gunther's steady support, the love of his partner, Sammie Martens, and Emma, the preschooler they parented. In a true reflection of his complex nature, Willy, despite such consistent support, remained braced for the day when they'd all tell him they'd had enough.

"You're one complicated guy," Sam had told him once, perfectly contented.

That was serving him well at the moment, sitting at the bar, posing as a social reject in false beard and stained clothes, a half-empty and untouched beer before him. Looking bleary and almost asleep in the midafternoon daylight, which was trying to penetrate the dirty windows bracketing the front door, Willy didn't have to stretch the imagination to sell a convincing portrait. No matter how bad he appeared here and now, he'd been in worse spots in the past. Calling on their memory to sell this image was no effort.

He'd already been waiting three hours for the giant who finally crossed the threshold, briefly allowing the accompanying sunshine to snapshot the establishment's hard-won tawdriness before the door slammed shut behind him.

He was also bearded, but for real, as Willy's informant had described him the night before in a clandestine meeting. Barrel-chested, close-fisted, narrow-eyed, and ready for a fight—whether it was available or not—the new arrival took in the sparsely populated bar like a polar bear eyeing a pod of seals.

But he was watchful, too, as Willy knew he'd be. Even a bear has its enemies, and for this one, that was the police. Gene McCoy was wanted for killing a man, and Willy, true to form, had given himself the task of bringing him in alone—typically against the rules or, for that matter, common sense.

Reassured after his scan of the room, McCoy sat on a stool down from Willy and ordered a drink. He was here to see someone, Willy's CI had passed along, but that person would be a no-show. McCoy had crossed a line with his actions, and word had gotten out—including to Willy, whose listening posts were many and reliable—that the big man's stature within this large but shadowy netherworld would no longer extend him the protection it once had. Life was a hard-eyed exercise in this circle, not unlike in the bear's icy realm, and it paid to respect unwritten protocols of behavior.

By Willy's informant having passed along what he knew, a formal decree had been issued. Gene McCoy was no longer one of us.

The timing here was important. McCoy, Willy knew, wouldn't wait for long, perhaps not even the time it might take him to finish his drink. Willy therefore awkwardly removed a threadbare wallet from his pocket and opened it on the bar, making a show of his clumsiness in extracting a single remaining dollar.

"What'll that buy me?" he asked the bartender, holding it up between quavering fingers.

After barely a glance, the response was, "A glass of water."

Willy pretended to let that sink in, growling "Asshole," as much to himself as anyone listening.

He slipped off his stool, barely keeping his balance, steadied himself against the bar, and then aimed for the distant door—and Gene McCoy sitting halfway along the way.

Not being able to resist, Willy paused just shy of the man, as if seeing him for the first time.

"Hey, buddy . . . ," he began plaintively.

But McCoy wasn't interested. "Fuck off," he said without turning around.

Willy grunted once, but left it there, the wizened veteran of rejection, and resumed his shambling journey, cutting behind McCoy's hulking shape.

The psychology worked. McCoy made an issue of not turning in Willy's direction, allowing the latter to reach into his coat pocket, extract a Taser, and shoot the big man point-blank in the back, launching him face-first onto the floor.

Tasers have been poorly depicted on TV and in movies. They do not knock you unconscious, they do not leave you debilitated for half an hour afterward. They put you on your ass for a few seconds of paralyzing, air-sucking pain, and then you're fine, unless the shooter squeezes the trigger for another jolt. If that doesn't happen, however, you are good to go—with a powerful incentive to get even.

This is where the speedy application of some form of restraint comes highly recommended.

Willy chose that second option. He dropped the Taser to muckle onto the man's wrists and cuff him, in seconds flat and with one hand.

That's in part why he was still employed. He did it with practiced ease.

"Eugene McCoy," he then intoned in a clear voice. "I am the police and you are under arrest."

Joe was still working at his desk when Kunkle walked in, now clean shaven, neatly dressed, and with a spring in his step. For a man who spent as much time as he did in the grubbier sections of most towns, he was oddly fastidious.

"What's your story this time?" Joe asked, watching him cross to his desk, wedged into the far corner like a foxhole. "You just happened to be loitering in a bar in full disguise, drinking beers and toting a Taser, when the one man a four-county dragnet can't find just wandered in?"

Kunkle smiled. "Dumb luck, right?"

"Dumb's the operative word."

"Word travels fast," Willy observed. "I just got back from booking him."

Joe considered keeping it going, but they'd been here before, and had always ended in the same place, with Joe covering for his colleague in some way or another.

It wasn't all pure indulgence on Joe's part, like the doting parent of a spoiled child. There was an element of jealousy, if Joe was to be honest. He recalled being Willy's age when he'd pulled some similar stunts. In simple terms, he missed those days, despite acknowledging their carelessness and folly.

He decided to move on.

"You interested in something a little less headline-grabbing?" he asked.

Willy had settled in by now and placed his crossed feet on top of his desk—a signature pose. "Sure. I gotta ticket a few parked cars?"

Joe was amused by the reference. "Damn, I don't miss those days. Nope, I just had a tale of ancient homicide walk in here a couple of hours ago, in the form of Scott Jezek, Esquire."

"He doesn't do those," Willy said with authority, as well he might, knowing something about the local legal trade.

"He didn't shop for this. He hired Sally Kravitz to find something warm and fuzzy about a four-time drunk driver—to keep him out of jail—and instead discovered the client's brother had just died of a possible beating twenty-eight years ago, when he was a baby."

Willy raised his eyebrows in appreciation. "Far out. Sally Kravitz? Good for her."

That had extra meaning for Willy. Dan Kravitz, Sally's father, had been one of Willy's best informants for years. Dan's peripatetic ways hadn't merely benefited his daughter's social awareness, Willy knew. They had also exposed the twosome to hundreds of people of unusual and unappreciated backgrounds, all of whom liked Dan for his generosity, courtesy, discretion, and helpfulness, and had taken to his offspring as well—which helped explain her choice of profession as a young adult. Both Sally and Dan, if for different reasons and starting from different places, had become "go-to" people when you were in a jam, and the last folks on earth to betray a confidence.

More interesting yet—and only dimly suspected even by Willy—was Dan's alternate life as a data thief. Playfully—arrogantly, in Willy's opinion—the man had once advertised his fondness for high-end illegal home entries by leaving behind Post-it notes saying, *You're it*, earning himself a moniker in the news as "the Tag Man." He'd never stolen objects, however, or vandalized anything or assaulted anyone—all of which had only resulted in the break-ins appearing that much more mysterious and creepy.

But those times were long past—or at least the Post-its were—and no one outside of Sally herself knew the real scope of Dan's current activities—or of the small fortune they had netted him. He'd kept even her in the dark on many of his innermost methods. Willy, in fact, was probably the closest to imagining the truth.

The basis of their cop-informant bond, therefore, was that Willy left Dan to his own devices, in exchange for Dan occasionally making himself available for a useful conversation—as long as it didn't violate his eccentric rules of conduct.

Gunther rose from his desk, walked two yards, and dropped a slim folder beside Willy's outstretched feet. "It ain't much, but it's what we got so far. The purported child abuser is named Daryl Hicks. And here's the catch: Given the source of this, I want to make sure we're not being maneuvered. I like Jezek, but you know what they say, 'Trust, but verify.' Maybe the kid was hit, maybe not; maybe Hicks did the hitting; maybe he didn't. Until you nail down the details independently, I'm not even saying we have a homicide."

Willy leaned in to pick up the file and began leafing through its contents. "Cool."

CHAPTER FOUR

Searching the Weeds

"*Brattleboro Reformer.* Rachel Reiling speaking."

"Hi, Rachel. It's Anne Proctor, from Proctor and Harris? Remember me?"

"Sure." Rachel pulled up her contacts on the screen and rediscovered that Proctor and Harris was a funeral home in Westminster, and thus the source of some biographical tidbits in the past—not that she'd ever actually met Anne Proctor. Theirs had been a phone relationship exclusively.

For Rachel, that was mostly a reflection of Anne's location. Westminster was a township she'd rarely visited or could characterize. Almost fifty square miles in area, located just below Bellows Falls, it had a minimalist town center and only a couple of major roads cutting through it. The rest was trees and fields. There were dozens of such tiny municipalities across the state, remnants of days when a few farmers had clustered together to keep each other company.

Rachel slipped on the demeanor of a long-absent friend. "Anne. How're you? It's been a while."

"Not since the Ferguson funeral," Anne reminded her brightly. "You did such a nice job describing that, and the pictures you took were just beautiful. The family talked about them for weeks after. It was so appreciated."

"Glad to help," Rachel said, glancing at the newsroom clock on the wall, marking a starting point and praying this wouldn't go on too long. As with every reporter she knew, time loomed overhead like a threatening schoolmarm of old, equipped with a willow switch and a short fuse. "What can I do for you?"

"Well, it's kind of along the same lines," her caller explained. "But a lot sadder than the Ferguson story. That's for sure. I mean, that was just an old lady, loved by everybody, whose death was a tragedy, of course, but she was ninety-five. I mean, how long can you live?"

"Right," Rachel agreed, hoping her sigh hadn't been audible.

"So this is a completely different situation," Anne forged on. "And because of that, Henry and I were thinking maybe you'd want to write a human interest story about it. It's got so much sacrifice and generosity to it."

"Could be."

"You ever hear of Peter Rust?" Anne asked her.

Rachel blinked. "Should I have?"

"Well, no. Probably not. Anyway, he's the one who died. Just twenty-eight years old. Isn't that terrible?"

Depends, Rachel thought, before responding, "Absolutely. Was he ill?" She suddenly fantasized about the headstone reading, "I told you I was sick," and pursed her lips not to smile.

"Born that way. I don't know what they call it, but he was in really bad shape his whole life. His mother died, his father walked out. That left his brother, John, to take care of him."

Rachel stopped fiddling with the pen she'd idly picked up. "How long ago was that?" she asked.

"Twenty-two years."

"The brother took care of him that long?" Rachel asked. "On his own?"

"Pretty much. He had a house, but that's what I'm telling you. And you should have seen that poor boy. Only sixty pounds, all curled up, pale as a ghost. But he was beautiful. I mean, you hear of these things all the time, how the sick person gets covered with sores and develops problems and has to wear a diaper. It's heartbreaking. Well, believe me, I looked at Peter all over, top to toe, 'cause that's what we do, including the cremation cases, and even Henry was saying how perfect he was. Not a mark on him. Hair washed, clean shaven, nails neatly clipped. That was all John. He dedicated his whole life to the boy. I just thought you'd find that interesting."

"I do," Rachel admitted, by now entertaining various approaches to the story. "What's up with John now?"

"Well, that's it, isn't it? Can you imagine? All of a sudden, he's got nothing. He never married, never had kids. Peter was his whole world."

Rachel, hardly a veteran newswoman in her mid-twenties, had nevertheless developed what her boss called a bullshit meter. "What're you not telling me, Anne? If I do this, I'll find out anyhow."

Proctor was clearly embarrassed at being caught out so bluntly, not knowing that Rachel came by her candidness genetically. Her mother, Beverly Hillstrom, was the state's medical examiner, and famous in her rarefied world of cops, politicians, and funeral directors for her frankness, impatience, and high standards.

"Oh," Anne said, "was I that obvious? I'm so sorry. I don't want to speak ill of anyone, you know."

Rachel tried to coax her along to the point of her call. "I realize that. I won't tell a soul. We protect our sources. You know that."

"I know, I know. Well, it's nothing horrible. And it never had a bad effect on Peter. But truth be known, John could take a drink now and then. And who can blame him?"

"Not me," Rachel quickly threw in, hoping it might undercut her caller's yearning to say more.

It didn't. "Can you put yourself in his place? Day in and day out? Caring for every little detail, and for someone who can't even say thank you. I have kids, and I tried to give them everything, like a parent naturally does, but there's feedback, you know? They laugh and hug you and give you joy in a hundred different ways, every day. But John? With Peter? Everyone needs to escape a little, now and then."

Rachel decided to pull the parachute cord. "I gotta go, Anne. Give me John's contact information. I'll check this out."

"He lives in Westminster," Anne said. "Just down Route 5 a ways from us." She delivered the street address and phone number.

"Got it," Rachel told her. "And thanks for the tip. Bye."

"Of course. Now, you'll be sure not to let John know that I . . ."

But Rachel had hung up.

Anne Proctor smiled and did the same at her end before replacing her cell phone carefully into her purse. "Was that all right?" she asked. "I hope I didn't overdo it. Henry says I can be a real ham."

Scott Jezek patted her shoulder. "It was Oscar-quality stuff, Anne. Assuming this reporter takes the bait, John'll only benefit. You did good work for a friend and neighbor. Trust me."

To Sally's way of thinking, she should've submitted her final invoice to Jezek by now. But, to his credit—and according to him, at the urging of his client—he was keeping her on. John Rust had been stunned by her discovery, Scott reported, since he'd supposedly been fed the same line as everyone else about Peter's being born handicapped. Now he wanted as many details as Sally could dig up.

"This is still on his tab, correct?" Sally had asked Scott protectively, knowing the lawyer's propensity for impulsive altruism.

"It is," the lawyer had reassured her, which made her again wonder where this money was coming from. Maybe, along with probing for details of Pete's trauma, she'd try taking a peek at a few financials.

First things first, however, which is why she was parked on Route 5, in Westminster village, studying the neat lineup of homes along the street. Laid out on a straight, flat, four-thousand-foot stretch of road—itself an oddity in the well-named Green Mountain State—the village felt a little prefabricated, like an antique Lego town grown to human proportions. What made the impression more remarkable was the place's claim of being the oldest "existing" such town in the entire state, citing a birth date of 1735, forty-two years before Vermont came into being.

Regardless of any debate surrounding this assertion, it did establish Westminster as a very old place, which ran completely at odds with its almost suburban appearance now.

Sally had never made sense of it.

Today, however, its small size and orderliness played to her advantage. Without having to sneak up and down narrow alleys, or among ancient, heavily intertwined buildings, she could at a glance get a feel for how John Rust's home was situated amid his neighbors, and which of them had the best sightlines of the family's daily comings and goings—and perhaps the best insights.

She was, after all, in the business of peering behind the veil of day-to-day life, be it the camouflage of social behavior, or any facts and figures only supporting the appearance of normalcy.

Scott Jezek had hired her to supply an alternate image of his client, who was going to be portrayed by the prosecution as a drunken menace to society. People in John's position normally fell prey to the system's nuts and bolts—the arresting officer's affidavit, the blood alcohol content, the video of the arrest, and usually an overtaxed public defender—unless they had a team like Jezek and Kravitz.

But what if Sally was about to lay bare a man less savory than either

Scott or she had been expecting? Every time she set out on a mission of defense mitigation, that possibility had to be considered.

Pondering this and more, Sally exited her car, took in a deep breath of the spring's awakening warmth, and crossed the road to the house just south of John Rust's home to begin her process.

She'd already conducted some research, dropping by the town offices to discover who lived where in the neighborhood. As a result, she was half expecting the young woman who answered her knock, and inquired, "Yes?"

"Are you Peggy Munroe?" Sally asked, pretending to consult a clipboard she'd brought along as a prop.

"That's me." Munroe had long brown hair, tied back in a ponytail, and was wearing an apron over a work shirt and jeans.

"I'm really sorry to interrupt," Sally said, smiling, pulling a business card from her pocket and handing it over. "Did I catch you in the middle of something?"

Munroe was caught between reading the card and maintaining eye contact. "Not really. Just cleaning. Who are you? I don't want to buy anything. Or find religion."

Sally stuck out a hand. "No, no, no. Sally's my name. I work for a firm that's settling some estate business for John Rust. Do you know John?"

Munroe looked confused and glanced again at the card, which had a name only printed on it, over INVESTIGATOR. "John? Not really. To exchange pleasantries, but that's about it." Her voice lowered sympathetically. "I do know what happened to his poor brother, of course."

Sally was encouraging. "Then you understand why I'm here, to fill out some of the details that come up with these transitions. It's really to help John get to a better place, emotionally and financially. Tough times, as you can guess."

Munroe's reaction was thoughtful. "Yes. I had to explain to the kids what was going on when the funeral home came and took him. Actually, I didn't, really. I kind of lied about that."

Sally dropped her voice slightly. "What did you tell them?"

"I said John was having a piece of furniture moved out. My son Jack asked if it was a sofa—the gurney, you know? So I just went along with it."

Sally touched the woman's hand. "Oh, good Lord. Don't feel bad, Peggy. I think you were really smart. Why do they need to know so much, so soon? Did you ever get to meet Peter?"

Peggy made an apologetic face. "No. I mean, it would've been hard. You know he was in a coma, don't you? Or whatever they call it."

"Well, yes." Sally gestured with the clipboard. "My firm's trying to help John sort out his life after all that, so I knew Peter wasn't well. Still, after so many years . . ."

She let the sentence die suggestively. Sensing the other woman's lingering resistance to invite her in, however, she fell back onto some well-practiced acting skills and suddenly changed her expression to help force the issue. Using a slightly pleading tone, she said, "Peggy, I'm really sorry, and I know it's not professional, but could I use your bathroom—superfast? I totally understand if you don't . . ."

But the door had already swung back on its hinges and Peggy was urging Sally inside, saying, "Of course. Oh, my gosh. Sure. It's just down the hall and to the left. You can't miss it."

Thanking her profusely, Sally took her directions, closed the bathroom door behind her, stood there for a couple of minutes, flushed, ran the tap, and reemerged, still looking contrite.

"I am so sorry," she repeated. "I should have prepared better for the drive, but I was running late."

They were standing by the kitchen, which was separated from the living room by only a barlike counter. Now facing a guest rather than someone at the door with a clipboard, Munroe indicated one of the stools and said jokingly, "Now that you've done that, would you like to refill with some coffee?"

Sally accepted with a smile. So far, so good.

She circled to the living room side of the counter and sat on a stool, surrounded by a scattering of toys and children's clothes decorating the floor and furniture in a comfortably lived-in way.

"How do you take it?" Peggy asked.

"A little milk, if you have it," Sally replied. "How long have you lived here?" she inquired.

Peggy had her back turned as she prepared the cups. "Oh, about eleven years. Brad got a job at the plant above Bellows Falls."

"You like it?"

"Sure. What's to dislike? The shopping's pretty convenient, and across the river, so there's no sales tax, and Keene's not too far away. The only thing I don't like is the way some of the kids drag race down Route 5 at night."

She sat opposite Sally, cups and milk spread out between them.

"Eleven years," Sally mused aloud. "That's a pretty good stretch. What do your neighbors say about the traffic?"

Peggy shrugged. "Oh, what're you going to do? We can't put out speed bumps. The snowplows won't stand for it. It's always something."

"Did John Rust complain, too?" Sally asked. "He strikes me as a quiet sort."

"No," Peggy allowed. "I never saw him at any meetings. Of course, I'm sure he had his hands full."

"I bet. Not only his brother, but the whole homeowner thing. My understanding is that he's not married and has no other siblings, so everything fell to him. That can be a lot."

Peggy looked equivocal, and silently took a sip of her coffee.

Seizing a possible opportunity, Sally filled the gap, again touching Peggy's hand. "I don't want to put you in a spot, but I can tell you're a little uncomfortable. Let me say one thing really clearly, Peggy. Everything I learn is confidential. My boss is a nut about that. But by the same token, I do need to know what there is to know, to avoid any surprises at the end. You hear what I'm saying?"

Her hostess was sympathetic. "Of course. I don't want to get you in trouble. You're just doing your job."

"So what's on your mind?" Sally pressed her.

Peggy made a face before admitting, "It's not anything huge. It's not like we ever suspected he was running drugs out of there or anything. But what you said about the homeowner thing being a lot to handle kind of rang a bell inside here." She tapped the side of her head.

Sally primed her for more. "Really?"

"Brad works hard so I can stay with the kids and give them an old-fashioned upbringing, you know? And he does pretty well. I'm not at all complaining. But living next door to John has been a little weird. He has people in and out all the time. Not funny people. I mean house cleaners and yard maintenance guys and health-care types. And we'd see big TV sets getting moved in, and a fancy van that could handle Peter's chair, and new furniture. He's had the house worked on several times, and either painted or touched up every year, which we sure can't afford. I think John's into something having to do with computers, 'cause there're cardboard boxes at the curb for recycling sometimes, with high-end computer logos on them. But whatever his job was—or still is—it didn't seem to take much of his time, considering how much activity goes on over there. We just never got the feeling that John was ever hurting, if you get what I'm saying."

"I do. The guy was loaded, in other words."

"It sure *looked* that way. There's no crime in that, of course," Peggy stressed. "But the few times we have talked, sort of neighbor-to-neighbor, I never got the feeling he was anything special. He doesn't speak like an educated man, or seem particularly clever."

She suddenly straightened, swinging her ponytail. "Listen to me. That sounds awful."

Sally moved quickly to bring her back. "Not at all. I think it's fascinating, and really insightful. You're a great reader of human nature. So there was a disconnect between how he presented personally and how he lived?"

Peggy's eyes opened in surprise. "Yeah. That's it exactly. It was like if you put me in a formal gown and had me walking around some English garden party. Brad and I used to joke sometimes that John was maybe in the witness protection program, or Peter didn't really exist, but was some life-sized doll John moved around to put on a show."

She shook her head in wonder and stood up, signaling to Sally that it was getting time to leave. "I shouldn't be saying this. The guy probably had some insurance policy that paid for it all, and was just doing his best to make his poor brother as happy as possible. I should've kept my mouth shut. I didn't tell you earlier, probably out of guilt, to be honest, but Brad and I actually attended Peter's service at the funeral home. We just felt we should do something, especially after thinking those terrible things."

Sally rose as well, circling around into the kitchen to give Peggy a two-handed shake. "You did nothing wrong," she soothed her. "There's no malice in having a little fantasy about the neighbor. We all do that. It's not like you called the cops on him. Come on. And, for what it's worth, right now, you've helped me a ton. Some of the hardest things I wrestle with are gaining the kind of psychological insight you just supplied. You've been a huge help."

The embarrassed woman's body language was still suggesting a desire to retreat from what she'd said. For Sally's part, however, her own last statement was the most truthful thing she'd uttered since knocking on Peggy's door.

There was more going on with John Rust than anyone presently knew, and Sally—out of loyalty to Scott Jezek if nothing else—felt a heightened obligation to bring it out.

CHAPTER FIVE

Scott Jezek's Best-Laid Plans

Willy Kunkle's interest in John Rust's background was different from Sally's, but like two golfers playing on parallel fairways, catching glimpses of each other's progress was sure to spark curiosity.

That turned out to be true when Willy dropped by the state police's fancy new barracks in Westminster, to see an old friend, Wes Thibodeau. Wes didn't get out on the road as much as in the early days, which for Willy's sake was a good thing. Instead, the old trooper, happily and forever locked in rank at senior sergeant, had found a comfortable niche within the building that made him the indispensable go-to guy of lore. He knew the people, the procedures, the history, and where to find the paperwork. His was a friendship that Willy had nurtured for years, always acknowledged, never abused, and always found dependable.

Looking as comfortable in his uniform as a cat in its fur, Thibodeau looked up as Willy entered his office, smiled, sat far back in his chair, and linked his hands behind his neck. "William W. Kunkle, scourge of thieves, ne'er-do-wells, abusers of children, and stalkers of old ladies. How the hell are you?"

Willy scowled and took a seat uninvited. "Who wound you up? You just eat somebody's pet canary?"

"Nah," Thibodeau replied. "But I am having a good day. Tangled up some lieutenant from another barracks in his own red tape. I love it when they think the gold on their shoulders makes them smarter than we little people. You texted me you were looking into Daryl Hicks? That's in connection to the John Rust deewee, I bet—Hicks being Rust's old man. John's a popular guy, all of a sudden."

There was that glimpse of the other player in the distance.

"Oh?" Willy asked, feigning ignorance despite Joe's earlier briefing regarding Sally Kravitz. "I didn't mention Rust."

"Rust. Hicks. Makes no difference. All the same family. That lawyer Rust hired—Jezer, or something—"

"Jezek."

"—turned around and hired a private eye I heard was studying the video of Rust's arrest. Guess he's gonna put up a fight. I don't blame him. He's facing serious jail time, the way he's going."

"You catch the name of the private eye?" Willy asked, in part to test his source's capabilities.

Wes hesitated, thinking back, hoping to rise to the challenge. As with many cops from different agencies, there could be some competitiveness stirred into the cooperation, regardless of friendship. "Kravitz, I think."

"I know her," Willy commented, mentally awarding Wes a thumbs-up. He gestured at Thibodeau's desktop with his chin. "You find anything on Hicks that didn't make it into the computer?"

Wes turned to the business at hand. "It was good you gave me a heads-up. Most of his interactions with us were left in old paper files when we put everything online. Too dated; too ancient history. You probably found out yourself that there's nothing about him recently."

"Correct."

"You mind my asking why the interest now?" Wes inquired. "All this predates the existence of the VBI."

"He *may've* assaulted a kid who took twenty-eight years to die of the injury," Willy summarized. "John's little brother. But I don't have proof of it yet."

The sergeant pushed out his lips thoughtfully. "That would do it, *and* it connects the dots. Daryl certainly had the personality for a stunt like that."

"Bad boy?"

"More run-of-the-mill jackass," Wes countered. "I'm warning you, I don't have a lot to work with. But I can confirm that according to how we documented involvements back then, Hicks did have a wife or domestic partner and two kids the last time he came up on our radar."

"Involvements" was police jargon for incidental details, memorialized alongside any criminal charges.

"Names?"

Wes was scanning his paperwork. "John, you know about. The baby's name, I have no clue. It's just listed as 'infant.' The partner's Karen Taylor." He looked up to add, "I ran her name, too, out of curiosity. She was no saint, either, which implies she could also be your bad guy, but she died of an overdose twenty-five years ago."

"When John was sixteen," Willy said half to himself.

"I'll take your word for that. I don't do math. Hicks has a juvie record I can't get into, but his first available appearances have him misbehaving in cars, drinking, disturbing the peace, blah, blah, blah. The kind of kid you'd like to flush, in other words. As he gets older, drugs start coming in, along with some suspected burglaries, con jobs, robberies, assaults."

"What's going on personally?" Willy asked.

Wes riffled through more papers before answering. "Like I said, not much. There's mention of a kid aged eighteen. Karen comes up as his wife later on—says she was two years younger—but I wouldn't necessarily take the spouse label to the bank. Check county records, if it's relevant."

"Where were they living then?"

"Just up the interstate. Springfield. And not the ritzy section. I got some jail time for Daryl, too, by the way. Ag assault with a weapon, probably attempted robbery. Cooled off for a while at state expense."

"When?" Willy asked.

"Got out last time . . . Jeez, again with the math . . . Twenty-nine years ago."

"About right," Willy observed. "Pete was twenty-eight when he died, so born about a year after Daryl's release. There's your happy homecoming."

"Whoopee. Doesn't sound like it did Pete much good."

Willy briefly massaged his temple. "Okay. To that very point, it's right after the birth that Daryl—or somebody, maybe Mom, or even John—supposedly messed up."

Wes didn't argue the point. "Fresh from jail, squalling kid, a twelve-year-old probably not being a saint, and, if any job at all, a lousy one. We've all seen that recipe before."

He paused, holding up a sheet for extra scrutiny.

"What?" Willy asked.

"Nothing, I don't guess. Just unusual. At about the same time, there's a change of address, to Westminster."

Willy checked the file he'd brought along from Joe and recited John Rust's current address. "That it?"

"Same one," Wes said. "Right in the village. Not swank, but way better than the Springfield digs."

Willy made a note to check into Karen Taylor's background. "Maybe she was doing all right while Daryl was banging a tin cup against the bars."

He gave Wes a thoughtful look before asking, "You got anything else?"

His colleague closed the file and slid it over. "Those're copies. You can keep 'em. But that's about it, minus the fine details you can read for yourself."

Willy leaned forward and picked up the file, placing it on his lap to open it. "You include known associates, family, that kind of stuff?"

"What there is of it," Wes confirmed. "But great minds think alike. If you really want to find out what was going on back then, you're going to have to visit a few old folks' homes. I have no clue where Mr. Hicks is now, but he can't be any spring chicken."

Willy glanced up from the paperwork. "Sixty," he said.

"The way most of these guys live, I bet he looks more like eighty, if he's still breathing."

Willy wasn't about to argue.

"Still," Wes continued, "you're doing what I would. Chat up the mopes of yesteryear, reminisce about fighting, fucking, and ripping folks off, and read what you can between the lines. My bet is Karen and Daryl saw themselves as Bonnie and Clyde at some point, surrounded by outlaws who'd be only too happy to talk about old times. Who knows? Maybe you'll actually find a witness to your crime."

"Stranger things have happened," Willy said, rising to leave. "I owe you."

Wes waved at him. "It's on the house. The hard work's ahead of you."

Rachel had driven north to the Rusts' home in Westminster, from Brattleboro, to meet a woman who'd been Peter's secondary caretaker, behind John. What she didn't expect as she pulled to the curb was seeing a tall blonde crossing the road, heading for her own car.

"Sally," she called out, stepping into the street.

Her friend tossed the clipboard she was carrying onto the passenger seat and walked over, smiling. "Rachel Reiling, ace reporter. What're you doing up here?"

The two women met in a hug. Sally Kravitz had first been recommended to Rachel as a source of local contacts by her boss, back when she'd joined the *Brattleboro Reformer* as a fledging photojournalist out of college. However, the two of them, despite very different temperaments—Rachel, outgoing and trusting to Sally's reserved and watchful—had quickly found an unexpected middle ground of mutual trust and instinctive warmth.

Rachel indicated the house beside the one Sally had just left. "I'm here to do a feel-good feature piece, at least I think I am. I got called out of the blue about a handicapped boy who just died after being cared for by his brother his whole life. Supposedly, it's the real deal, and a nice story. It would probably make you want to throw up. How 'bout you? On a case?"

Sally smiled, feeling bad about withholding her true purpose here. There were a few times when she regretted the confidential trappings of her job, and this one was further complicated by her sudden suspicion about who'd stimulated the phone call to Rachel. In Sally's world, there were few real coincidences. But there sure as hell were lawyers who would pull any strings to bring sympathy to their client.

She just wished Jezek had told her.

"You know me," she answered lightly. "Always skulking around on somebody's behalf. You up for a pizza tonight? It's been a while since our last Netflix brain drain."

She moved back toward her car, as if sensitive to the time. Rachel got the hint and waved. "Deal. Eight o'clock?"

"Cool. Good luck with the story."

Rachel watched her get into the car and drive south on Route 5, before ducking into her front seat for her bagged camera equipment and recorder.

• • •

Despite Scott's subterfuge, Sally had to admire his machinations. Rachel's appearance in Westminster was the last in a classic three-part hat trick, consisting of a background check for Sally, a criminal investigation for the VBI, and this public relations piece that he'd orchestrated for Rachel. It wasn't as cynical as it might have seemed. Sally knew that. Scott's efforts to reduce the charges against his client were just one aspect of his job. An additional goal was that with all this stirring of the pot, anything might emerge to catch everyone by surprise.

CHAPTER SIX

Researching John Rust

The door to John Rust's house opened before Rachel touched the bell. The woman framed before her was older, short, compact, and friendly, exuding an aura of competence. "No nonsense" was the caption that flickered in Rachel's mind as she was swept up in the woman's enthusiastic greeting.

"You must be from the paper," she exclaimed, gesturing for Rachel to enter and reaching to unburden her of her bag.

"No, no. That's okay. I got it," Rachel stammered, before introducing herself.

"I'm Martha Wallace Jones," the woman said. "John phoned me that you'd be dropping by."

"He's not here?" Rachel asked, surprised. He'd been the one she spoke to on the phone after being given the number by Anne Proctor.

"No. He apologizes for that," Jones told her. "He got tied up and couldn't get away."

Rachel studied her, trying to read more into the statement. Finding nothing, she settled for forging ahead. This was simply an opportunity to gain insight for now, although into what she didn't know, which was part of the appeal of her job.

"This is such a nice house," she began, removing her camera from the bag. An admitted icebreaker, it was also the truth, reflecting a detail she hadn't been expecting. Somehow her concept of intensive care for an invalid had precluded equal care toward that person's environment—as if one would suck all the energy from even thinking about the other. But here the walls were clean, newly painted, and decorated with artwork, the floors carpeted and immaculate, the furniture fresh as in a showroom.

"Oh yes," Martha explained. "John believed that everything Peter saw should be bright and clean and cheery. That was one of the things he stressed when I was hired. It really surprised me, until I got used to it. He even wanted to know if I was ever moody or downcast. It meant more to him than my nursing skills, I think. He never wanted Pete to be exposed to any anger or ugliness."

They'd been progressing down the hall, Rachel taking in her surroundings, until they reached an unusually wide door to the right, leading into a large room with an elaborate hospital bed in its middle, surrounded by counters, cabinets, comfortable seating, and one of the bigger flat-screen TVs Rachel had ever seen, mounted to the wall.

"Before he got to where it was hard to tell," Martha continued, "Pete loved old movies. He and John would watch them for hours. Not really my thing, to be honest, so John let me watch the soaps sometimes."

"How often were you here?" Rachel asked.

"Five days a week, eight hours a day. The rest of the time was all John. You know, as dependent as Pete was, I couldn't complain. He was always washed and tended to when I got here, in clean clothes, and any decubitus ulcers dressed and dated. John made things so this was one of the easiest jobs I ever had. He was an amazing brother."

Rachel had taken a couple of reference shots already, to use if and when she wrote her article. "Lucky he had the wherewithal to afford it," she said.

"Yes and no," Martha replied. "A lot of this came through state programs and support networks. You should write about that, too. John does have a job, and makes money at it, but he couldn't have done all this on his own." She then added, "But you'd have to ask him for details. That part of the business is lost on me. I just know he used to talk about how he had to be careful to make it all work.

"People think this kind of patient care is tough because of the so-called medical stuff. But that's just half of it. I'd see John sitting at the kitchen counter for hours, working on financial things. It was nonstop. I don't know how he did it."

Or why, Rachel wondered privately, hoping that wasn't callous.

"On the phone, there was reference to a photo album?"

Jones's eyes widened. "Right. Birthday pictures, Pete as a baby, family and party shots. We got a bunch of those."

She crossed to one of the cabinets and pulled out a thick volume, but as she was placing it on the now empty bed, her cell phone rang. She answered it, begged forgiveness, mouthed, "Another job," to Rachel, and stepped out onto the rear deck, beyond the living room, to talk freely.

Rachel seized the opportunity not to flip through the album, but to quickly check out the rest of the house.

It was a rewarding if perfunctory tour, rich in additional insight. From Pete's surgically clean room, she climbed the stairs to what was clearly John's domain—messier, dirtier, neglected, and hosting remnants of fast-food containers and empty liquor bottles. Not an excess of either. It wasn't extreme or alarming. But it certainly told Rachel about a life bifurcated between a mission of mercy and its pent-up costs. Also, regarding the feature article floating in her head, it was indicative of the deeper pathos she was hoping to portray.

She got back downstairs before Martha ended her phone call, and was just opening the album when the nurse entered Pete's room.

"Sorry about that," the older woman apologized. "The assignment I had here was a treat, professionally. John was a saint, and it was steady work for two years. Now it's back to the usual of a few days here and a few days there." She smiled, looking around. "I was spoiled rotten. Now, where were we?"

They began with the photos, with Martha describing the various people pictured. Using the clear light from the window, Rachel took copies with her camera of major events in Pete's life, all of them featuring him looking detached and uninvolved, surrounded by smiling and laughing people. The only one who most often matched Pete's remoteness was John himself, whose expression showed the strain of navigating each day.

There was something else, however, transcending that initial impression, that also caught Rachel's trained eye. In addition to the often fabricated gaiety portrayed in these pictures, she noticed the two brothers exchanging glances, usually surreptitiously, when the photo's center of attention was elsewhere. In those few instances, Rachel saw a real communication, even slight smiles being traded, as Pete seemed to acknowledge and offer thanks for John's efforts. It suggested to her at least a partial answer to her earlier question about John's degree of commitment—Pete was not in fact the virtually inanimate patient people had reduced him to. Up until the end, it seemed, there lay hidden a sentient, expressive, thoughtful young man inside the frail, curled-up, and featherlike body that everyone except John seemed to overlook.

While seemingly ignorant of this one telling subtlety, Martha Jones remained a good guide, lending personalities to the faces they leafed through together. She still lived in Springfield, so, while having worked here for only two years, she nevertheless knew the general gossip, had seen the Rusts in the old neighborhood, and heard many of the rumors attached to them.

"How did Pete end up like he did?" Rachel finally asked, now that the two of them were comporting themselves as old friends. "And why did John take on so much?"

"The first one's easy," Martha told her. "He was born that way. And I told you how they used to live in Springfield, with things pretty rough and Daryl scraping by, so maybe the second question answers itself. I mean, Karen died when the boys were still kids—Pete, four, and John, sixteen or there'bouts. It was hard. Daryl wasn't going to take responsibility. He wasn't the type. Somehow, John just rose to the challenge. That's one reason I admire him so much. He didn't have any more reason than Daryl to make a sacrifice like that. But he did, and as a teenager. You have to admit, pretty incredible."

"Did you know Daryl and Karen personally?" Rachel asked.

"Not well. Just around town. They moved here a few years before Karen died, so there was a bunch of time when I totally lost touch."

"That's the part I still don't get," Rachel said. "If they were down-and-out, with this handicapped child, how were they able to move here? This is a nice house, in a good area. It's kind of surprising."

Martha was nodding throughout. "No argument from me. It was pure coincidence when I was assigned here by the agency, but I was amazed when I found out who the client was. Eventually, John told me there'd been a settlement of some kind after Pete's birth. And then, of course, he began to do well with his at-home website business after he turned eighteen and Daryl moved out. Plus, I mentioned the state assistance and outside support."

"Did John and Daryl have a fight? What happened?"

Martha shrugged in response, but she volunteered, "I think it was John turning eighteen, if you ask me. That's when John could care for Pete legally, all on his own. I always thought Daryl stuck around as long as he did out of some kind of responsibility—despite what I just said about him. Or maybe it was easier staying here than finding a place of his own. Either way, once he could cut out, he did."

"What happened to him?"

"Daryl? I don't know. He just disappeared."

"He and John don't keep in touch?" Rachel asked, adding, "Father and son. Seems sad."

"Well," Martha said philosophically, "you know what they say about not being able to choose your family. If I were John, I'd be thinking I was dealt a pretty poor hand in that department. Daryl was no prize."

Rachel checked her watch, having been here for over an hour. "Is there any chance John might be coming home soon?" she inquired. "It seems a little weird not to interview him as part of this article."

Martha did the same, glancing at a wall clock and tidying up quickly. "Oh my Lord," she said. "I totally lost track. I got to go—that phone call I got earlier. I wouldn't worry much about John. You probably wouldn't've gotten much out of him anyhow. He's real quiet. You can try calling him later, but he might not answer. It's just his way."

She stopped suddenly and stared at Rachel. "Oh. I didn't think. Does that mean you couldn't write about Peter? John not being a part of it?"

Rachel tilted her head to one side. "It'll be odd, like I said. But the story's good enough, and the pictures I copied strong enough, that I might still sell it to my editor. You have to deal with what you're handed, right?"

By this point, Martha was physically escorting Rachel out the door, and said as she locked it behind them, "Right."

They hurriedly exchanged goodbyes, and Martha left Rachel on the stoop, to half run toward her car in the driveway.

Rachel thought about her own parting cliché as she watched Martha drive off, and wondered what exactly she had been handed here.

It was a feel-good story, complete with a poignant ending. That's certainly the way she'd pitch it to Katz.

But there was something else about it. Something elusive and unacknowledged, that made her feel like the only one at a party who doesn't know the host.

Sally knocked on Scott Jezek's office door, having seen his car in the parking lot.

"Come in," he called out.

She stuck her head in only. "This okay? I should've called."

He took his eyes off his computer screen and gestured to her. "No, no. It's fine. Just doing grunt work. What's up?"

Sally settled into his guest chair as she spoke. "I don't want to take too much time. Something came up when I was interviewing John's next-door neighbor. I wondered if you could help me out with it."

"Shoot."

"It goes to finances," Sally continued. "I'm wrestling a little with what I see as a disconnect. John seems pretty well off, but I can't line up what he does for a living with that kind of income. Nice house, well kept, pretty new car, neighbor seeing big TVs going in, expensive renovations. You know anything about that? It's beyond my reach legally to get into his bank accounts without his permission. And I don't want to upset any applecarts. He's your client, after all, and you're mine."

Scott was shaking his head. "Haven't the ghost of a notion, Sally. I'm not his regular attorney. I know Rust because of his previous DUIs, but I don't have any more access to that kind of information than you do. Is it relevant to your research?"

"You asked me to come up with a tearjerker version of John and his late lamented brother. It's gonna be awkward doing that without knowing how the whole thing was financed, or at least enough to keep the state's attorney from surprising us with something we should've known."

"Okay," Jezek agreed. "Good point."

"Could I interview John?"

"Seems reasonable," Scott replied. "I'll ask him. Maybe he'll even give you a look at his finances."

Sally rose. "Cool. Told you it would be brief."

She moved to the door before looking back, one hand on the knob. "Oh, another thing. I ran into Rachel Reiling of the *Reformer*, outside John's house. She said she was chasing down a feature story. Did you feed her that?"

"Indirectly," he admitted.

Sally tapped the side of her nose. "Thought so. Isn't that a little risky, given what we know? Possible homicides and drunk driving aren't a good mix, if you're pitching a warm and cozy story and the DUI is already public record."

Jezek smiled. "There's an angle to everything. If the paper does tumble to the truth, they'll probably reach out to me. I'll suggest how they can have their pathos and a hard news story in the same bite."

She absorbed that before finally opening the door. "You're a devious man, Lawyer Jezek."

"Thank you."

Thinking of how her friend Rachel was being used, however, Sally had not meant the comment as a compliment, even if she did understand the strategy.

At the north end of town, surrounded by unstable piles of books, newspapers, clippings, and who knew what else, Rachel was sitting in the small, cluttered office of her editor, Stanley Katz, an old-school, curmudgeonly throwback to days of typewriters and press rooms, who'd recently been brought out of retirement to keep the newspaper afloat against dire financial reversals. More open to innovation than he admitted, in fact, Katz was trying his best to succeed in a challenging world.

"What've you got?" he asked his youngest, possibly most aggressive reporter, for whom he'd developed a genuine if unspoken soft spot.

Rachel laid a few sample photographs before him. "Call it an obit-slash-feature piece of love and sacrifice. Young man born handicapped; older brother gives him immaculate care till the day he dies at age twenty-eight. This despite mom dying young of an overdose and dad doing a walk-out on the older kid's eighteenth birthday, now twenty-two years ago."

Katz's first response was practical. "Where?"

"The ending occurred in Westminster, where they moved about twenty-six years ago. Before then, it was Springfield, outside our circulation, technically speaking."

With the practiced eye for a good story, Rachel's boss scanned the fanned-out pictures. "That's all right," he growled before looking up and asking, "Name?"

"Rust," she replied. "John's the older." She pointed him out. "Peter's the recently deceased. You can see how he interacted to a certain extent in the early years, before essentially becoming comatose. The woman in the pictures is Martha Jones, who helped out with the younger brother's care."

"John Rust?" Katz repeated. He swiveled in his chair toward the computer, which was almost inaccessible due to the clutter. He quickly brought up a recent online edition of their own paper. "Thought so," he said, twisting the monitor around so she could see it at an angle. "When did the kid die?"

She gave him the date, squinting at the screen.

"John got nailed for a DUI that same night," Katz reported. "I thought it rang a bell."

Rachel straightened, astonished by his memory, as well as by the revelation itself. "I didn't know," she said, thoroughly embarrassed by this rookie oversight.

"You were out doing your job," he said brusquely. "Not hanging around the office, reading. I don't think it does us any harm. Not if we do our homework, acknowledge the fact, and even use it. Adds to the sadness, if you ask me, and to the irony—free at last, the poor bastard's thinking, just before he gets busted."

He pawed through the prints again, on the hunt. "I don't see a recent picture of the older brother here. Just the woman caregiver."

"Jones."

"Whatever. Where's John?"

"He couldn't make it," Rachel reported. "He was supposed to be there, but she said he got hung up with something."

Katz gathered up her prints and returned them. "Get on that last part. Find out where he stands in the legal system, put an interview into him, and write me a rough draft. Nice work."

As she reached the door, he asked, "How'd you hear about it?"

"Funeral home woman called me. She was a friend of the family."

Stan Katz's eyes had already strayed back to his screen. "Okay, Rachel, write like a Pulitzer was hanging in the balance. And find the brother."

CHAPTER SEVEN

The Deeper One Digs, the Darker Things Get

"You knew Daryl Hicks," Willy stated.

"There's a claim to fame. You askin' or tellin'?"

Willy placed the red rubber ketchup bottle before the man opposite him as the latter peeled open his burger and stared balefully at what lay inside.

"You just answered your own question, Norm."

Norman Lane applied the ketchup and dropped the top bun back in place, smiling. "Guess I did."

They were seated at a fast-food restaurant on Washington Street in Claremont, New Hampshire, fifteen miles across the river from Springfield, Vermont—safe turf, as far as Lane might be concerned. Willy had pulled Norm's name from the list of known Hicks associates that Wes Thibodeau had given him, in part because he knew Lane, if not well. Willy collected people with criminal records like a good lepidopterist does butterflies. Not all were true prizewinners, but many kept the company of the rarities that were.

"So?" Willy pressed him.

Norm reached out carefully with both hands, took hold of the burger, and brandished it like a small pet. "This is not a French meal with all the fixin's, Detective. A burger'll buy you only so much."

Lane was older, gray-haired, and not recently shaved, dressed in clothes overdue for a wash and spin. But he was slim, relatively fit, and seemed to have spared his brains most of the readily available batterings of drugs and alcohol.

"I haven't gotten anything yet," Willy pointed out.

Norm took a bite and chewed for a while before swallowing and conceding, "Granted."

He lifted his pebbled red plastic glass of root beer and drank through the straw. Willy waited patiently, allowing Norm to establish the etiquette common to these kinds of conversations.

Willy presumed he'd passed at least the first mile marker when Norm wiped his mouth and stated, "Daryl and I used to hang out some."

"Still?"

"Nah. Not in a long time. We weren't buddy-buddy; just traveled in the same circles."

"You know where he is now?"

"I know he's not dead or moved to Utah," Norm conceded. "Beyond that . . ." He left the sentence unfinished to take another stab at his burger.

"Tell me about him," Willy requested after Lane had finished chewing. "He and I never crossed paths."

"You didn't miss much. He was a few chunks shy of a cord, if you ask me. Good guy for taking punches, or handing them out if his target wasn't too fast. Otherwise . . . I don't know. Not much to say."

"How 'bout his personal life? Wife? Kids? You ever know them?"

Lane surprised him by smiling softly, as if suddenly dipped into warm memories. "Karen. There was a wife. I could never figure what she saw in him. First time I saw her, I stopped dead in my tracks. She was a fox. More than that. She had these eyes. There wasn't a man I knew who didn't think she was hot beyond belief. Incredible woman."

"You're using the past tense," Willy said, playing dumb.

Norm returned to his soda for a long pull. He wiped his mouth and answered, "So's she. OD'd years ago. Big waste."

"You knew her well?"

The other man smiled. "Not well enough, not that it wasn't possible. Maybe it was just me, but I figured she'd be open to the right guy if he asked."

"And you knew such a guy?"

But Norm wouldn't go that far. "I'm just sayin'. Probably wishful thinking. Her being with Daryl was a crime against nature. I woulda hoped better for her."

"How did they get along?"

"Get along? How does any man get along with his wife?" Lane then paused to actually consider the question, and continued, "He had a temper, and he'd stomp around some, but if you ask me, if it came down to who really wore the pants in the family, my money was on her. Being a druggie didn't do her any favors, though, so it depended on the day who was the alpha dog."

"They both work?" Willy asked.

By now, the two of them had settled into an easy rhythm of give-and-take, with Lane less reserved about airing his reminiscences.

"Oh, you know the Daryl type," he said. "A bottom-feeder on his best day. He would get day jobs now and then, keeping an eye out for something to steal. Karen was more enterprising, but her bad habits would trip her up. Either she'd have to cop to having a past record when she was applying, or if she got a job anyhow, she might fuck it up by drinking or doing dope and getting fired. Still, I remember walking in on her when she was running the checkout counter at a grocery store, and you wouldn't believe the energy she put into it. Damn. She was like on speed, you know? Fingers flying on the cash register, putting stuff in the bags faster'n you could see. I figured some people were standing in her line just to see her work, but I'm probably making that part up."

Willy didn't respond, but apparently his expression betrayed his doubts, because Norm then emphasized, while reaching for the last of his burger, "It's not what you're thinking. Not a single screwup. She never hit the wrong button, never dropped a tomato, nothin'. It was like watching a machine. Perfect. *And* she made small talk with the customers. They loved it."

"But she didn't last," Willy suggested.

His lunch guest responded through a full mouth. "Nah, never . . ." He swallowed, adding, "I thought it was because she got bored too fast, like her brain always moved as quick as it did at the grocery. She didn't have the patience to act like the rest of us. That's probably what killed her, in the long run."

"She had kids," Willy reminded him.

Lane frowned. "Yeah. Two boys. That didn't turn out too good, either."

Again, Willy feigned ignorance. "How so?"

"First one was fine, if you like 'em to begin with, which I don't. But the second was born retarded. I don't know what it was—mom's drug habits trickling down, her age, maybe, not that she was really old. Coulda been just the way they lived. Who knows why this shit happens? Anyhow, wasn't long after that Karen OD'd. I always figured the kid turning out the way he did had something to do with it. Total waste, like I said."

"How did Daryl deal with her death? Must've been even tougher with the child being handicapped."

"He didn't," Norm said simply.

"Meaning?"

"The older boy took over. Daryl just sponged off him till he finally left for parts unknown."

"You said he wasn't dead or moved to Utah. How do you know?"

"I guess I don't, really. But you get a feeling when somebody's died, you know what I'm sayin'? It's like they leave something behind."

"Even Daryl?"

Norm smiled. "Good point. Well, then there you have it. He's probably dead and nobody cares."

Willy let that pass. "How did Daryl sponge off a kid who's just been saddled with a handicapped little brother?"

"I don't know the details," Norm said. "But that's the way it was for a couple of years after Karen died. I always figured there was an insurance payoff, or a government-assistance thing that kicked in for the little guy, because right after he was born, they got out of the dump they had here and moved to a house in Westminster. They weren't rolling in it, but they were doing better than before. A couple of years later, she dies, and about two years after that, Daryl splits. Then it's just the two boys, 'cept the older one was probably eighteen or older, since the state people didn't come knocking to collect the messed-up one, like they do when there's no adult."

There it was again, Willy thought. The party line. Or something murkier and more subversive.

Or not.

"Let me ask you, Norm. It's a little off-the-wall. This thing with the baby—I mean how he ended up. Are you sure that was a birth defect?"

Lane studied him. "You saying somebody made him that way?"

"I'm asking what you know for a fact."

The other man didn't respond.

Willy tried another approach. "You got a family with an ambitious, restless woman who had her first kid when she was a teenager; a father fresh out of prison who plays second fiddle to his wife; and the older boy, who's now probably resentful of the newborn competition. Introduce a baby who's maybe colicky at night, a drain on family finances, and has no hopes for the future, and you've got a scenario where the baby becoming a vegetable maybe wasn't so natural after all."

Lane looked at him sourly. "Man, I thought I was a hard-ass. You are one dark guy, Kunkle."

"Am I wrong?" Willy challenged him.

"I don't know," Lane replied. "What I knew of Karen, you can count her out. Daryl and the older kid? Could be that's why she overdosed, 'cause she knew one of them had done what you're sayin'. But I don't see her as the doer."

Willy watched Norm's features, seeing the blind prejudice stamped there by some long-gone heartthrob, and he moved on. "So Daryl sticks around a few years after the birth," he picked up from earlier, "and a couple more after Karen dies. My question is, why?"

Norm drained his soda before holding both palms up, his tone impatient. "Don't know, don't care. You're talking about people nobody gives a damn about, Detective." He leaned toward Willy slightly for emphasis and added, "You got lucky with me. I don't know how, but you found a guy who knew 'em both, Daryl and Karen." He pointed out the window. "I almost guarantee you, I could be one of half a dozen. Everybody else? They'd have no clue. I was still hanging with Daryl when Karen OD'd. That's the only reason I know what I know, irregardless of your half-cocked ideas. You think there was even an obit for Karen? That's what everyone thinks. You die, they write about you. Not true. The Daryls and Karens of the world? Me, too, for that matter? Nobody gives a rat's ass. People like us die, and it's 'What's the weather gonna be tomorrow?' And now you come pokin' around, long after you can do any good, and start smearing what reputation any of them might've had. Goddamned disgrace."

He paused abruptly, his face flushed by that outburst, and then pushed himself upright, tapping his chest and finishing with, "I'm Karen's obit, her walkin', talkin' gravestone, 'cause I promise you, you won't find one of those, either. A mother, a wife, a fine-lookin', decent woman who lit up the room. I'm all she's got to talk about her."

He stopped, breathing hard, suddenly looking embarrassed, stared at Willy and the remains of his meal, muttered, "Thanks for lunch," and walked out of the restaurant.

Sally Kravitz handed her friend the half-empty pint of Ben and Jerry's Cherry Garcia. Rachel, her spoon still in hand from her last bite, accepted it with an appreciative, "Hmmmmm," before carving out another portion.

They were in Sally's apartment, late at night, usually the only time they got to see each other. Sally had recently moved into the completely refurbished Brooks House building, in downtown Brattleboro, only a block or so from Rachel's older, more run-down place. Brooks House, a nineteenth-century, redbrick former hotel that once anchored the center of town with both its architecture and importance, had been gutted by fire a few years ago. A group of investors, deemed lunatics by most thoughtful local capitalists, had poured millions into restoring the building, and had actually pulled it off, filling it with apartment dwellers like Sally on the top floors, and a community college, several restaurants, and some businesses lower down. It had once more become a functional, contributing landmark, against serious odds. Sally, however, mostly liked it because, while from the outside it appeared blessed by antiquity, its inner trappings were all new, modern, and clean.

"Did you get what you were after in Westminster?" Sally asked casually, referring indirectly to their accidental encounter outside the Rust home.

Rachel expressed delight as she finished her mouthful. "I *knew* it," she stated. "You were there for the same reason I was. Admit it."

Sally hesitated, pretending to concentrate on taking back the ice cream and not dropping it on the couch between them. Their personalities weren't the only things that made them an odd couple. Rachel's upbringing couldn't have differed more from Sally's, either. Born outside Burlington of successful, accomplished, prominent—if now divorced—parents, Rachel had followed a conventional path that should have stamped her with a blandness approaching invisibility. But whether influenced by those parents—lawyer father, doctor mother—or her own powerfully independent and open-minded intellect, Rachel was anything but bland. In part, this may have been helped by Joe Gunther, her mother's romantic partner for years by now, who had put her budding photographic talents to use on a criminal case or two, despite her youth, and thus fired up her ambitions. But Rachel had also independently suffered a few traumatic experiences. Twice, she'd seen people killed in her presence, one a charming and hapless young woman on the run whom she'd taken in briefly as a roommate while still in college.

These rites of passage—exceeding what many a veteran cop could claim—had tempered her beyond her years, and imbued her with a maturity that Sally found admirable and, more meaningful still in Sally's eyes, reliable.

Nevertheless, Rachel tumbling so quickly to their mutual interest in John Rust echoed what Sally had asked Jezek. How best to thread the needle between portraying John as a vulnerable drunk with a heart of gold, against his family background of criminality and child abuse?

She decided to honor their trust over competing professions. This despite the fact that Sally's job was largely to extract selective facts, while Rachel's was supposed to be less discriminating, exposing everything she found to potentially harsh public scrutiny.

"Truth?" Sally therefore asked.

Rachel's smile faded a little as she read into her friend's expression. "Uh-oh. Here it comes. What've I stepped into?"

Sally didn't bother with how Rachel had been told about John in the first place. Jezek's cynical manipulativeness didn't need airing here. But she was going to be more honest with Rachel—despite her job—than she might have been with anyone else.

"I'm working for John Rust's attorney, trying to mitigate the DUI against him. When we bumped into each other, I'd just interviewed the woman next door about what kind of neighbor he was. That's why I was curious about what you found out."

Rachel looked thoughtful. "I heard about the drunk driving charge from my boss a few hours ago, and saw some dead bottles upstairs in John's part of the house. He got stopped the same day Peter died, didn't he?"

"Yes," Sally said, happy to no longer be so covert about her assignment.

"That explains a lot," Rachel followed up. "The house itself was almost bipolar. The downstairs all neat and pristine as a clinic, and the upstairs like a college kid's dorm room. I wondered about the emotional cost of all that devotion and care. The woman I was interviewing was Pete's caretaker, and she showed me a family album. I know those things rarely reflect reality, but John, especially, put his all into making his brother comfortable, and weirdly, I think Pete appreciated it. I could see it in how they looked at each other."

"You still have the album?" Sally asked.

Rachel got up and crossed the room to the front door, where she'd left her equipment bag. "I took shots of it. They're still uploaded."

She brought the camera to the couch, turned it on, and began showing Sally what she'd copied, identifying some of the faces. "I have no clue what you already know," she said, "but there's Pete . . . John as a young man . . . His mom—"

"Damn," Sally interrupted. "She's really striking."

"Yeah . . . And there's the dad—Daryl Hicks. That's a Beauty and the Beast matchup, if there ever was one."

"No lie," Sally agreed softly, scrutinizing the small pictures on the camera's screen as they scrolled past. "Who was the caretaker?"

"Martha Jones. That was a piece of luck for me. She worked for John only the last two years, long after Karen and Daryl were out of the picture, but it turns out she knew them from the old days in Springfield, at least enough to say hi."

"What did she say about them?"

Rachel glanced at the ceiling briefly to remember. "Nothing too exciting. They were down and out, scraping bottom, like so many others. We didn't get into details. She had to leave for a meeting or something. She was only there because John called and asked her to meet me."

"Did you talk about their finances?" Sally asked, very interested in the answer.

"We did. It's such a disconnect. In a way, it sounded like the only good news attached to all this. From what Martha told me, the state came to the rescue, along with some outside help, and John's at-home business. She also mentioned a possible settlement of some kind, but again, no details. I think that last part was just a guess."

Finished with the camera, Rachel placed it on the coffee table before them and crossed her legs. "If I were writing a different kind of article," she resumed, "I'd spend more time poking into that. It's not like I smell a scam exactly, but the whole downstairs of that house—even the house itself—sure looked better than you'd expect with that backstory."

She looked at Sally and tilted her head questioningly. "I mean, I believe John did what he did. There doesn't seem to be any doubt about how much he cared for Pete and the sacrifices he made. But I don't know . . . There is something missing."

"Including John," Sally commented. "Have you ever met him?"

"No. And I asked about his no-show," Rachel said, her interest matching Sally's. "He was *supposed* to be there. That was the deal when I set up the interview. But Martha said something came up."

Sally was caught on the horns of a dilemma. If she'd been a good pal only, knowing what she did, she would have confessed what she knew about Daryl's suspected role in Pete's condition. Her knowledge, however, had been gained while working for a client, and was wrapped in confidentiality. She had to keep it to herself.

On the other hand, Rachel was her best friend, in some ways a kindred spirit, and she was torn about withholding such a crucial fact, given Rachel's own professional obligations.

She tried steering for a passage through her dilemma. "That complicates things," she stated. "You can't write a feature about one brother caring for the other without even meeting him."

"Yeah," Rachel conceded. "That's what Stan Katz said. I've been leaving messages, but so far, John's been in the wind."

"I know what you mean," Sally agreed, taking another spoonful of ice cream, adding, for comfort's sake, "Still, you probably want to do some more background checking anyhow, just in case John isn't as straight up as you'd like when you meet him."

She knew she was taking a risk, but Rachel's comment had implied there remained some breathing room on the story's deadline—or even its being completed. Selfishly, Sally thought, news of Pete's true cause of death would leak out in the meantime, and get her out of her tight corner.

CHAPTER EIGHT

The Power of Institutional Memory

Willy was still in Springfield, having spent a good part of the night combing through ancient paper files in the local police department's basement—box after box of old "calls for service," as official outings by cops were referred to, especially in the days before computers and 911.

Following his interview of Norman Lane in Claremont, and fueled by the ambiguity surrounding how young Peter Rust had met his fate, Willy had decided to dive literally back in time and consult whatever historical paperwork still existed.

His first stop had been simple enough. The town records had yielded an address for Karen Taylor and family, dated thirty years ago.

His next move had been more onerous. Armed only with the last names, Rust and Hicks, along with that old address, he had set out to locate any official responses during the same time of little Peter's first six months of life.

It was an unlikely shot in the dark, reflective of Kunkle's obsessive drive. Hicks had vanished, John was proving elusive, and Karen and Peter were dead. As inspiring as the talk with Lane had been, it had told Willy that he had to do more than merely interview old acquaintances.

He needed a paper trail—a chain of evidence—if he was to satisfy Joe's assignment and Willy's own curiosity. Cops are trained to exceed simply asking about the past. The likes of Sally Kravitz can do that, to meet their clients' needs. The Willy Kunkles have to credibly document their efforts, to the point where some prosecutor can eventually carry their case to court, and expose it to the scrutiny of the legal system.

He got lucky at about three in the morning, and now, five hours later, he was sitting in his car, at the end of a dirt road, in front of a small, neat, well-maintained, remodeled hunting cabin northwest of Springfield, in a sparsely populated area of low mountains and woodland. It was the kind of setting that Vermont's tourism bureau seeks out for its postcards, far from Willy's usual haunts of trailer parks, urban back streets, and foul-smelling bars.

Looking around, he could see the appeal.

He was preparing to cross the road and knock on the door, thereby closing the circle on his marathon research, but first, he had something more important to do—a recent daily obligation that he'd come to credit as a major source in his improving mental health.

He pulled out his cell phone and hit the speed dial.

Sammie answered the call. "Hey there, stranger. Burning the midnight oil?"

"And how. Didn't want to miss the boss before she heads out to work."

Sam laughed. "Perfect timing. I'll put her on."

There was some noise in the background, informing Willy that he'd caught them in the kitchen. Moments later, after some prompting by her mother, a small, high voice came on the line.

"Daddy?"

"Hey, daughter. You having a good breakfast?"

"*Waffles*," was the shouted response.

"Holy smokes. I wish I was there. But since I'm not, I wanted to wish you good morning."

"Where are you, Daddy?"

"I'm about to have a talk with a man. Do you know what you're going to do in preschool today?"

"*Field trip*," she exclaimed again.

"That'll be fun," he replied. "Do you know where?"

There was a thoughtful pause, during which he could faintly make out, "nature museum" in the background.

"Nature muzem," came the answer.

"Far out. Well, I gotta go, and so do you. I love you a bunch and I hope you have a terrific day."

"You, too, Daddy. Love you."

"Love you, too," he answered, but he'd already recognized the phone being dropped on a tabletop.

"You good?" Sammie asked seconds later.

"Not as good as if I were there," he told her.

"Take care of yourself," she ordered him. "Precious cargo."

"You, too."

With that gentle hitting of his emotional reset button completed, Willy swung out into the early-morning coolness, casting a glance down the miles-long valley to his right, now clotted with morning fog as dense as a captured cloud.

"Like what you see?" a voice called out from the front porch of the cabin.

An older man was standing there, cane in hand and a benign smile on his face. Arnold Griswold, retired Springfield police, who now lived here year-round with his wife, Charlotte, according to the dispatcher who'd given Willy directions before dawn.

"I do," Willy replied, crossing the dew-dampened and slowly greening yard to the steps leading up. The place did indeed have it all—a wall of trees as a backdrop, a burbling stream running alongside the property, and that long, open view across the road.

"I'm sorry to barge in on your peace and quiet," he said as he approached. "I'm Special Agent Kunkle, from the VBI."

"Oh, I know who you are," Griswold said with another smile, gesturing to Willy to join him on the porch. "Not too many people carrying a badge who look like you."

It wasn't the subtlest reference to Willy's limp left arm, but it was said in such an accepting fashion that no offense could have reasonably been taken—not that Willy was inclined to be thin-skinned in any case.

"Yeah," he therefore responded in kind. "A little hard to miss, which can be good news or bad, depending. It *can* be the ultimate undercover disguise."

"I bet," the man said, shaking hands and introducing himself, "Arnie Griswold, which I figure you already know."

"I do. Call me Willy."

Griswold turned slightly and called out over his shoulder, "Charlie. We have a guest. Fair warning."

He then nimbly stepped aside and indicated the open door with his cane, explaining, "My wife. You first. We have coffee on, if you got the habit."

"I do, thanks."

They entered a spacious, log-lined room with a trestle table on one side and a sofa on the other, positioned before an open fireplace. There was a loft overhead and a hallway to the back, which presumably led to a bathroom and some storage space. It wasn't large, by any means, but seemed so from its open concept and cathedral ceiling.

As Willy was looking around, a woman appeared at the upper railing above him and said, "Hello. Welcome."

"Hey," he replied briefly.

"I'll be right down."

Griswold in the meantime had pulled out a chair at the table for him, and now went to pouring a mug of coffee, asking, "You take anything with it?"

"No, thanks," Willy replied, sitting down.

The woman from overhead reappeared from the back. "Hi, again," she said, holding out her hand. "I'm Charlotte Griswold. Charlie for short."

"Willy Kunkle," he said. "I'm just here to pester your husband about an old case. Sorry to barge in."

"No, no, no," she protested. "Happy for the company. Not many people drop by. Would you like something to eat, along with your coffee? I have pound cake in the fridge. Or maybe you'd like breakfast."

"No thanks," he said. "All set."

The niceties concluded, Charlie took them both in, as her husband settled into another chair, and announced, "Well, you two have fun reliving the past. I'm going outside to patrol the perimeter and see if anything's showing in the garden yet."

She mussed Arnie's hair as she walked past him, collected a canvas bag of tools and seed packages at the door, and left.

"She does love that garden," he commented. "I prefer working in the woods myself."

"Sounds like retirement's working out for you," Willy said, taking a sip of his coffee and wondering, given his phone call of minutes earlier, whether he and Sam would ever enjoy something like this. It wasn't in his nature to think happy thoughts, so the notion caught him off guard, like an unexpected flashbulb in his otherwise dark and suspicious mind.

"It is," Griswold admitted. "I missed the action at first, but not anymore." He pointed at the TV set in the far corner. "What we see on that thing every night convinces me I left at the right time."

Willy balanced maintaining this pace for a while longer, exchanging platitudes, versus getting to what he was after. If pressed, he could certainly do the former. But it didn't come naturally, and the good coffee notwithstanding, he was already looking forward to getting back on the road.

"So, Arnie," he therefore began, "I was hoping you could go back in time a little and tell me about something I'm looking into."

Griswold gave him a steady gaze and asked, "Is that your way of telling me I'm fucked?"

Willy smiled at the response, so at odds with their setting, and studied his host in a different light.

"I don't know," he answered honestly. "I'm going to have to rely on your memory, and then your integrity, to answer that. Maybe you'll get lucky, and find out I'm here for something besides what's eating at your conscience."

Griswold's poker face didn't change. He blinked once, slowly, before saying, "Okay. Ask."

"Twenty-eight years ago," Willy said, extracting a slip of paper from his inner pocket and laying it on the table, "you responded to a call for service. A child had phoned it in, saying he'd just witnessed a fight, and that his baby brother had been injured."

Willy slid the call entry sheet across the table to where Griswold could read it. This the older man did, although without actually touching it, as if it might be hot.

Cops throughout their careers will respond to tens of thousands of calls before they're done, especially if they have stayed in patrol work, as had Arnold Griswold. It was hoping beyond reason that such a veteran could reach back almost three decades to recall something as mundane as a domestic complaint that had resulted in no formal charges.

And yet, Arnie responded without hesitation. "Little Peter Rust."

Instantly interpreting why Griswold's recall had been so fast, Willy controlled his emotions, saying, "Tell me about it." But inside, he was roiling. Confusion, anger, frustration, all assaulted him simultaneously, as a cop and father both. It took extraordinary effort to simply sit and wait for Arnie to explain.

"It's eaten at me ever since," he began, addressing not Willy, but some middle distance between them. "I knew in my bones that something had gone wrong, even as a rookie. It was a low-profile call. The kid was calm on the phone, Dispatch told me no alarms went off in her head. I thought it might be a dead end, like so many of them are. Also, in those days—not to sound like a fogey—nobody cared much about domestics. Not like they do today. Now, it's almost set in stone that you have to cuff and stuff somebody, regardless of how crazy it might feel. Back then? There was a ton more leeway."

"You blew it off?" Willy asked neutrally, still in check.

"No," Arnie replied, finally reaching out and barely touching the call slip, now a talisman of past guilt. "I went there, met the family, divided them up like you're supposed to, put the interviews in. I did it by the book."

"Tell me," Willy said, his initial outrage settling down.

"Well," Arnie sighed. "That was the start of it—that gnawing feeling that never let me go. Karen Taylor, Daryl Hicks, John and the baby, they all seemed okay on the face of it. I'd already come to expect that with the parents in these cases. The doer always lies, the spouse always backs them up out of fear or misguided loyalty. It was John I spent the most time with, trying to get him to open up. He'd made the call, after all. He had to be my best chance to get inside this story." Arnie sighed heavily at the memory. "But he wouldn't come through. He said it was a mistake, that his dad had just been yelling, and had hit a door, which had made the baby cry. Same story as what the adults had told me. Rehearsed and memorized. I knew it was. But I had nothing to go on."

"What about the baby?" Willy asked. "Did you examine him?"

Arnie's voice was sorrowful. "Yeah, but what can you tell, if there's no blood or a bruise? Peter was flushed, but that was explained by the crying. I tried to see where it might've been a slap, but there just wasn't anything there."

"How did he seem when you were looking at him?"

"Asleep by then. Karen said he was a really sound sleeper, especially after a crying fit. I lifted up his shirt, checked under his diaper. Charlie and I had a baby in those days, too, so I knew the drill. I didn't cut corners, Agent Kunkle. But I found nothing. No marks, no sores, not even diaper rash that might've told me he'd been neglected. I spent an hour and a half in that house—way beyond normal. Dispatch radioed me twice, to ask if I was okay, and the sergeant later told me not to take so long again."

Willy was now in a completely different mood, interested as much by the man before him as the tale he was telling. "Arnie, if there was nothing to it, why do you remember it so well?"

"You've been at this a long time, too," Griswold replied. "I know you have. How many times have you closed a case, knowing there was more to be done? Maybe it wasn't all that important. Maybe you knew the right people had gone to jail, or whatever, but still, there were unanswered questions. How many times?"

"A lot," Willy conceded. "This sounds like more than that."

"It was. I did forget about it for a while. A few months, even, and then I heard through the grapevine that Peter was known to be delayed. Completely disabled. That really bugged me. I couldn't get it out of my head. I know the kid was asleep when I checked him out, and that there'd never been complaints from that address before or after. But still, it was enough that I went back there one day, making sure Hicks's truck wasn't parked out front, and I asked Karen privately if Pete had been born the way he had been. Stone-faced, she said he was."

"Did any of them call Pete's condition a birth defect the first time you were there?" Willy asked.

Arnie grew excited as he stressed, "*No*. That's the biggest thing. Why didn't they? I'm spending all this time, talking to them, looking at the baby, asking questions. You'd think one of them would say, 'Oh, by the way, he's handicapped.' But it never happened. Only afterward did they close ranks around this story."

"Did you ever contact a family doc or anything?" Willy asked. "Just for the hell of it?"

"I tried. Karen said there was no such animal, and I wasn't in a position to push. For what it's worth, I did visit the next-door neighbor on another occasion. They'd told me she was Pete's usual babysitter, and I asked her the same question. That was the only thin crack in this whole mess, and the reason I've never been able to get it out of my mind."

"What did she say?"

Arnie straightened and slapped his hand on the table softly for emphasis. "That Pete was a perfectly normal little baby, until the night John called for help."

"But you couldn't do anything with that," Willy suggested.

"Not a thing. The woman left within a year, who knows where, and I had nothing. Not that I had much even if she *had* stuck around. Pete was a newborn, she wasn't a doctor, she only cared for him a couple of times. Anyone could've and would've shredded her story in three minutes."

A silence fell between them then, as each man contemplated Arnie's tale. A clock over the mantelpiece, unheeded until now, made a ticking sound that felt like it was filling the room.

"Why are you here?" Arnie then asked. "Something must've happened."

Normally, that wasn't a question Willy would answer. But this was a special situation, and much of this had already been released to the papers, although without fanfare. Willy wasn't going to begrudge the poor man just because of some standard protocol.

"Pete died," he said simply.

Arnie absorbed that before saying, "Ah." He looked down at his hands, clasped before him on the table, and asked, "Because of having been beaten?"

"We think so. Something like that."

Arnie suddenly looked as old as he had to be, which his speaking style and movements—even with a cane—had belied until now.

He sighed again and said, "Damn. I'm glad I don't do what you do anymore. I don't think I could take it."

Willy stood up, to leave the guy alone with his newfound mourning, but had to say nevertheless, "Arnie, given what you've just told me, we're gonna have to call on you again, get all this sworn to."

"I know." Griswold looked up at him, his face etched with sadness. "Not a problem. Least I can do."

Willy walked out onto the porch and descended the steps, giving Charlie a wave from afar, as she stood in her nascent garden. He remembered Arnie's fatalistic reaction to the start of his questioning, but even now, he doubted that the call to Pete Rust's house had been the sole cause of it. That's not to say the man's pain concerning Pete wasn't real, along with his sense of guilt. But Willy knew in his bones Arnie had other, unrelated ghosts in his past—the extent of which he took as a given.

Willy shook his head slightly as he reached his car, the view now ignored. What veteran cop couldn't lay the same claim, reaching back over decades of service? Those thousands of calls, of snap judgments and choices. Was there a single retiree that wasn't haunted by a few doubts, and others who lay awake at night, still fearful of being caught in a long-dormant lie?

God knows Willy had a closetful of such secrets. So here and now, Arnie's remorse trailing behind him, Willy wasn't about to sit in judgment for any sins he hadn't come looking for. He would carry the story of Pete Rust forward, and leave Arnie to guard his own troubled soul.

Sally recognized the outline of the man from the end of the long hallway, leaning casually against the wall opposite the front door to her apartment. She wasn't sure she liked Willy Kunkle, despite his friendship with her father. She found him cynical, uncaring, perhaps even unethical. Her father, Dan, had warned her that he was far more complex than that, and actually hid behind those unpleasant traits more than he embraced them. To Sally's mind, if that was true, then he did one hell of a convincing job.

"Mr. Kunkle," she greeted him stiffly as she drew near, her keys already out.

"Ms. Kravitz," he replied with a small smile, not moving.

She turned her back to him as she worked the lock. "I'd invite you in," she said without turning her head, "but I'm not really inclined."

"Oh, be a sport," he mocked the cadence of her voice. "It won't take long."

The door swung open. Neither of them made to walk through it.

"Peter Rust," Willy said. "That help?"

It did make her face him, still with distaste. "Guess it'll have to. Don't make an effort to stretch things out."

"Wouldn't dream of it," he said, following her inside.

She didn't offer him a drink or something to eat. She didn't even suggest he have a seat. He sat anyhow, however, on a kitchen island stool, to watch her circle the apartment, turning on lights and removing her shoes.

"Speak," she said, avoiding eye contact. In fairness, she was willing to cut Kunkle a little slack, knowing how he'd trusted her father for years as a confidential informant—although pressuring him sometimes to an unpleasant degree. She was also fully cognizant that the only reason Dan wasn't currently behind bars was precisely because Willy had run effective interference. "What about Peter Rust?"

"Tomorrow, I'll be making official what you dug up for your boss, Mr. Jezek, Esquire. Rust is a homicide."

"He's my client, not my boss."

"Whatever. Your boss being the one who got us into this mess, I'm hoping you'll tell us how you two reached your conclusion. If you show me yours, though, I'll show you mine, which I guarantee can't hurt Jezek's defense of *his* client."

That wasn't necessarily true, of course. Willy might have been convinced that someone indirectly killed young Peter, but he couldn't say for an absolute fact that it hadn't been John.

He expected Sally to continue showing resistance, even though she'd be on tenuous ground if she did. Scott Jezek was an officer of the court who'd already passed along to law enforcement what she'd uncovered. For her to play coy at this stage would be ill-advised and wrongheaded.

Her response to his offer, however, caught his inborn cynicism completely by surprise. She stopped her wandering, settled onto the stool beside his, and addressed him seriously and openly, presumably having reached the same conclusion.

"I tracked my way back to the midwife who delivered Pete," she began. "Marcia Ethier. She's living at Maple Tree and is probably older than God, but she's as sharp as ever and remembers delivering Pete Rust like it happened last week. She's the one who told me Pete was completely normal at birth, and became the way he was because of a beating—or a smothering or shaking—she couldn't swear to what. But she's convinced he was abused."

Sally further impressed Willy by reaching out and touching his forearm for emphasis, adding, "She went back to check on him—something she apparently did with all her babies. That's when she discovered he'd changed radically, from the normal kid she'd help deliver to the rag doll she saw then. She's no doctor, and knows some forms of Pete's condition develop over time. She made all that clear to me. But she said she was essentially escorted out of the house by Hicks after that visit, and that he emphasized he knew where she lived if she ever mentioned her suspicions to anyone else."

"He threatened her?"

"Subtly. But here's the kicker. Ethier said she didn't get bad vibes just from him. She told me all three of them—Hicks, Karen, and even John—seemed united against her. The last two maybe out of fear, maybe something else, but she got the message and she kept silent."

Sally straightened, almost done. "It's bugged her all this time. I think she was scared half to death by the whole thing."

Willy had been hoping for something more concrete. "How did the family explain what she found?" he asked.

"They didn't," she replied shortly. "Another reason she had nothing to go on, nothing to report. But she convinced me—enough that I brought it to Jezek."

Willy gazed at the floor thoughtfully. "Convincing is one thing," he said. "Proving is another."

"What did you find out?" Sally asked.

He was under no obligation to tell her. Protocol was clear that he shouldn't. But he'd said he would. He honored and respected both her and her father, despite the latter's eccentricity. Plus, he didn't feel he had much to risk by being honest. Quite the contrary, if Sally was to be helpful to him in the future. That's in part what oiled these relationships.

"I found the cop who responded to the domestic where Pete was most likely shaken into a stupor," he said.

"Holy crap," said Sally.

"Yeah, well," Willy went on, "it also wasn't cut-and-dried. Like you with Marcia, what I ended up with was a feeling, an interpretation—not proof. Together, they point in the same direction, but it's still a circumstantial case."

Sally looked disappointed. "Does that mean you won't pursue it?"

He was surprised. "Hell no. Maybe just the opposite, at least in my opinion, and I bet in Gunther's, too. It's not much different than the classic he-said-she-said rape case. Physical evidence is nice, but it doesn't mean we quit because of the lack of it."

He checked his watch and stood up. "Speaking of which, it's late enough now that I can probably wake the old man up and tell him what we found."

"That's mean," Sally said, unexpectedly enjoying his humor.

"The price of being top dog," he corrected her, smiling. "You have to put up with jerks like me."

She saw him out the door, still underwhelmed by his crude style, but struck also by his commitment and sense of purpose. She would never want to find herself standing between him and any goal.

Which in turn made her think of a phone call she needed to make herself.

Not surprisingly, when Rachel picked up, she sounded as if she'd just stepped in from outdoors.

"Hey," she said. "What's cookin'?"

Sally smiled at the tone of the greeting. One thing she could rely on with Rachel, the girl was rarely in the dumps. And never there for long if she was.

Sally chose her wording carefully, not wanting to reveal that she'd withheld this information earlier. "I wanted to give you an update on John Rust."

"Cool. What's that?"

"Not sure how cool you'll think it is," Sally cautioned. "And I'm giving you this on deep background. I just bumped into Willy Kunkle, since he knew I was working for Rust's lawyer, and he told me they'd be treating Peter's death as a homicide, probably tomorrow morning, after he and Gunther put their heads together."

A moment of stunned silence was followed by Rachel saying, “No way. Holy cow.”

“What’s that do to your story?” Sally asked.

Rachel’s response was refreshingly unsentimental. “You kidding? Katz’ll love it.”

CHAPTER NINE

Evel Knievel

"Damn," said Stan Katz, reacting to Rachel's news. "Talk about ducking a bullet. We almost printed a fluff piece, complete with violins and family snapshots, without casually mentioning that—oh, by the way—the younger brother in this love story was actually murdered, and the older one can't be ruled out as the culprit. Christ on a crutch." He looked balefully at her and added, "Yesterday, John was a drunk facing jail time. Today, Pete's a suspected homicide. What else don't we know about this story?"

"You've got to admit, it's becoming a better piece," Rachel countered, startled to hear her thoughts out loud.

But they had the desired effect. Katz paused to stare at her. "Okay. I buy that. But what's our new pitch?"

"No more fluff, no more violins. It's all hard news, like an obit with attitude, complete with family background."

He gave her a thumbs-up. "Just what I wanted to hear. Put something together and get it to me before deadline."

He stopped as she was halfway out of his office. "And get an interview into John Rust."

She looked back at him. "I'm trying. He's disappeared."

• • •

Joe glanced up from reading Kunkle's latest summary. Willy was across the room, flipping through a magazine. Also in the office was Sammie Martens, wrapping up an unrelated case on her computer.

"Who's your money on?" Joe asked.

Willy answered indirectly. "The midwife thinks it was the dad. That would fit. But while the brother and mom are wild cards, I wouldn't rule them out."

"Except that the mother's dead," Joe countered, adding, "She is dead, isn't she?"

"Yeah. Nobody seemed to care much at the time, judging from newspaper clippings. But the official records are solid—ME's office, funeral home files, county and town clerks. It all checked out. I chased 'em down myself."

"Any idea on Hicks's whereabouts?" Joe asked.

"Not specifically."

Joe sighed, the response being typical of Willy. "Meaning?" he asked leadingly.

"Meaning," Kunkle explained, "I think he's still in Vermont."

"Why?"

"Call it a lack of imagination. In my experience, and I bet in yours, too, guys fitting Daryl's profile don't have the brains to leave the state. They confuse familiarity with safety, and run to the caves they know instead of the big, wide world outside, where they really might vanish without a trace."

Joe couldn't disagree.

"You going to start with John?" Sam asked, looking up. "Potentially, he knows Hicks historically better than anyone."

"I would if I could find him," Willy told them.

"Great—that doesn't sound good," Joe said.

"I don't think so either," Willy agreed. "But there you have it. Are you tight enough with his lawyer that you can ask him where John's hanging?"

Joe reached for his desk phone. "Tight or not, I'll find out what he has to say. John's disappearing would be an interesting development. In the meantime, you better keep hunting for Daryl. Sam?" he added, to which she looked up at him. "If you've the time, maybe you could help. I'm getting a nasty feeling this is about to get complicated."

"Where *is* John?" Sally asked Scott Jezek.

Sitting at his desk, Jezek cupped his chin unhappily. "I just fielded a call from Joe Gunther asking the same question."

"What did you tell him?" Sally inquired, settling into the seat across from him.

"Not what I'm about to tell you. I told him I'd let John know about the VBI's interest in having a chat."

"What's my version?"

"Same thing, except that you have to find him first."

Sally frowned. "Terrific. He's skipped?"

"I don't know. I can't find him and he's not returning messages."

"And he's got to be next to you at the arraignment," Sally guessed.

The lawyer gave her a thin smile. "It'll be awkward if he's not."

Sally asked, "What've I got? A couple of weeks?"

"It's not set in stone yet, but let's say that, for safe measure."

Sally pushed her lips out thoughtfully. "Any ideas on where I start? I've only given his background a once-over lightly, but I haven't picked up on a raft of relatives or drinking buddies. The man's a walking advertisement of a loner."

Jezek gave her a blank look. "Damned if I know. I helped him a couple of times. It's not like we hung out. For what it's worth, he never spoke about close friends or family, at least beyond what you already know. I got the feeling his world was pretty small—not much beyond a few neighbors and people like Martha Jones—which I guess is now being borne out."

"All right," Sally said with emphasis, pushing herself up and out of the chair. "Time to earn my keep."

She walked to the door before stopping there yet again, and asking, "How exactly are you going to justify billing him for my services from here on?"

Jezek shrugged, and then said what she hoped he would, "I'm not. You're on my tab now, so be gentle on an old sentimentalist."

"Consider yourself on the friends-and-family discount, Scott."

"From what I read," Sam said, her face just visible in the darkness, "Springfield was the seventh most likely bombing target in the country during World War Two."

Willy gave her a look. "You're kidding."

"No. I looked it up."

"So why didn't it get blown up?"

"The question is," she countered, "why was it a target? That's what you should ask."

"I don't care. I just think somebody missed a good opportunity."

Sammie scratched her forehead. "Yeah . . . I guess you would."

They were sitting together in Sam's car, near midnight, backed into a side alley, where they could watch the front of a sorrowful residence on one of Springfield's older, more battered streets, behind an empty factory building along the Black River, once the source of most of the town's hydro energy.

Sam was right, of course. Springfield, Vermont, had once been a powerhouse in the machine tool industry, peaking during the Second World War, when plants operated around the clock. She'd heard stories about those heady years, fueled by patriotism, hubris, money, and the feeling that the entire country was both fighting for its life and becoming a world power.

But as with most such places propelled by intoxicating, if passing enthusiasm, the town she grew to know in her lifetime had found itself victimized by the same specialization that had generated its fame. The economy, the industry, diversification, and competition from overseas had combined to throw the onetime champ against the ropes. Echoing Willy's dismissive comment, many people from outside Springfield now saw it as a throwback to a vanished era. To Sam, on the other hand, Springfield was a town on the mend, relying on its old can-do spirit to reinvent itself into something it had yet to fully formulate.

"Did Emma have fun on her school trip?" Willy asked, seemingly out of the blue.

"She did," Sam reported, well used to his often unpredictable thought process. "I wasn't sure how the museum was gonna bear up under a bunch of preschoolers, but it was a hit. She had a blast, especially seeing their stuffed moose."

"Sorry I missed it," he said. "I hope Louise didn't have too hard a time putting her to bed tonight."

Louise was their steady, almost omnipresent babysitter. An ex-cop herself, and now a widow, she'd taken to Emma like an adoring grandmother, paradoxically fueling Sam's guilt while comforting her to have someone reliable to care for their child.

"Nah," she said. "I texted her a while ago. Your daughter went out like a light as soon as she lay down. Busy day for her."

"Sounds nice," Willy said meditatively, his eyes on the house opposite. They'd been staked out for several hours, waiting for one of the men mentioned on Wes Thibodeau's list of old associates of Daryl Hicks to appear. Headed for a second sequential all-nighter, Willy appeared as sharp as ever.

Sam glanced over at him. He'd come a long way since they'd met as fellow cops working for the Brattleboro police. She'd actively disliked him at first, a rough-hewn transplant from the NYPD, with more attitude than even she'd been used to. He was brusque, judgmental, and transparently beset by inner demons. Initially, she'd even wondered—without merit, it turned out—if one reason for his frequent disappearances while on the job was because he was using brutal and illegal methods to produce an extraordinary string of successful arrests.

But she'd learned. And, to his credit, so had he. Over time, and certainly through the additional trauma of losing the use of his arm, Willy had worked hard to gain firmer footing. He hadn't done so alone. Sam and Joe had been there without hesitation, and more recently, Lester, after the VBI was formed. Joe had even forced the issue over Willy's arm, cajoling the state into making an exception for Willy's condition by essentially making him Joe's ward. Willy had recognized what that must have taken, and it had made him forever after a loyalist of the older man—not that he'd ever admitted it out loud.

For Sammie, witnessing this from close quarters had been equally life-changing. Military trained, the product of a largely neglectful upbringing, and with a predisposition toward self-sabotage, Sam had not been headed for safe shores when she signed up as a cop. But whether it was the discipline, the camaraderie, the daily challenge, or Gunther's influence again, she'd started becoming more reflective, less impulsive, and more trustful of her better instincts. When she began to warm toward Willy, to most people's astonishment and disappointment, it had been at once Willy's own response and Joe's unequivocal support that encouraged her.

Now, living with Willy and bringing up Emma with him, she had the benefit of hindsight as proof of her judgment.

Reflecting on this, and acting on impulse, she suddenly leaned over and kissed him on the neck.

Willy reached for her leg. "Stakeout sex? Cool."

But of course, it was then that a flash of movement drew their attention to the house under scrutiny, where a car had pulled up.

Willy had brought along his night-vision scope, and now balanced it on the fingertips of his right hand to see through the gloom. A single profile got out of the car and made its way up the walkway to the front door.

"Got anything?" Sam asked.

"Fits Boris Ryder's mug shot," Willy confirmed.

Sam checked her watch. It was close to one in the morning. "He look sober?"

"Good call," Willy replied. "I don't know if it's his liver or that he's been up to something else, but he's walking as straight as a judge."

"Too bad," she said. "Be easier if he was shit-faced."

"No lie," he agreed, lowering the scope and opening his door. "Shall we do the honors and render him a visit?"

They crossed the street stealthily, eyes on the house. One light came on toward the back, implying the newcomer was alone inside. As they drew abreast of the car, Willy ducked down and checked its ignition switch. Seeing the keys still in place, he reached through the open window, pulled them out, and dropped them under the seat to impede any quick departure.

Now in the front yard, Sam whispered to Willy, "Want me to go round back, just to be safe?"

"Yeah," he agreed. "I'll give you one minute before I knock."

This was not a typical move. There was nothing in Boris Ryder's recent profile to suggest he might fight or run, but instincts were something neither Sam nor Willy tended to ignore, and both of them sensed something about this situation urging caution. Traditionally, when visiting another agency's patch, VBI agents informed their host that they'd be in the neighborhood. Sam had done so here, downplaying their mission. Now she was wondering if she shouldn't have pushed for a little company.

It took her all of the allotted sixty seconds to get into place. The alleyway alongside the house and its backyard were clotted with garbage and debris, including a large Harley motorcycle resting on its kickstand, not far from the back steps.

Still, she made it in time to hear Willy's loud pounding on the door.

What she hadn't truly anticipated was the reaction from within, despite having circled around to the back. Rather than the predicted calling out of a response and a shuffling toward the front entrance, there was the sound of a crash, just before the rear door exploded back on its hinges, knocking Sam aside, and a dark-clad man blew out onto the small wooden deck.

"*Stop*," Sam shouted, fighting to regain her balance. "*Police*."

The man paused just long enough to finish what he'd inadvertently begun, placing his hand against Sammie's chest and shoving her over the railing behind.

"Fuck," she gasped, toppling backward, as the man, whom she'd just recognized as Ryder, leaped down the stairs, straddled the motorcycle, and brought it to life with a roar.

Sam fought free of a tangle of trash cans and yelled, "*He's a runner. Motorcycle*," hoping Willy might somehow improvise a roadblock. But Ryder was already skidding and fishtailing down the driveway toward the road out front when Willy came pounding down the alleyway to check on Sam.

"You good?" he asked breathlessly, grabbing her upper arm in his powerful hand.

She was already moving toward where they left her car. "Yeah. Never saw the son of a bitch coming."

They ran back across the street, hearing the motorcycle's harsh rattle bouncing off the hard walls in the darkness.

Sam had the engine on before Willy slammed the door, and the two of them squealed out of their hiding spot, slithering on the pavement as the rear tires grabbed hold.

Willy keyed the onboard radio to contact the Springfield police and ask for their assistance, giving them Ryder's identity and, as best he could, that of the motorcycle.

As for where they were headed, however, he could be of no help. Given their starting point, within a crisscrossing of narrow, residential side streets, Sammie was reduced to simply following the bike's raucous howl until she finally caught sight of its single gleaming taillight, just as it engaged Park Street, heading toward the hospital and the edge of town beyond.

"He's got nowhere to go if he turns left or right along here," Willy said, grabbing hold of the dash to keep his balance. "He's gotta be heading for Route 11."

"That's not good," Sam replied.

She was right. Park T-boned into 11, with a right turn being easier to negotiate for Ryder. After that, they both knew a large motorcycle had a huge speed advantage on the open road.

Luckily, bikes were also unstable by design. Now in pursuit with their blue lights and siren alive, they saw Ryder almost fly down the last incline of Park Street, to confront Route 11's tricky choice of options. Left was the better one, heading away from civilization, but it angled back more harshly than Ryder's speed could safely accommodate. He was forced to follow the lesser of two evils and swing right, toward a bridge over the Black River and a complicated intersection with River Street just beyond.

At any other time of day, that probably would have put an end to the chase. The intersection also marked the town's shopping mall entrance, not to mention several other businesses. Even during non–rush hour, it was a bottleneck for traffic, made worse by two traffic lights.

But not now. There wasn't another vehicle in sight. As a result, Ryder tore through the lights, leaned over into a left lane designed for opposing traffic, and almost skidded onto River Street, now heading northwest out of town.

That route wasn't completely free of complications. A miracle mile along this portion, River Street, also called Route 106, was lined by more businesses and driveways. But they, too, were clear of cars, and Ryder paid little attention to them as he hit the throttle, approaching a hundred miles an hour.

"Damn," Sam let out, both hands knuckle-white on the wheel.

"It won't last," Willy replied grimly, interpreting what he was hearing over the radio. "He's about to get the surprise of his life."

That happened beyond the commercial stretch, officially in North Springfield, just as they were approaching a long, smooth, left-hand curve in the road, near where the small local airport's paved runway ended on the right.

Where the curve began to announce itself, aiming straight at them from the opposite direction, was the patrol car that Willy had heard responding to their call for help.

The dazzling blue lights ahead cost Ryder his concentration. Sam and Willy saw the bike wobble ever so slightly, overcompensate, and then lose control, as Willy had predicted. Already, Sam was applying her brakes as they saw the bike's taillight shudder, bounce, and sail off into the field on the curve's outside edge.

"This is gonna be ugly," Willy commented as their car half skidded to a halt, alongside the cruiser in the other lane.

Yet again, however, things didn't go as expected. The fence separating the field from the roadside was in disrepair, and right where Ryder left the pavement, it was out entirely. Sliding, slipping, his legs flying out to both sides for stability, Ryder managed to keep upright, churning up grass and dirt as he headed toward the distant airfield.

Sammie didn't hesitate. As Willy opened his mouth to speak, she crushed the accelerator and threw their car back into pursuit, forcing Willy to focus instead on not smashing his head against the roof.

The field looked smoother than it felt driving across it, and here the car proved to have the final advantage. Lit from behind by the pursuing headlights, Ryder's flailing outline, at times only barely in contact with the machine beneath him, eventually gave in to superior physics shy of the chain-link fence surrounding the airstrip. The motorcycle going in one direction and his body hurtling off in another, Ryder landed in a heap just as Sam ground to a second halt, just short of running him over.

Both agents got out, slightly shaky, and walked up to the figure sprawled in the grass. In the distance, they could hear the police officer heavily pounding along to join them on foot, having wisely chosen to leave his vehicle on the pavement.

Willy placed his boot hard on top of a gun they could see shoved into Ryder's waistband, causing the other man to wince.

"That hurt?" Willy asked him, carefully watching his hands in case he chose to make a sudden move.

But Ryder was out of fight. "Yeah. A bit."

"Good."

CHAPTER TEN

History Lesson

Willy gave Boris Ryder a cardboard cup of coffee before making himself comfortable in the other chair. "Cream and sugar, as requested," he said.

They were in an interview room at the Springfield Police Department, fresh from the hospital, where Ryder had been given a clean bill of health after treatment for several scrapes and cuts.

"You're in amazing shape, given what you put yourself through," Willy observed.

Ryder slowly reached for the cup, wincing for theatrical effect. His other hand was cuffed to the concrete wall beside him. "Easy for you to say. I almost died out there, thanks to you. I'm thinking about suing you guys for assault."

Willy only encouraged him. "Good idea. Someone hanging by a thread should do everything he can to piss off the only people who can help him."

Ryder scowled. "What're you talkin' about?"

"Why do you think we knocked on your door?"

Ryder seemed to see that as a trick question. He gave it considerable thought before admitting, "Don't know."

"You think it was the drugs we found on you?"

"Maybe."

"The gun, in violation of your parole?"

"Sure."

"The assault I heard about that put your girlfriend Lexi Nugent into the ER last week?"

"Who?"

Willy looked at him without saying a word.

"I barely touched her," Ryder then said. "And she hit me first."

Willy was slowly shaking his head. "Nope. It wasn't any of those."

"What?" Ryder asked plaintively, looking increasingly confused.

"We just wanted to talk."

He left it at that, again allowing Ryder enough time to weigh his reply's significance.

"Talk?"

"That was it."

"'Bout what?"

"Well, that's the point, isn't it? You didn't wait to find out. Instead, you brought the roof down on your head, because you didn't just open the door."

"What're you sayin'?"

"That we're right back where we were early this morning, only now, you're in a bucket of vomit you could've avoided."

Ryder tried sorting out what Willy was slowly revealing. "So I'm outta here?" he asked.

"There's the tricky part, Boris. See, I'm from the VBI, not the local cops. You know what we do?"

"Sure. You're plainclothes guys. Detective stuff."

"It's a little more specialized than that." Willy moved his chair closer, as if imparting a secret he didn't want overheard. "We investigate murders, Boris."

Ryder stared at him a while before Willy's meaning sank in. "What're you sayin'? I didn't kill nobody."

Willy smiled. "There you have it. Maybe you did; maybe you didn't. That's what I have to figure out. So let me lay it out for you. There are three parts to this. Pay attention. If you get them right, I'll get lost and you never have to see me again."

As hoped, Ryder misinterpreted that to mean that he would end up going free. "Okay," he said.

Willy held up a finger. "First, I'm the murder police. I wouldn't be talking to you if this wasn't wicked serious, and that you'd put your foot in it somehow."

"I didn't kill nobody," he repeated.

"Quiet," Willy ordered him, holding up another finger. "Second, you've already got charges against you of a lesser nature that might go away if you help me out."

Ryder nodded, his eyes on Willy's.

"Third, what I want to do right now is have the conversation I was trying to have before you turned all Evel Knievel and went flying cross-country. But," Willy emphasized by poking Ryder in the chest, "you gotta be straight with me. You screw around with this third part, the other two come in to bury you. Is that crystal clear?"

The lead-in had been easy enough. All that remained was what magicians referred to as "the reveal."

"Sure," Ryder said, his tone saying otherwise.

"I want to talk to you about Daryl Hicks," Willy said.

After all the buildup, Ryder was suitably nonplussed. "*Hicks?*" he exclaimed. "What the fuck's *he* gotta do with anything?"

Willy sat back happily, his point made. "See? That's what I meant. It's the only reason we came knocking. Tell me about Daryl, and all the rest of this goes somewhere else."

To the Springfield police, for instance, he thought.

But Ryder was on board. Recovering from his surprise, he let his posture relax as he asked, "What's to tell? He ain't around—hasn't been for years. I can give you what I got, but it won't be much."

"Let's start with where he is now," Willy resumed.

"Now? That's what I just said. Who knows?"

You probably do, Willy thought, but he wasn't going to press the man—not at first. These conversations assume their own pace, and Willy had time.

"Take a wild guess," he suggested. "In state? West Coast? Somewhere in between?"

Ryder laughed. "Right. West Coast. I can really see a woodchuck like him out there. Wouldn't know what to do with himself. Nah, if I took a guess, I'd say in the area. Daryl's a Green Mountain boy."

Willy moved on. "When did you last see him? Or talk to him? I know you two were tight back in the day."

Ryder looked bemused. "Us? We maybe hung out with some of the same people. But tight? I wouldn't say that."

Willy dropped his voice to a more threatening register. "Eighteen years ago, you and Daryl were arrested while you were living together, for running a scam fleecing people on bogus driveway paving projects."

Ryder paused before saying nonchalantly. "Oh yeah. Forgot about that."

"A year before, the two of you were caught stealing copper from a Keene, New Hampshire, roofing company at night, and selling it on the black market."

"We did a few jobs together. Doesn't mean anything."

Willy rose and paced the small room, occasionally brushing uncomfortably close to the man attached to the wall. "I don't know, Boris. I'm thinking this might be a bad idea. You're so on the edge of habitual-offender status and getting tossed in the jug for the rest of your life, maybe it just doesn't matter to you anymore. Maybe the idea of three hots and a cot has become easier to accept than the hassles of making it in the real world."

"Oh, come on," Ryder protested. "I can't remember every mope I've hung out with. I forgot."

Willy stopped so close to him, they were almost touching, forcing the seated man to press up against the cinder blocks and crane his neck to see Willy's face.

"I think you're forgetting the high wire you're on. You tell me Hicks is nothing to you, and yet here you are, risking your freedom forever by not being straight. It makes me think you know more than you're saying, and since I'm working on a murder case, that means you gotta be tied into it somehow."

"Bullshit," Ryder protested angrily, squirming. "You're making that up."

Willy bent at the waist, putting his face inches from Ryder's. "You *really* want to see if I'm serious?"

The man swallowed. "No."

Willy straightened and sat back down. "I'll make this easier for you. Let's go back in time. Tell me about Daryl's home life."

Ryder knitted his brow. "Really?"

"Yeah. Wife, kids. Fill me in. Who was he married to?"

"Karen Taylor. Good-lookin' woman. Knew it, too."

"I heard that," Willy prompted him. "She ever step out on him? He was no catch."

Ryder didn't reject the idea, which Willy found interesting. "She might've. I wouldn't know."

"She ever bat her eyes at you?"

"What?"

"Nothin'. Was Daryl ever jealous?"

"Nah. He couldn't believe his luck. Kept his mouth shut."

"Rumor has it she wore the pants, anyhow," Willy suggested.

"She had more energy than anyone I ever met" was the indirect answer.

"The question's still out there, Boris. What did she see in Daryl?"

"She got knocked up."

"And had John?"

Ryder looked surprised. "Yeah. I forgot his name."

"Still," Willy persisted. "Why sleep with Daryl in the first place?"

"He'd do anything she wanted."

"Okay," Willy encouraged him. "And what did she want him to do?"

"Huh?"

"You made it sound like she put him to work. At what?"

"Stealin'."

Willy smiled. "There you go. Now we're talking. Tell me about that."

"Jeez," Ryder complained. "It was a long time ago. She was the brains and he was the muscle—him and anybody else she needed."

"What kind of jobs did they pull?" Willy asked.

"They started with homes. Karen figured out flatlander second-home owners hired locals to be caretakers sometimes, you know, to mow the lawn, plow during winter, maybe do repairs now and then. So she tapped into that crowd to get the inside scoop."

"How'd she do that?" Willy wanted to know. "No caretaker I know would be stupid enough to blab to a local bad girl and put himself out of a job when the place got robbed."

Ryder was getting into the flow of his story, as Willy had hoped, and snorted at the suggestion. "Duh. That's where she showed her smarts, and probably flashed her boobs. That would've persuaded most of 'em. But she was real careful, and didn't target just one guy. She moved around. Took her time."

"Where did Daryl come in?"

"Like I said, muscle. We're talkin' heavy stuff sometimes. You gotta put it on trucks or trailers, move it around, hock it to the right people, store it in barns and sheds before that. There's a ton of manual labor there."

"And they did this a lot?"

"Yes and no. They started to, but it's high risk/low yield, and she got hinky about too many people knowing what they were doin'."

"Like you," Willy guessed. "How many jobs did you pull with them?"

"A few," he admitted. "I came in toward the end, after she figured out another scam—less labor, better profits, not as many people in the know."

"Which was . . . ?"

"Old-fashioned moolah," Ryder said. "She started going for money."

"Banks?" Willy asked incredulously.

"Nah. Too much attention. The FBI gets in on those. I told you. Karen was a thinker. She figured there was a mess of money out there that wasn't in any bank. That's what she went for."

"Smart," Willy conceded, playing along. "Don't tell me she started knocking off retail stores."

Ryder took him seriously. "No. That was the thing about Karen—what made her stand out. She didn't do fast and flashy. She didn't need people to know how cool she was. That's why she always had a legit day job, and made sure Daryl did, too, even if they weren't much and didn't last long. That way, any extra money got disguised about where it came from."

"Got it," Willy replied, some of Ryder's respect for this woman rubbing off. "How did she go about it?"

"Same as before, in a way," Ryder explained. "She did research. She found people who knew other people. She liked finding the kind of folks everybody else looks right through, like janitors and clerks. And she really knew how to lay on the charm. Even the women ate out of her hand. They'd tell her what she wanted, give her keys sometimes, the layouts of places, security systems."

"You're talking companies, in other words."

"Companies, sure. Or anywhere that kept money overnight. I can't give you specifics, 'cause I was out of it by then, but I kept up with Daryl, and he'd give me little bits when he got tanked up."

"How much money are we talking about?"

Ryder reacted eagerly. "See? That's what I mean. Better than before, but not as much as it sounds. Not at first. Karen knew enough to keep it light. Don't go for the headlines. A few thousand here, a little less there, *maybe* more, now and then. The trick to this was staying under the radar. Some of these rip-offs were so subtle the people who'd been robbed thought they were being embezzled, and not robbed. Ya gotta admit, that's genius."

Not the word Willy would have used, but clever enough. "You just said, 'Not at first,' when it came to how big her hauls were. How much did she generate later on? And why did she break her own rule?"

Ryder's expression turned equivocal. "Yeah. Well, she must've, you know? She got knocked up again, they moved outta that dump here in town, got a nice place. That's the jackpot, right? Everything comin' up roses."

Willy's voice became less conversational. "Meaning you don't know or you're starting to play games again. Which is it?"

Ryder sat back, all innocence. "No, man, no. Come on. I ain't sure. I'll give you that. Like I said, I wasn't with them no more. *But*," he emphasized, "there was talk about a job—a payroll heist—that did the trick. Don't know who; don't know what; don't know a thing. But that was the rumor."

"You're saying Karen and the gang, including Daryl, made off with a company payroll, with nobody the wiser?" Willy asked, his voice rising.

But Ryder's response seemed open and genuine. "Hey. It's what I heard, okay? And it's all I heard. It does explain the whole move-outta-town thing, don't it? After all those years of sloggin' along. Course, it turned to shit right after, so, another case of beware what you wish for. But it looked good for a while."

Willy played it by the book, asking, "Explain the last part—the downside—just so we're on the same page."

Ryder shrugged. "You know, the second kid comes out weird, then Karen OD's. Daryl dumps his boys, and the older one gets stuck with the dummy. That's no fairy-tale ending."

"Okay," Willy replied. "Let's go back to this supposed payroll robbery. I know you said you don't know nuthin', but did you get a sense of how many were involved, beyond Daryl and Karen? It couldn't have been just the two of them."

"Don't know what to tell you, man. I got no argument with what you're sayin', but I got zip. I do remember there wasn't a peep afterward. If it happened like the rumor says, then not a word came out in the papers or on the street, or anywhere else. Dead silence. That's what was weird about it. Everybody talks, sooner or later. Otherwise," he added with a grin, "why do it? Ya gotta have bragging rights."

Willy rose and moved toward the door, stimulated by those last words. Boris Ryder, all appearances of stupidity aside, had hit a buzzer in Willy's brain.

Oftentimes in police work, the best move is to wait for events to unfold. Ryder was right. The worst enemy of most crooks was their need to brag. Sooner or later, cops knew, somebody rats out somebody else—to cut a deal, win some influence, or exert some pressure—and word leaks out.

For a major theft to go completely unreported, as Ryder had just detailed, was as rare as the proverbial hen's tooth.

Somehow, Willy thought, Karen Taylor had put together a perfect combination—the right target, a big haul, and utter discretion. And Daryl Hicks had been in the thick of it. The same Daryl—described as little more than a lummox—who had, immediately before and after Karen's death, comported himself according to character.

What, in Willy's mind, was therefore the single most attractive suggestion in all that?

The unknown identity of at least one missing key player with brains enough to have met Karen's needs.

CHAPTER ELEVEN

Crunching Data

"I don't care," Stan Katz told her. "Write it."

Rachel showed her disappointment. "How 'bout just one more day?" she pleaded. "He's got to be somewhere in the area. He has to show for his arraignment."

"That's too far off," Katz argued. "I already let you miss one deadline, after you first told me about this. You expect us to hang fire on a suspected homicide because John Rust decided to go on a bender, or whatever the hell he's doing? Get real, Rachel. Peter's already in the ground. I will not have this paper running what you've got after somebody else has already stolen our headline. It's idiotic. Just work John's absence into the piece, and use a quote from Jezek to explain it. I've already waited longer on this than I should've."

She knew he was right. She'd even started her piece, leaving room for quotes from John, after finding out from Sally—on deep background—that it wasn't likely he'd show up anytime soon. Sally had gotten back in touch with the missing man's neighbor, Peggy Munroe, and been told that the house had been deserted for days by now.

It was okay with Rachel. The story had started soft, progressed oddly, and was only now building toward something with real teeth. Writing what she'd gathered so far, with or without John weighing in, struck her as merely the start of a story that was bound to keep her busy for a while.

Willy and Sam were already in the office when Joe arrived, their heads together as they sat at her desk, studying her computer monitor.

"You two look like a couple of hunting dogs sniffing the breeze," he commented, moving over to the coffee machine. "What's up?"

Sammie, typically, saw the possibility of an error on her part in the comment. "We haven't had a chance to fill out our dailies yet, boss. Sorry."

Joe smiled and waved it off. It was a perfect snapshot of Sam's warring personalities—one hard-charging, confident, and utterly responsible, the other self-doubting and insecure. "Not to worry. You'll get to it. You're obviously at full speed. What d'ya got?"

Her partner may have been even more complicated, but apologetic, never. "You ask me," he said without looking up, "we've got a couple of nice, big juicy felonies growing like storm clouds on the horizon."

Sam cut him a surprised look as Joe laughed outright. "Damn, Willy," he said. "I never heard you so poetic."

She rubbed Willy's back protectively. "Sleep deprivation. He was up all night with Boris Ryder, ex-pal of Daryl Hicks and acquaintance of Karen Taylor, and the night before that finding Arnie Griswold. Willy's pretty sure the money that allowed John to take care of his baby brother all this time wasn't government handouts or John's computer business, but probably stolen."

"Nice," Joe said, moving behind them to look over their shoulders—a position he could tell immediately made Willy uncomfortable. "You know where from?"

Sam tapped the screen. "This is feedback from the fusion center on everything they got on Daryl. We ordered it as soon as things started ramping up against him, but they were swamped and our request got bumped because it was low priority."

Out of empathy, Joe moved toward his own desk near the window, where Willy could keep him in his peripheral vision. The things we do for the paranoid among us, he thought fondly. If nothing else, he'd once told Beverly Hillstrom, if there really were some pearly gates awaiting everyone at life's end, his continued support of this irascible, quirky man was going to be his ticket in.

Sam was still speaking. "From what Ryder told Willy, Karen was doing a Ma Barker, running Daryl and a small gang, sometimes including Ryder, ripping people off. The implication is she may've finally hit the big time by stealing somebody's payroll, just as she became pregnant with Peter, and right before they moved to Westminster. That would explain the finances we've been wondering about."

"But no word about the target," Joe filled in. "Which, if this is true, had to have been a major employer."

Willy spoke up, still scanning the information before him. "That's the kicker—not a sound, which tells me he, she, or it was in on it and benefited, or kept it under wraps to duck any bad PR."

"Unless," Sam added, "they collected on insurance, which we might be able to discover. Either that, or, if their cash cushion was thick enough, they just swallowed the loss."

"It's interesting, I'll give you that," Joe said. "And we don't even know what state this might've happened in."

The silence from his two detectives sadly confirmed that statement.

"Too bad we can't get a court order for anybody's financial records," he added, "beyond whatever information the local town clerks might have. Be nice to take a peek at Karen's income for that watershed year."

There, he didn't need a response. For now, the only suspect they had was Daryl, for possible child abuse—not anything involving money.

Willy was thinking along similar lines. "So we keep poking at Mr. Hicks and see what it gets us." He sat back and pointed at the computer display. "Like what I just found."

Sammie had been looking at her boss and now read what Willy had discovered. "Cool."

Joe asked Willy, "You want me to come over there and stand behind you again?"

Kunkle laughed. "Nice one. No. Hang on." He hit a couple of keys and brought his screen onto the wall-mounted monitor they used for squadwide discussions. Appearing there was a fragment of Hicks's fusion center report.

Sam interpreted, "We already knew DMV had no current license for him, but this looks like a whole list of nothings—no property deeds, current motor vehicles, businesses, hunting permits, utility bills, voter registration, on and on."

"You can see his old address in Westminster," Willy pointed out, "which is ancient history. Then you can follow him for almost fifteen years, moving from place to place, job to job. Finally, like a door slamming, four or five years ago, it ends. *Bam*."

"Implication being," Joe filled in, "he's either dead, which we're thinking he's not, for no particular reason, or he's worked hard to erase his tracks."

Sam ventured, "Somebody was or is after him?"

"That's my guess," Willy agreed. "People die, they leave a trace; they choose to disappear, not so much. Still, we may have a thread to follow."

"What?"

Willy moved the cursor to a vehicle listing. "Ford Bronco. Probably crushed by now, given the date, but look at the co-signer."

"Diane Wrinn," Sam read aloud.

Willy ran the cursor rapidly up the fusion report in a blur, stopping in the properties section. "And up she comes a second time," he said, "as co-owner of a trailer—like before, lost in the mists of time. Here's where I'm going with this." Once more, the image blurred, almost to the end of the document, where he froze it again. "Right here."

His colleagues studied the image. Listed among "possible relatives" was Diane Wrinn.

"Sister?" Joe asked.

"That's what I would say, given her appearance at the very top, among family. His parents are both deceased. Diane seems to be it."

"What's your thinking?" Joe asked him.

"That Daryl's on the lam. Somehow, he went back to his old tricks, without Karen calling the shots this time, and he got jammed up. Here, back when John turned eighteen, it looks like Daryl just left home, abandoning Pete, which he could now do legally. Maybe he and John weren't getting along. Whatever the case, he splits and diddles around for years, like he did before meeting Karen."

He snapped his fingers. "Then, just like that, he's gone. I say because somebody's hot on his heels for a deal gone wrong. But where's he go? Who does he trust?"

The question was rhetorical, but Joe voiced it anyhow. "Family."

"That's what I'm thinking," Willy said, sitting back. "Sister Diane, who appears to be alive and well, just outside Saint Johnsbury, in Peacham. Nice farm country, if memory serves."

Joe reflected on that. "Works for me," he finally said. "If nothing else, talking with her might give us another lead. Worth a shot."

Sally cradled her cup of hot cocoa and watched her father studying a linked array of five oversized computer monitors, arranged side by side along a stretched-out, curvilinear worktable. They were sitting in an immaculate, white, windowless room, below the level of Brattleboro's Main Street, in the bowels of one of the many ancient redbrick buildings that helped define the town's former industrial identity. Dan Kravitz had operated out of this room even before semi-retiring from his previous career of specialized house burgling.

Nowadays, he largely concentrated on managing the assets he'd accumulated then, primarily the personal information from over a hundred cell phones, laptops, tablets, and desktop computers.

His had been a lucrative run. He'd since used the data to enrich himself, put his daughter through school, and—because of viruses he'd planted in each machine, which replicated wherever they went—to monitor an exponentially expanding communications network. Through his ability to track the keystrokes of an increasing number of users, if he sensed a financial opportunity he could invisibly exploit, he took it; if he noticed something illegal, he passed it along anonymously to law enforcement, often Willy Kunkle; but otherwise, he simply kept up, amassing people's activities, indiscretions, and investments like a lexicographer acquiring new words.

For Sally, while it had all the makings of a potentially subversive espionage enterprise, she wasn't worried, trusting in her father's integrity and well knowing his peculiar psychology. It did, however, make her think of all the others out there, doing roughly the same thing for unsavory and cruel purposes.

The recent hubbub in the news about foreign governments trying to contaminate the nation's voting system was only one example she could cite. Her father had no such ambitions, she knew, but he was certainly active in a world on the edge of an end-to-privacy plague.

That notwithstanding, she was also this practical, problem-solving progenitor's natural daughter, and was therefore here not just to enjoy what she considered the best, most mysteriously concocted cocoa on earth, but also to use Dan's abilities and tools to her own advantage.

By her lights, she had a job to do, a client to serve, and the contents of this room and its occupant to supply her, she hoped, with what she needed to go forth. She wasn't inclined to cloud her horizon by considering just how disturbing Dan's actions truly were.

Nor was she about to consider the likelihood that her best friend Rachel, now vaguely aware of Dan's prowess as a researcher, would be horrified to learn of his methods.

Perhaps we all accommodate the devils that serve us best, consciously or not, she pondered.

"He's certainly wrestled with Mr. Barleycorn over the years, your John Rust," Dan said, scrolling through pages of information. Like the police across town, he, too, had access to reams of data on individuals; but his was in real time, raw and unfiltered, and most definitely not reliant on legal channels for access. Sally had once peered over his shoulder during such a search, and not understood a thing about how he organized it for retrieval and reference. User-friendly, it was not. Intimately invasive? Absolutely.

"You hit his DUI records?" Sally guessed.

"Well, yes, that, certainly," he replied. "But I see also that he's attended AA several times, albeit without much success. At least he's been trying."

Sally had been here for over an hour already, and hadn't been given much more than she'd arrived with. That wasn't Dan's fault. Just as his information gold mine ran deep and far in some respects, it wasn't without limitations. Back in his burglar days, he'd exclusively targeted homes of the megarich—at least by Vermont standards. Given his modest background and life habits, Rust had no particular reason to have featured much within such a collection of wealthy, ambitious, aggressive business types.

However—and in part why Sally was here—the nature of Dan's unique archive reflected the commonality of most people's being six, or fewer, social connections apart from one another. He may have only picked on an elite few, but by gaining covert access to their cross-communications, he'd caught a ride on an electronic pinball careening among and between phones and computers across a huge, growing spectrum. As a result, Dan had gained intimate access to the lives, thoughts, and actions of thousands of people he'd never even considered.

Including John Rust's.

"Interesting," he now commented, half to himself.

"What did you find?"

He faced her to answer, "Your man John has just suddenly gone from living what appears to be a predictable if sometimes messy life, to vanishing altogether. No credit cards, no phone or emails or internet presence at all. Even his power usage at home is maintenance only."

"Starting when?" Sally asked.

"A couple of days ago. He's pulled the equivalent of switching off the lights upon leaving a room. Could be a glitch, but it doesn't look like it."

"Gone dark," she rephrased.

Her father smiled. "Very James Bond. And that's not all."

"Oh?"

"I used the word 'predictable.' His life became so years ago, according to his bank statements, when generous, regular deposits started appearing from his eighteenth birthday onward, helping with his upkeep, but mostly used for the care and maintenance of someone named Peter Rust."

"His brother."

"Huh," Dan reacted. "What's going on there? Peter has no electronic footprint whatsoever."

"No," she said thoughtfully. "He wouldn't. He was never particularly active. Did that money appear yearly in John's account, or in monthly installments?"

"Monthly."

"The mother's trust in her son may have extended only so far, it seems."

"I would say so," Dan agreed, "assuming that the mother set this up. There were indeed times in John's history when he probably would have burned through the whole pile had it been available. That's just a guess, of course."

"You have no way of finding out where the cash came from?" she asked.

"No. My gremlins have their limits."

"Did you pick up on why John's pulled a vanishing act?" Sally asked. "Any 'Farewell, cruel world,' departing email, or anything?"

Typical of the man, he weighed that philosophically first. "Interesting world we're becoming, isn't it? Messages in a bottle; suicide notes; ransoms and death threats—I supposed they're all becoming electronic." He then addressed her question. "No. He wasn't overly chatty to begin with—mostly communications with someone named Martha Jones, and then the usual business-related stuff with an array of clients and the web-crawling everyone does in their spare time."

"Does it look like he has anything approaching an actual income?" she asked. "Or is the mysterious trust what's been keeping him afloat?"

His eyes returned to the screen. "I would say, looking at his expenditures, that you are primarily correct. John's independent income is visible, but modest. I'm presuming from what you said that Peter was incapacitated in some way, because he stimulates a very large number of medical bills, which the trust does adequately cover. But John makes a little money on his own, especially given that his house is owned outright, which is most people's biggest financial drain."

"How's he paying his way right now?" she asked. "Now that he's covering his traces."

"I've accessed his bank account, obviously," her father said. "But that doesn't mean he didn't start building an alternate universe earlier, and simply shifted funds over. He could have a bag full of greenbacks. Very traditional."

"Damn," she said in reaction. "I hadn't thought of that. He may've been planning this Houdini act for a while, which raises the question, why? What did he know before his brother died?"

Dan Kravitz looked at her proudly. "That's why you're the private eye."

She smiled. "Fair enough. Then tell me, O Oracle, what guidance can you impart about my other curiously missing person, Daryl Hicks?"

That had been the other half of Dan's assignment from his daughter. He swiveled into position before a different monitor, Captain Kirk at the helm.

"He's more a dyed-in-the-wool bad boy," he said. "Basically in trouble from the age he became mobile, committing most of the usual offenses. This, you said you already know, including his marrying Karen and siring two children. Unfortunately, I think I may fail you completely after that. Perhaps not surprisingly, given his history, he apparently never became too fond of computers or smartphones. Either that, or he stuck with burner units, which I can do little about."

Sally sighed. "Okay, then I'll stick to chasing John. Can you do me a favor?"

Dan gave her a wry smile. "You have to ask?"

She conceded the point. In fact, she only rarely requested his help. Aside from the time-honored issue of filial independence, there was a professional consideration. For her, a licensed investigator, gaining knowledge via the likes of Dan could be an ethical and legal nonstarter. Fortunately, this time, she was after information only. In her mind at least, she felt on safe ground to continue—for the moment.

Besides, she reasoned, she really had nowhere else to turn.

"Can you put out an alert on anything associated with John?" she therefore asked. "Some kind of alarm bell that would tell you if, when, and how he resurfaces?" She gestured to the equipment in the room. "I don't really understand the ins and outs of all this, and don't want to, for your sake, in case I'm ever sworn to tell, but I'm hoping you have an alert system—like stringing empty cans around a campsite at night."

"I can and will try," he replied, smiling at the image. "I know what I do unsettles you. That helps keep me at least partially honest, just so you know. But I might be able to set up a couple of things that could work. Let's put it that way."

Sally raised her cup to him in gratitude.

CHAPTER TWELVE

Family First

Vermont is famous for its cows, and proud of the oft-quoted observation that there are more of them in-state than people.

That hasn't actually been true for many years. Not even close.

It is an understandable if nostalgic holdover. The Green Mountain State seems permanently stamped, correctly or not, as the symbolic cradle of colorful leaves, fancy ice cream, maple syrup, and opinionated, plain-speaking politicians. That cows and farms have in reality slipped down on that list counts for little, given old-fashioned sentimentality and the state's real-enough sylvan backdrop.

Peacham, therefore, is postcard-perfect. It's a charming town, without being precious, and is surrounded by enough farms and trees and hills to seductively fill a camera frame.

It was certainly compelling enough to stimulate Lester Spinney, a native-born resident of postindustrial Springfield, to tilt his head into the warm, lightly manure-scented breeze wafting through the car window, and say, "Damn, this is pretty."

To which Willy Kunkle unsurprisingly responded, "Fresh cow shit? Whatever. What's that address again?"

Lester, well used to his partner's general outlook on life, merely pointed ahead. "Next left, then up half a mile."

Lester was the newest member of the VBI's southeastern branch office. Joe, Sam, and Willy had worked together for so long they were like family. However, despite having come to them from the state police, Les had never felt excluded. An outsider within his old organization for his original thinking and sense of humor, he'd fit into this squad from the first day. By design, the VBI had been structured for self-motivated free thinkers, and the Brattleboro office, especially—largely because of Joe—had become emblematic of how such teams could work best.

Having a colleague like Kunkle, therefore, whose antics wouldn't have survived a week inside the state police, merely added to Lester's enjoyment.

The farm they pulled into was more trim and tidy than either of them was used to. Farming in Vermont, especially the small-family version, had been suffering for decades. Spending time and money on keeping the dooryard neat and the clapboards freshly painted fell victim to more pressing necessities. But that wasn't a given, as this place certainly proved.

They got out and looked around, the sun warm on their shoulders and the smell of hay, grass—and yes, manure—hovering about. A woman in jeans and a denim shirt, possibly in her early sixties, appeared at the farmhouse's door, drying her hands with a dish towel. She had short hair, a body built for hard work, and an expression encouraging brevity and directness.

"I help you?" she asked.

"Diane Wrinn?" Lester asked, taking the lead, even though her gaze was warily fixed on Willy—the man to watch, in her practical assessment.

"We're from the Vermont Bureau of Investigation," Lester continued, displaying the badge clipped to his belt. "We're involved in a case in

Windham County where your name came up, just in passing, and we were hoping you could spare us a few minutes."

Wrinn hadn't taken her eyes off Willy. "What's up with him?" she asked, lifting her chin slightly at the sight of his atrophied arm.

Willy gave a half smile and imitated Lester's gesture, revealing his previously covered badge, saying, "Shot on the job. They still let me hang around."

It proved the right approach. Her expression didn't change, but her features softened slightly. "That's Vermont for you," she said. "You want to come in? I'm cleaning a bird in the kitchen."

She turned on her heel and returned to the house. The two men filed in behind her, entering a large, functional kitchen with a row of windows above the sink overlooking the green fields behind. Wrinn was already back at her task, eviscerating a fresh chicken in a bowl with the water running. She didn't offer them refreshments or chairs to sit in, although Willy didn't hesitate to make himself comfortable, settling at the wooden farmhouse table in the room's center. Lester remained standing.

"So, talk," Wrinn ordered over her shoulder. "What's this about?"

Lester stayed on as their spokesman, easing his way into the conversation until he got a better feeling for the woman before them. "We're on a research trip, trying to reconstruct a period about twenty years ago, more or less, in Springfield and Westminster."

"Never been to either one," she replied, keeping at her grisly task, her back still turned.

Spinney moved until he could lean his hip against the counter beside the sink, and thus get a view of at least her profile.

"But you've got family from down there," he stated.

"You mean Daryl?" she asked without pause.

"Yeah," he said casually, "and his kids. I am sorry about poor Peter, by the way."

"Didn't know him," she said, eyes on the chicken, which Lester noted was receiving a very thorough job.

"You knew he'd died, though, didn't you?"

"He wasn't going to live long anyhow," she commented, in a tone more fatalistic than harsh.

"No. Still . . . Did you get to meet John, the older boy?"

"Once or twice. Couldn't say I knew him."

"Did he and Daryl get along?"

"I wouldn't know."

"How did you get to meet John?" Lester asked. "Did he come up here, or did you travel south?"

"Here," she answered shortly. "When his mother was still alive."

"Karen. Right. What did you think of her?"

Diane Wrinn finally twisted around to stare at him. "What do you care?"

"We're trying to reconstruct what the family dynamics were like," Lester told her, keeping things vague. If she wasn't going to ask precisely why they were here—which he found interesting in itself—he wasn't going to volunteer anything.

Diane returned to her work. "Didn't like her much."

"Why was that?"

"Didn't think she was good for Daryl."

"He seems to have stuck with her, though, all the way to the end."

She didn't respond.

"What was that like?" Lester asked. "The whole family suddenly losing her? We heard she was a pretty energetic person."

Diane paused again. "What's that supposed to mean?"

"That she worked a lot," Lester said innocently. "I mean, just on a practical level, that must've been a kick in the head, losing a breadwinner with a special needs kid in the house. Had to be tough."

"I wouldn't know anything about that."

"What did Daryl do to cope?"

Her efforts on the bird became a little more furious. "He just did, I guess, like we all do."

"Until he left," Willy said from his place at the table.

His blunt tone stopped her. She straightened, turned off the water, and swiveled around to face him. "What's that mean?"

Lester wasn't unhappy with the change of mood. In their line of work, and in such roundabout circumstances, it could often be helpful.

"It means he left," he answered, adding, "Didn't he?"

She studied them both before at last getting to where most others would have started. "Why are you here? Really?"

"We'd like to talk to Daryl," Willy said.

"He's not here."

"When will he be back?" Lester asked.

"I don't know."

"So he's living here," Willy suggested.

"I didn't say that. I haven't seen him."

Lester joined in. "Since when?"

She pressed her lips together, scowling, before saying, "I want you to leave. I got nothing to say."

Neither man moved.

"Diane," Willy asked, his voice softer, "how did Pete end up the way he did?"

Instead of answering, she crossed to the door and opened it, turning to face them. "Leave. Now."

Lester stayed put while Willy slowly rose, pushed his chair up to the table's edge, stamped his feet gently to straighten the drape of his trousers, and only then walked slowly toward her, Lester in tow.

Willy paused with his face inches from hers. "There are questions to answer, Diane. Daryl's got things to answer for. You know it. We know it. This is just beginning. We'll be back."

"It's only going to get harder," Lester added as Willy stepped outside.

"Fuck you," she said in an angry whisper.

They drove until the house disappeared behind a curve in the road and pulled into the parking lot of a store, tucking in behind some other vehicles.

"You think she'll go for it?" Lester asked. "It's not like we're on a TV show."

"Where do you think they get that crap?" Willy argued. "She's either gonna go to him or call him, and I don't see Daryl Hicks as a big cell phone user."

"*Everybody's* a cell phone user," Lester replied. "What planet are you on?"

"This one," Willy said, pointing toward the road. Sure enough, the same truck that had been parked in the Wrinn dooryard drove by, with Diane at the wheel, wearing a bright red baseball cap, her face set.

"Nice," Lester laughed. "I'll never figure out how you do that."

They slipped in behind the truck, leaving ample room between them, and followed Diane as she circled the entirety of her farm, to eventually turn up a dirt road on its far boundary. At that last corner, they stopped, conscious of becoming conspicuous.

Willy held up a pair of binoculars.

"Lucky," he reported. "She stopped."

Both of them got out and began walking quickly up the road. As they topped a small rise, now even Lester could see that their quarry had stepped onto the edge of a field and was waving to an enclosed, tinted-window tractor that had been wending its way back and forth along the furrows. At her gesturing, instead of making its turn as normal, it continued to the road, meeting up with Diane's truck.

Lester and Willy crouched low, watching. They saw the distant profile of a heavyset man wearing a brown jacket descend from the cab and confer with Diane before the two briefly vanished behind the truck.

"Giving him the bad news?" Lester surmised.

Willy had been looking through the glasses again. "The mug shots we have are old, but he fits the profile."

The couple reemerged and parted ways—Willy distinguished Diane in her red hat from Daryl in his coat. They returned to their respective vehicles and drove off, with Diane continuing in the same direction she'd taken to get here, away from the two cops.

Willy turned back toward their car, saying, "Guess we'll go have a chat with Daryl, talk about the old days."

They drove to where Diane had parked, walked into the field, and waited for the tractor to reach them on its return journey, waving down the driver once it drew near.

The unit stopped, facing them like a rumbling monster, uncertain of their intentions, until its driver finally killed the engine.

The men walked up to the bottom of the cab door. Lester reached up and rapped on it with his knuckles. It opened to reveal Diane Wrinn looking down at them, hatless and dressed in her brother's bulky coat.

"I help you?" she asked, smiling for the first time.

Willy gave his partner a withering look. "Not like we're on TV, huh?"

"What did you think?" Rachel asked Sally, standing in the latter's doorway and holding up a copy of the *Reformer*, turned to her full-page feature on Peter Rust, complete with photographs.

"I liked it," Sally replied, stepping back to allow her friend in. As usual with them, it was almost midnight, which was often the only time either one even considered stopping work long enough to entertain sleeping—which they then put off to socialize together. The rapid evolution and strength of their friendship had caught them both by surprise, and continued to be rewarding every time they met.

"I especially liked that John Rust's mug featured prominently," she continued, crossing to the fridge. "It should help get more people to watch for him. Want anything?"

Sally's apartment, like her father's, was spare, neat, surgically clean and organized, and accessorized with only the bare minimum of furniture, decorations, dinnerware, and the rest, to make it all appear almost normal. Rachel had—after making sure it wouldn't be taken wrong—suggested that Sally was perhaps an alien in human form, who'd copied how people live by leafing through catalogs. The response had been an enigmatic laugh.

"I'd actually go for cereal," Rachel answered. "You're always tracking folks. What do you think he's up to?"

Without comment, Sally was preparing two bowls, complete with a plastic tub of sliced fruit. "Could be he's scared of being locked up, like most runners. If I were to lay money on it, though, I'd say it's something else."

"Involving Peter?"

Sally fetched two boxes to choose from and laid out spoons beside the bowls, placing them on napkins. "Too vague," she replied. "Everything involved Peter until a few days ago. His death was a trigger. That's probably safe to say. But was it a release or a stimulus?"

"What's that mean?"

They settled down to dig in to their midnight breakfast. "You know—you're living with an invalid for thirty years, and then he dies. So you buy a motorcycle and become Easy Rider. That's a release. Finding out somebody actually murdered him when you thought it was a natural phenomenon? I'd call that a stimulus. You might go out and kill somebody. Question is, which one fits John?"

CHAPTER THIRTEEN

A Roadside Discovery

Joe heard about Daryl Hicks while in Beverly Hillstrom's bed in Windsor. She primarily lived outside Burlington for her job—the ME's office was located in the basement of the University of Vermont Medical Center on Colchester Avenue, downtown—but she'd purchased this second home, on the other side of the state, between Hanover, New Hampshire, and Brattleboro, after accepting a part-time teaching job at Dartmouth's medical school in Hanover. The house was a good investment and allowed her to spend more time with Joe—a benefit he found to be working out beautifully.

Except at times like this.

"Yes?" he answered his cell phone, disentangling himself from her, which she was making purposefully difficult.

"Special Agent Gunther?"

"Speaking."

Beverly, as playful in private as she was famously not before others, draped a naked leg over his waist and curled her arm under his, making it difficult for him not to react.

"This is Bob Brewster at VSP Saint J dispatch. We have a notification order to contact you in case we get a hit on Daryl Hicks."

Joe's sudden tension caused Beverly to desist and raise herself up on one elbow, so she could look over his shoulder at the phone's screen. "Correct."

"He was found dead by a passing motorist outside Peacham; actually west of Pasumpsic, on County Hill Road."

"How?" Joe asked, swinging his legs off the bed as Hillstrom did the same on the other side. He put the phone on speaker.

He could almost hear the dispatcher smiling as he said, "Little embarrassing, I guess. The guy stopped to take a leak. Damn near pissed on the body in the process. Managed to stop just in time."

"Who do you have responding?"

"Troops are there already. We can roll BCI, but because of the notification order, my lieutenant said to call you first. I'm about to get the local ME rolling, too."

Joe glanced at Beverly, who was already getting dressed and gave him a cheery thumbs-up, mouthing, "Field trip" and smiling.

"Do that," Joe told Brewster, "and let him or her know as a courtesy that the chief medical examiner will also be responding to the scene."

"Wow" was Brewster's reaction. "The big guns. Will do. Your travel time?"

"About an hour."

"Roger that" was the response, followed by a more precise address on County Hill Road.

Beverly and Joe had met decades earlier, when she was married to a lawyer and he was involved with a woman who later became governor of the state for a time. Their initially professional relationship had evolved quickly through the years, developing into a bond between kindred spirits.

And so it had remained for a long time. Beverly knew that when bodies came up from Joe's part of the world, they'd be accompanied by paperwork reflective of his or his team's thoroughness and care. Joe knew that anyone undergoing her analysis would benefit from the best and latest forensic science that Beverly could locate or afford on her budget, and that, if necessary, she'd work off the clock to get what was needed to satisfy her own curiosity. Together, in case after case, they lent each other unspoken support and encouragement, reaping the extra benefits that come from working with the best of friends.

Perhaps inevitably, given how long this status had been maintained, other factors in their lives, like her divorce and changes in his life, had finally encouraged them to expand this affection into something openly heartfelt.

So far, it had been a more natural and rewarding progression than either of them could have imagined.

The spot along County Hill Road to which they'd been directed was a different image of quintessential Vermont. Not the verdant mountains version, with fields dotted with hay bales, and countless white clapboarded villages, but the less photogenic one of dirt roads, weed-clotted ponds, and endless miles of low hills crowded in by trees.

As they slowed to a stop near a couple of state police cruisers and two pickups, the trees made room for a stagnant pond pressed up against the edge of the road, and a narrow embankment leading down to the murky water.

There, reminiscent of a small, beached dory, was the body of an overweight, supine man, his sightless eyes fixed on the passing clouds high above.

"Who found him?" Joe asked one of the troopers.

The man checked his notepad. "Nathaniel Johansson. He was driving along here and found him when he got out to relieve himself."

"It looks like Hicks. You confirm it beyond a description?"

"He might have a wallet that'll do that, but we haven't touched him yet—beyond making sure he was dead. Waiting for you." He indicated Beverly.

"Yeah," Joe replied as Beverly stepped away to take in more of the overall scene, already applying her professional skills. "Much appreciated. Thanks." He studied the ground around the body. "Those your footprints?"

"Just mine," the trooper said. "Went in and came back out. The rest is the way we found it."

"I asked Dispatch on the way up here to get the evidence search team on the way. You know if that happened?" Joe asked.

"It did. Last I heard, they're about an hour out. Maybe less."

Of the many unwritten rules hovering over most scenes of unexplained deaths, a key one is always, Don't rush. They take hours. Many hours. During which everything is left as found, including the body, which, even if it was remotely fresh to start with, is allowed to slowly stiffen and cool, seemingly ignored. There are checklists, logs, hundreds of photos to take, measurements by the dozen, canvasses. A command post is established—usually the search team's truck—communications set up, a strict pecking order of who does what and how.

All of which Joe appreciated. Not when he was cutting his teeth at the job, so long ago. Then, he was all impatience and eagerness—both of which routinely stood ready to ruin a case on its slow and methodical way to court. He had since learned, sometimes the hard way.

Everyone involved has done this many times before, often working together, despite being from different agencies, so the mood is rarely awkward, but it is influenced by the rigid rules of procedure. There is a resulting odd mixture in the air of familiarity and formality.

Beverly, in stark contrast to her playfulness that morning, fit right in, adding her own element of severity to the proceedings. She was conferring with her local death investigator, of which there were approximately forty sprinkled across the state, when Joe approached to ask, "Are you where you can give me some insight?"

"Yes," she replied with the hint of a smile. "Jill?" she addressed the young woman by her side. "Why don't you give Special Agent Gunther an overview?"

Joe felt for the girl. Generally drawn from medically related jobs like nurses, PAs, paramedics, or volunteers from local rescue squads, these so-called assistant medical examiners, or AMEs, were expected to perform to rigorous standards, while being paid only on a case-by-case basis. Being an AME took a special kind of outlook. It was a job people either tried for a year or so, or stayed with for decades.

Jill was new, nervous, and not happy to be put on the spot by her boss, whose benchmark for quality was well known and intimidating.

"According to the documents we found in his pocket," Jill began in a quavering voice, "the decedent is Daryl Hicks. None of those is a photo ID, however, so we're just going by that until something better comes along, including a familial DNA match, if necessary."

"Cool," Joe encouraged her, not bothering to mention that Daryl's identity wasn't really a question. "Can you tell how he died?"

"Not how he died, but some of what he went through." She smiled tentatively at Beverly, adding, "She's the one to tell you what really killed him."

Joe went along. "Okay. I'll settle for best guess right now."

By this point, there were some fifteen people milling about, and half as many vehicles. Some individuals were in Tyvek suits, others in uniform, a few more in civilian clothes. Joe, Jill, and Beverly drew closer together to maintain the privacy of what the young AME was about to impart.

"As far as I can tell from an external exam only," Jill reported, "Mr. Hicks was stabbed, strangled, some of his fingers broken, and maybe drowned, because of where he was found and a small amount of foam at his mouth."

"There are also burn marks on him," Beverly added, "consistent with a cigarette being applied to his skin."

"Damn," Joe replied.

"Joe," Beverly said, "there were additional indicators on his wrists that I've seen before in bondage cases."

Joe knew how she disliked reaching beyond what the evidence clearly revealed. "He was tied up?"

Jill couldn't resist speaking, her enthusiasm stamped on her face. "We think it might've been duct tape."

"There was a sticky substance at both sites," Beverly confirmed, frowning slightly.

Her modest mentoring over, she took Joe by the forearm, thanked Jill, and steered him over toward the far side of the search team's green-and-gold truck. "You did get that he was probably tortured, I'm assuming," she said.

"Yep. Was there more than Jill just relayed?"

"There was a subtlety in the findings I think you should be prepared for when I report on the autopsy."

He smiled slightly at her language, which tended to get more rigidified as she became serious. "Such as?"

"Jill accurately reported on signs of stabbing and strangulation, but from my experience, I doubt either one will be proven lethal when I pursue them on the table, and I have reservations that he was drowned."

He knew better than to press her. "Okay," he said. "Will you be doing this one yourself?"

"Oh, yes."

He left her to finish up with Jill, and crossed to where a woman in white Tyvek was logging something into a binder by the open back of the truck. She was a senior crime lab tech he'd worked with before.

"Find anything interesting?" he asked.

"Like the driver's license of this guy's killer, dropped in the mud? Nope."

"It is a dump site, though, correct?"

"That's what we're seeing," she agreed. "And 'dumped' may be the operative word. From the impressions in the moist soil outlining where he landed, it's looking like he was tossed from the back of a pickup or some other truck. Also, there are no drag marks, no footprints, and the position he was found in looks disorganized, not arranged, like it might if someone stretched him out. The indentation under the body suggests a drop of a few feet."

"No signs that he moved at all?" Joe asked.

She looked surprised. "The ME saying he was still alive when he got here?"

"No, no," Joe reassured her. "I'm guessing her findings will match your own. I was just asking."

She was visibly relieved. "Nope. I think he crashed pretty much like a sofa—*thud*."

Joe looked up at the approach of another car, and saw Willy Kunkle pulling off the road.

"Thanks," he said to the tech, and walked over to greet his colleague.

"You drive all the way from Bratt?" he asked as Willy stepped out of the car, looking grim.

"I wasn't gonna miss this," Willy growled. "Not after the asshole gave us the slip." He pointed toward the scene with his chin. "I'm guessing you're confident that's Daryl."

"The one and only, and it's looking like somebody tortured him before dumping him here."

"Fuck," Willy complained. "Two days ago, we *had* the son of a bitch. I hope his sister's gonna be happy with this. Talk about being too clever for your own good."

Joe didn't disagree, even if he saw Diane's earlier deception in a more charitable light.

But Willy was already over his outburst, observing thoughtfully as Daryl's body was at last removed from the edge of the pond and placed into a hearse.

"Two reasons for doing that to somebody," he mused. "You either hate the guy or you want him to tell you something."

"Or both," Joe suggested, recalling the list of abuses Jill had rattled off. "Well," he continued, "I think we've got two options. We can either wait for Beverly's bottom line on cause of death, or, since you're already here and we're in the neighborhood, we can break the news to Diane Wrinn and see if it'll open her up more."

Willy turned to look at him, deadpan. "That a trick question? I'll lead. I know where she lives."

Breaking the news of a death to family members can be tricky, more so when the person receiving it has been less than candid and might even be a suspect. As they neared the Wrinn farm, Willy in the lead, Joe pondered his choice of approaches. He'd read the report Lester and Willy had filed about their encounter with Diane Wrinn, and so knew his options were that much more complicated. Diane, according to their description, was no sentimentalist, not to mention that she'd cared enough for her brother to run interference with the police.

As things turned out, he needn't have worried. Willy took care of it by grinding to a halt ahead, getting out as the dust was still swirling, marching up to Diane, who was hosing down a manure spreader in front of the barn, and shouting over the power washer, "The day before yesterday, Diane, the last words you said to us were, 'Fuck you.' Well, we just found your brother in a ditch, tortured to death. That's on you. So, while it might be too late in your book, we'd sure as hell like to catch the son of a bitch who did that, unless maybe you don't give a good goddamn."

He then kicked the power washer's switch with his foot, dropping silence onto the scene like a hammer.

Joe stopped in midstep, choosing to let his colleague keep running with the ball.

Diane stood still, the wand dripping in her hand, her mouth partially open.

"Come on," Willy pressed her, standing almost face-to-face. "Give me a good one-liner, Diane, like after the switcheroo with the tractor."

Diane swung at him with her other hand, but he'd been waiting for it. Fast as a snake, his muscular right arm flew up in time to ward off the blow, making her stagger and clutch her wrist in pain.

"You prick," she said in a half sob.

"Don't throw stones, Diane," Willy warned her. "I'm not the one who put him in harm's way." He took one step closer. "Think about it. Daryl didn't do a disappearing act up here because *we* were after him. *We* could've thrown him a lifeline."

Already partially doubled over, nursing her arm, Diane simply yielded to gravity and sat in the mud like a sack of flour, her booted feet sticking out before her. Her head bowed and her body shaking, she started to cry.

Willy crouched before her, still crowding in. Joe quietly approached and stood nearby. A hen appeared from the yard, walked over one of Diane's legs, and began pecking at the mud.

In contrast to moments earlier, Willy pulled out a bandana and slipped it into Diane's hand. Without looking up, she wiped her eyes and nose, whereupon Willy grasped her farm coat under one armpit and easily helped her back to her feet. He then slipped his arm around her waist and escorted her to the farmhouse's front porch, where he eased her to a sitting position onto one of the steps and sat close beside her.

"This is my boss," he said.

Diane looked up into Joe's face, her eyes damp and cheeks flushed. "Hi," she whispered.

"I'm truly sorry," Joe said, now standing before them both.

She blinked a couple of times before blowing her nose and wearily replying, "Yeah."

"You did what you could," Willy now spoke supportively, his arm still loosely draped across her lower back. "My guess is Daryl was always a handful."

"No joke," she confirmed in a whisper.

"Can we go back a few years?" Willy asked. "So maybe we can figure out what happened?"

"Unless you already know," Joe ventured, hoping they might get lucky.

Willy didn't mind. It was a truth of this kind of conversation that sometimes, trying to cover everything, you missed the obvious questions. Joe's attempt was like twisting the knob before kicking in the door.

But not this time.

"I knew he was scared," she said. "I didn't know why."

"Okay," Willy resumed. "Maybe we can figure that out. How long's he been living here under wraps?"

"Four—five years."

The men exchanged glances. That fit their interpretation of Daryl's fusion report. But what had made him so paranoid? And did it have anything to do with his old life, Karen, people like Boris Ryder, and whatever shenanigans they'd been up to? Daryl was prone to following a troubled road. Who knows where he'd ventured recently?

"Why?" Willy asked. "From what we know, he never went invisible like he did here with you."

"It was always something with him," she replied. "I told you I didn't think Karen did him any favors. But honestly, he could fuck things up pretty good on his own. It was in his blood. Our dad was the same way."

"How 'bout these last few days? Did anything make him twitchier?"

"Besides you guys showing up?" she asked bitterly. "No. I thought things were getting routine. We hadn't talked about him keeping his head low in a long time. What happened, anyhow? What made you come looking for him, all of a sudden? Something must've changed."

"It always does," Joe said, hoping to stave off any rant holding them accountable. "You know that. It's part of that life."

"We wanted to talk to him," Willy followed up. "But we have no clue why he was killed."

Thankfully, she left it alone. They'd spoken the truth, after all, at least in general terms. Who knew, half the time, whose toes were going to be stepped on because of a quantum shift like Pete's death, its motive, and what ripples might result? Diane might not have participated in Daryl's old life, but she'd been no stranger to it.

"What about those days?" Joe asked. "What was that gang up to, that he hung out with?"

"Careless, stupid, destructive things," she said. "Daryl was a follower. He did what people told him. He was big and strong and not too bright, and when Karen latched on to him—for what reason, I'll never know—he pretty much died and went to heaven. She wiggled her assets at him and what brains he had went into the freezer."

"John was born around the same time," Joe suggested.

"Yeah. That sealed the deal."

"We've read their rap sheets," Willy said. "Not much surprising, but that's only what we caught them for. We're hearing lately that they may've pulled off bigger jobs we know nothing about, and at least one that may've set them up with a decent nest egg. You know anything about that?"

She let out a sad chuckle. "A nest egg? If there was one, either Daryl missed out, or he pulled a big fat one over on me, 'cause I sure as hell never saw it. That was one of the things when he came up here to hide out. He was broke, or said he was. That's why I put him to work here. I got free labor and he got protection, room, and board."

"It was just the two of you?" Joe asked.

"My husband died fifteen years ago. Stupid. He was reaching backwards off the tractor trying to fix something with the tedder while he was still going down the field. Fell off."

Both men were temporarily silenced by that gruesome image, Joe envisioning her husband being stabbed by the machine's dozens of icepick-like tines at once.

"You have any other family?" Willy asked.

"Not now," she answered simply.

"Were you and Daryl close as kids?" Joe wanted to know, hoping to get back to events that might lead somewhere.

"We were okay."

"So," Willy picked up his cue, "you probably kept in touch, more or less, when you and your husband were up here and he and Karen were in Springfield with the kids?"

"We didn't make a big deal of it, but sure."

"You ever go down to visit?"

"Maybe a couple of times."

"When they were in Springfield, or later?"

"Both."

Willy pressed her, remembering that earlier, she'd claimed not to have made such a trip. "Then you saw the transition, from their days in the pits to better times in Westminster."

"Yeah."

"How did Daryl explain that?" Joe asked. "Or Karen, for that matter."

"Karen wouldn't explain squat to me," Diane said.

Willy spoke leadingly. "Okay . . ."

"Hell," Diane swore. "You're talking thirty years ago, almost. Who can remember?"

"You can," Joe suggested. "This is your big, dumb, loser little brother, hitting it rich for no reason. Sure as hell you noticed."

Until now, she'd been poking at the dirt with her boot, her elbows on her knees. At Joe's comment, she straightened and looked straight at him. "I figured they'd robbed a bank."

"And you asked him about that," Willy said, "'cause that's what big sisters do."

"Yeah," she conceded. "He gave me some bullshit about it being an insurance settlement. I knew in my gut it was her behind it."

"Why?"

"The way she was watching what he said. She knew who she was married to, and that he'd blab if I opened him up. She was having none of that."

"Diane," Joe asked her, "when you went down there to visit, did you ever see other people hanging around? Friends of theirs, perhaps?"

She gave him a pitying look. "Right. Three decades ago. Want their addresses and phone numbers, too? What they were wearing?"

Willy briefly returned to his earlier persona, leaning against her and saying in a low voice, almost whispering, "You want to remember why we're back here today, Diane—and your role in it."

She stared at him, her eyes filled with tears once more.

"We showed up before whoever got him," he reminded her unnecessarily. "You made a choice."

Joe watched in silence. Under no circumstance would he have used the same strategy. He had interfered with Willy in the past, but only rarely, when he'd feared a law was being transgressed or the rules of human decency glaringly trampled.

Certainly, this had veered close, but he'd kept silent based on experience and trust.

While he was Willy's boss, he was not the keeper of his soul. The man had his demons, a past that had molded him uniquely, and money in the bank when it came to integrity, devotion to his family, and loyalty to service. Joe might not have always liked his tactics, but he honored the man's instinct for the truth, both in himself and in others.

It also didn't hurt that in cases like this, Willy got results. Diane hung her head, sighed deeply, and said, "I know. I have to live with that."

"Yeah," he agreed, "but you can do something about it now. We came up because we found Daryl was probably responsible for Peter's brain damage. Now we know somebody else was after him, too, and not 'cause he smacked his kid. Daryl did something bad four years ago, Diane, and he did bad things thirty years ago, too. That's how he lived. He made crappy choices. You just told us that."

He bumped her shoulder gently with his own. "You loved him. I get it. That's why you pulled a fast one on us two days ago. And now he's gone, which was going to happen anyhow, sooner or later. So do your mourning, and then help us find who did it. Any way you can, including reaching back into ancient history and giving us whatever you got."

Her tears were dropping on the dry wood of the steps between her blue-jeaned knees.

Willy stopped speaking and let the sounds of the chickens, the breeze in the treetops, and the hum of passing bugs settle in.

Joe spoke at last, laying a business card beside her. "We're going to leave you right now, but please think back all you can. The cell number on that card works twenty-four hours a day. Call us, even if it's something minor."

She didn't respond, but she did pick up the card.

CHAPTER FOURTEEN

The Things He Left Behind

"You gonna eat your pickle?" Rachel asked.

Sally nudged her plate an inch toward her. "Have at it."

They were sitting at a window table at the Works Café, overlooking Main Street in downtown Brattleboro. A single large, sunny room, popular, with lots of wood and art on the walls, a casual feel, and a ringside view of the passing population through a row of oversized plate glass windows.

"Any feedback after the John article?" Sally asked before popping a potato chip into her mouth. Her father still hadn't gotten any alerts from the traps he'd set out across the internet, looking for traffic linked with Rust, and she was becoming concerned. In her world of devious dealings, complete silence across all "platforms," as some called credit cards, cell phones, and internet traffic, usually implied only two grim conclusions: The person of interest was either dead or had decided to disappear—something John Rust, with his computer knowledge, would likely know how to do.

Her mouth half full, Rachel tapped her ever-present phone with a fingertip, replying, "I got a possible hit less than an hour ago. The VBI's investigating an unexplained death outside Saint Johnsbury. I'm hoping a source'll give me a name soon."

"It's not John, is it?"

"Apparently not. Someone older and fatter. I know it's a stretch, but it's Gunther and his squad at the scene. I'm betting they wouldn't be way up there, out of their area, unless it was somehow connected to Hicks's killing of Peter Rust."

"Do you think the dead body is Hicks?" Sally asked, happy to be chatting as equals, instead of feeling so conscious of the private eye–reporter divide that often stretched between them.

Rachel shrugged. "That would be surreal. Along similar lines, though, I think I found another puzzle piece. You hear about the chase in Springfield?"

Sally indicated her own phone, lying facedown opposite Rachel's, like two toy vehicles parked nose-to-nose. "The motorcycle? Yeah, I did."

"The guy they caught is named Boris Ryder. I was told by a contact at the PD that he's an old associate of none other than Daryl Hicks, speaking of the devil, going back thirty years."

Sally paused, another chip halfway to her mouth. "Really."

Rachel was pleased with herself. It wasn't often she got an informational jump on her friend, who seemed cross-connected to every known source in the universe.

"Yup, which is why I'm working on a follow-up article suggesting the VBI is going deep into past history to sort out Peter's death. Why else chase down an old pal of Hicks's? This afternoon, I plan to head up to Springfield to interview a few witnesses to that chase, and see if I'm right."

Sally was amused by Rachel's glee. Despite their mutual interest in establishing both Pete's fate and John's whereabouts and intentions, their approaches were remarkably different. Rachel's incentive was more pursuit than acquisition—she wanted the story, especially if it included tantalizing bits for her readers. Sally labored to satisfy a legal process, and accumulate an increasingly sturdy pile of evidentiary building blocks. She was only mildly interested in the VBI's travels down memory lane, preferring what they actually found. With Rachel, the more soap opera elements she could introduce, the better.

And how could you improve on a high-speed chase on a motorcycle in the middle of the night?

Rachel's phone made a small chirping sound. She flipped it over to read the screen before relaying, "It is Hicks and it is a homicide, pending an autopsy. Wow, my mom was there, too. She never goes into the field anymore."

Sally's gaze drifted outside to the passing traffic while she considered the ramifications of this news.

"The murderer could've been John," she mused.

Rachel made a face. "But why? And how did he know where to find him? Did you know where Hicks was living?"

Sally shook her head.

"Me neither," Rachel continued. "And that's true for all my sources. Which means that if John knew, and killed him only now, he must've been keeping tabs on him all along—maybe biding his time depending on how things finally worked out with Pete."

The comment prompted Sally to confess, "My father and I were kicking some of the same thoughts around. Makes you wonder if John was planning to vanish *before* his brother died, in preparation for the inevitable, like you said."

"Making this premeditated." Rachel abandoned picking at the food on both plates to sit back and cross her arms. "If we're right."

"About whether he did kill Hicks or not?" Sally asked. "It would make things fit nice and tight, minus a few details to fill in the blanks. It would be the old story of a bad man being punished once his avenger is free to take action, which in this case was after Pete's death."

Rachel raised her eyebrows. "Isn't that the catch, though? Did John know about Daryl making Pete the way he was? Most people're claiming Pete was born delayed."

Sally considered the point. "Maybe, although nobody said John didn't know the truth from the start."

"Damn," Rachel said, staring off into space.

"What?"

She leaned forward with the thought she'd just conjured up. "Karen overdosed pretty soon after Pete's birth."

"Within a couple of years, yeah."

"This sexy, impatient, take-charge woman with a head full of plans and dreams."

"She must've known, too," Sally filled in. "She *knew* Daryl had damaged Pete and it knocked her feet out from under her. She hit the dumps."

Both women stared at each other as the next reasonable scenario dawned.

"Or . . . ," Rachel began.

"Daryl or someone else supplied the overdose, because everything was finally coming to a head."

Rachel rolled her eyes. "Man. No wonder John's worked up. If any of it's true, it would be one hell of a motivator."

"We have to go back to Diane's," Joe stated.

"Agreed," Willy said without hesitation.

They'd repaired to a St. Johnsbury motel after conferring into the evening with colleagues at the local VBI branch office. It was the smallest of the organization's outposts, given the so-called Northeast Kingdom's sparse population, which had obligated them to call upon the region's tried-and-true mutual response system, where different organizations—including federal agencies sometimes—quickly and readily cooperated in a crisis.

The squad, thus enhanced with several troopers and sheriff's deputies, had coordinated canvassing for any suspicious or remarkable activities around Peacham in the last few days, as well as any statewide unsolved major crimes four years ago, when Daryl Hicks might have had a falling out with confederates that had stimulated his going underground at his sister's.

In the end, all these efforts had boiled down to old-fashioned procedural work—the equivalent of raking through leaves in search of possible clues. This also meant that Joe and Willy, now sharing a room, were in dire need of something more concrete and immediate, beyond merely following fundamentals. That this hunger exceeded simple frustration became clear after Joe pondered aloud, "You feeling the same way I am about our trip to the farm today?"

"That we didn't push her hard enough?"

"Yeah."

For Joe, that was one of the many appeals of an elusive case like this. It twisted around like a book suspended from a string, allowing glimpses of one page or another, but without enough time to absorb its contents. Random thoughts occurred like inspirational flashes. In this situation, however, they'd each reached the same conclusion, that Diane Wrinn, regardless of what they'd put her through, had more to tell them.

They didn't wait until morning, but pulled up to the farm that same evening, after sunset. There was a light on in the room leading to the porch, and the sound of approaching footsteps after Joe had knocked on the door.

Diane Wrinn looked out at them tiredly in the glare of the porch light. "Again?"

"We'd like to see Daryl's room," Joe said.

"Don't you need a warrant for that?"

Willy avoided answering. "You went to all that trouble to protect your brother. Now you're being coy about finding out who killed him?"

In response, she stepped back, widening the doorway. "Top of the stairs, room to the right."

She didn't accompany them. As they started up, Joe saw her return to a glass of amber fluid parked on the kitchen table.

Daryl's were spartan quarters. They made Joe think of some farmworker dorms he'd visited long ago, where the basic amenities of a bed and small side table were barely softened by personal touches like pictures, magazines, or even the presence of a colorful blanket. The walls here were unadorned, the single lamp by the bed a harsh bare bulb stuck on the top of an empty wine bottle. Even the clothes were piled on the floor, or stuffed into a laundry bag. There were no books, one newspaper, an empty coffee cup from Dunkin' Donuts. The bathroom held only a toothbrush, toothpaste, a plastic comb, and a bottle of generic aspirin.

Joe had seen more clutter in a rent-by-the-hour motel room.

Willy dropped to his knees and pulled out a small flashlight to peer under the twin bed.

"Anything?" Joe asked.

"A herd of dust bunnies," Willy reported, standing again and moving to the bed's foot. "Help me move it."

Joe took hold of the other end. "Why, if it's all dusty?"

"'All' is the operative word," Willy answered as they coordinated to shift the bed. "Half of it's been swept aside."

Sure enough, they could see not only where the dust had been disturbed, but even how a large object—like a man's body—might have wiped across the wooden boards by sliding over them.

They studied the floor carefully. Not surprisingly, they found where a single section of board showed a distinct gap around its edges.

Joe crouched down, a penknife in hand, and ran its blade along the board's length. As if on a hinge, it flipped back to reveal a cavity.

Willy threw some light into the void. Before them appeared a bundle of cash, a handgun, a dusty manila envelope, and a cell phone.

"Hello," Willy said, his voice flat.

Donning latex gloves, they used the bed's surface to display the envelope's contents, which came to a small assortment of photographs and a folding knife with blood on it. The phone, they left alone, preferring a more controlled environment in which to open it. That was more Lester's expertise, which they were happy to let him practice.

They also had other things to hold their interest.

The pictures caught them first, the most striking of which—dog-eared and obviously decades old—showed a young woman in a striking pose, wearing a bikini and a wide smile.

"Damn," Willy said appreciatively.

They had seen mug shots of Karen Taylor on the computer, during their earlier research. The impression had been of an attractive woman, certainly, but one memorialized looking hard, worn, older, and angry, as befit the circumstances.

Here was the girl who'd so struck Daryl Hicks. There was a luminescence to her that transcended physical attractiveness, which was as considerable as they'd been led to believe. To Joe's eye, she resembled a precocious, mischievous child, while exuding the sexuality of a woman in her prime.

"I can see why he was pole-axed," Willy said.

Joe laid down the photo and fanned out the remaining three. One was of a boy, helpfully labeled *John* with a pen, one portrayed a small family gathering of two grim-faced parents and two kids, one looking like a teenaged Diane Wrinn. It appeared to be a cheap group shot one used to get at department stores during Christmas, and indeed was stamped J. C. PENNEY COMPANY on the back. The final picture showed a commercial building, as if taken from the road while driving by, with the indistinct and blurry profile of two men walking toward its entrance, and the name of the company partially blocked but clearly legible—WILKINS.

"That mean anything to you?" Willy asked his more experienced boss.

Joe studied not just the large, austere, concrete structure, but the little of its surroundings that were visible at the edges, as well. "Looks like Vermont," he said eventually. "But it means nothing to me. Guess we'll have to let Google do our footwork, for starters."

Willy referred to the photos generally. "Why keep these four? Specifically?"

Joe considered that before answering. "You're on the run, dispossessed, broke, maybe in fear for your life, it makes sense you travel light, ready to move in a flash. But you want reminders of a life left behind. Talismans. In this case, the people who meant the most to you." He reached out and touched the images in turn. "The sister who took you in, and maybe the parents who threw you out, for all we know. Your firstborn child, the woman who lit up your life."

He paused, allowing Willy to add, "And some butt-ugly building."

"Yeah," Joe agreed meditatively. "Not only, but no picture of the second kid. Two mysteries."

"Don't guess I'd keep a shot of somebody I'd messed up, either," Willy mused, "assuming we're right about that."

Joe straightened at the comment, looking thoughtful. "Now that we've got Daryl's DNA," he said, "it might not hurt to compare it to something containing Peter's, like an old hairbrush."

"Right," Willy dragged out the word. "If the kid's not yours, why not take out a little pent-up rage? We did do the math on his getting out of jail and her delivery, didn't we?"

Joe held up his hand with the palm down and wobbled it from side to side, saying, "More or less. That might be another question for the doting sister, when we get to it." He tapped one latex-gloved finger on the picture of the building. "What about this?"

Willy checked Google for the name on his cell phone, soon shaking his head and saying, "Nothing, at least around here. It'll have to wait till we find out where it was, what was made there, and who worked inside."

Both men then looked at the knife, without touching it. It was a folding model, with a four-inch blade—certainly enough to be lethal if applied to the right target.

Willy said, as if in confirmation, "Nasty."

"Another job for the lab," Joe concluded, "along with that money and the gun."

He got to his feet, adding, "I think another chat with Diane is in order."

Willy smiled. "Blowtorch time."

Joe grimaced, unsurprised.

Diane was still at the kitchen table, the glass before her. Joe noticed that its level hadn't lowered, however, as if she'd been waiting for the inevitable.

He let Willy assume the lead he'd established earlier, sitting down at the table across from her while Joe leaned against the sink.

Willy studied her silently for a few seconds, forcing her to look up.

"What?" she asked.

"Your brother's been murdered, you've told us diddly, we just found a gun, a bloody knife, and some cash hidden under his bed, and you ask me that?" He sounded incredulous. "You're jerkin' us around."

"I told you. I didn't know anything."

He acted unoffended. "Okay. Let's talk about what you do know. You knew enough to help Daryl head for the hills when we showed up the first time."

"I was being protective."

"You *were*," he emphasized supportively. "But in reaction to us. The police. You see, that's what's sticking in my craw, Diane. We aren't the bad guys, unless that's how you see us. You wouldn't have gone to such trouble unless you knew he'd done something crooked, *and* that it was recent. Otherwise, you would've just said, 'Oh my goodness, Officer. What's he done?' But not you. You aided and abetted like you *knew* he was wanted. See why I have a problem with that?"

She didn't answer, returning her gaze to the glass before her.

Willy reached into his inside jacket pocket and pulled out a small paper evidence bag, which he upended onto the table between them. It was the large folding knife, its blood stains garish under the light overhead.

She stared at it as if it might move.

"Yeah," Willy commented. "Ouch, huh? You know the story behind this, Diane?"

Her voice was barely audible. "No."

"Doesn't look good. Somebody got stuck. And Daryl thought enough of it to not clean it off *and* hide it under a floorboard, under his bed." Willy pointed at it. "You add that to what you did after we came calling, and you can see why we're thinking you know more than you're saying."

She didn't speak. Willy shrugged, saying, "Well, what the hell? You're a practical woman. You run a farm single-handed, kill things to keep alive, struggle to make ends meet. You did what you could for your brother, despite his making a career of dumb choices. Now he's dead, so why get all worked up? The past is past. That sorta your thinking?"

"I didn't do anything wrong," she said softly.

"Meh," he equivocated. "Not sure the prosecutor would agree with that, but let's say he does." He took out his pen, reached out, and poked at the closed knife as it lay on the table, making it spin in place a couple of times.

"The problem," he said at the same time, "is that whoever contributed the blood on that thing may not be so forgiving. Or—if he's dead—then the people associated with him. And if *they* think, like I do, that you know more than you're telling, they may be the next ones to come knocking. After we're gone," he added after a pause.

Throughout this conversation, Diane had been leaning forward, her elbows on the table and her hands cradling the glass. At Willy's conclusion, she released the glass and buried her face in her open palms, sighing heavily.

Neither cop said anything, waiting her out.

She finally leaned back in her chair, dropping her hands to her lap, and said, "He just couldn't stop. No matter how deep he got in. It was like a sickness, even as a kid."

"Talk to us about the knife, Diane," Willy requested. "The fact that he kept it, after a lifetime of tempting the devil, tells me this screwup was maybe worse than anything he'd pulled before."

"I don't know the details."

"Tell us what you do know."

"It was a few years ago," she said. "When he first came here to stay. He was living in Burlington back then, doing the same dumb stuff he always did, but this time, it was worse. Like you said. Somebody got hurt—crippled." She pointed at the knife. "With that."

"Daryl did it?"

"No," she said forcefully, but then quieted as she added, "at least, that's what he said. But he was involved, and people were after him because of it. The knife was insurance, supposedly."

"How so?"

She shrugged. "I don't know. Fingerprints, maybe? DNA? He just said it's what he needed for a rainy day, in case they ever found him."

Willy opened the evidence bag and scooped the knife back inside. "No names? Details?" he asked.

"No," she answered dully.

Joe stepped forward and used his handkerchief to remove a photograph from a larger envelope he'd been holding.

He laid it faceup on the table, where the knife had been. "How 'bout this building?" he asked. "You know anything about it, or a company named Wilkins?"

This time, her ignorance struck both of them as genuine. "I don't know," she said. "Never heard of it."

"How 'bout either of the two men in front of it?"

"They're hard to see, but no."

Joe pulled out another chair and sat down to get at eye level with her. "Okay. Diane, I need you to listen carefully, all right? If what you said is true, about Daryl being in fear for his safety for so many years, then it's reasonable to think you might also be in danger. We don't know who killed him or why. It may've been this mysterious Burlington bunch, in which case you're probably off the hook, or it may've been somebody else. But whoever it was, you need to be aware that some risk is still associated with your brother's past activities."

He shifted in his seat to heighten his emphasis. "I hope for your sake that you've told us everything you know. We're not in a position to offer you protection. We can have the local police drive by now and then to check on you, but that's not going to be very effective. So our options are limited. Is there anywhere you can go for a while? Anyone you could stay with?"

"No," she said without pause. "They want me, they can find me here. I told you what I know. Daryl's dead. I'm not going to have his ghost fuck me over like when he was alive. I've had enough of this shit."

Joe placed his business card on the table and retrieved the photo he'd shown her. "Okay," he said. "I understand. I already gave you one of those, which you probably threw out. Keep that one, and call me if anything comes up. You remember something; someone unexpected contacts you; you feel threatened in any way. Anything at all. You understand?"

She nodded.

There was nothing left to say. Leaving her as they'd found her, they drove back to St. Johnsbury.

CHAPTER FIFTEEN

Analyzing the Evidence

"What d'you want?"

Rachel looked into the bruised, bearded, hostile face of the man who'd just opened up to her knock.

"Mr. Ryder?" she asked, half hoping he'd slam the door.

But, sadly and predictably, he apparently liked what he saw—at once the blessing and the curse of Rachel's gender, youth, and appearance. "Yeah."

"I'm Rachel Reiling, from the *Brattleboro Reformer*. I was hoping I could ask you a couple of questions about the other night."

There were more wily ways of slipping under people's defenses. But she suspected, now that she was confronted with the man behind the name, that perhaps she was subconsciously hoping to sabotage her chance for an interview. She'd been leery of this Springfield neighborhood, the house hadn't helped, and now here was its actual owner.

She hadn't worked as a reporter for long—certainly not proportional to the high number of scrapes she'd gotten into over her brief career—and now another looked to be looming nigh.

She was hopefully preparing for rejection, therefore, when of course he responded, "Damn right you can ask. Those fucking people think they can do anything they want. Damned cops. Bunch o' Nazis. And my bike—totaled. Come on in."

Impressed by her own sudden self-protectiveness, she gestured to a couple of crates upended on the derelict, trash-strewn porch. "Mind if we talk out here? It's a nice day."

He chuckled. "Smart girl. You're probably doin' me a favor. I bet they're watchin' me right now; I bring you inside, they'll throw a rape charge at me. That'd be typical."

Comforting, she thought, glancing across the street, hoping he was right about the surveillance.

"So," he began as they settled down, "what d'ya wanna know?"

"I heard it was quite a ride through town. Normally, we get the police blotter about something like this, and pretty much plug it into the paper without question. When I heard you weren't under arrest, it got me curious. What was it all about?"

She had to give him marks for honesty. He admitted straight out. "Oh hell, that was my own stupidity. I'm no virgin when it comes to the cops, so I figured it was something I'd done. They pounded on the door, I split out the back instead of asking. Turns out, they just wanted to talk."

"They had nothing on you?"

He laughed, a man at ease with his lot in life. "They do *now*, but I'm out on my own recognizance for once."

"What did they want?" she asked, getting to the point of her visit, if much faster than anticipated. Her plan had been to put up with twenty minutes of outrage and claims of innocence first. The man's almost professional lack of guile was refreshing.

"That was the craziest thing of all," he admitted. "It was all old stuff. They were major-case cops and they wanted to talk about the dinosaur days, and I mean *really* long ago, back when I had some spring in my step."

"Really?" she asked, she hoped enticingly.

"Well," he began nibbling at the bait. "It wasn't like we were the Hole-in-the-Wall Gang or anything, but things were a lot livelier than now. It's all drugs and cybersex today. Getting off on your phone, feeding your habit. Disgusting, if you ask me. We were more into stealing and causing trouble. And booze. Damn, there were a lot of bars around. Bratt, here in Springfield, Bellows Falls. You name it, there were six bars to a street in some of those places. Now it's all those stupid phones everyone's got."

He dug into his pocket and fished out an iPhone, admitting cheerfully, "I got mine. It's turning my brain to mush. I heard emergency rooms across the country are getting patients 'cause they're walkin' into phone poles and growing little bones in their eyes, or heads, or somethin', and stuff like that. It's on the internet. Unbelievable."

"Did these police officers ask about anyone in particular?"

"Yeah," he resumed, unfazed by the course correction and repocketing his phone. "There was a kind of gang I hung out with way back. That's what made me think of Butch and Sundance. They were a couple. Karen Taylor and Daryl Hicks. She was the brains and he was the muscle. We pulled a bunch of stunts. It was fun, didn't hurt anyone, and kept us busy."

She wasn't about to debate the moral issues with him. "Karen and Daryl came up in the news recently," she said leadingly.

He pointed at her, grinning broadly. "Not in your paper," he said. "You got scooped. Daryl was whacked yesterday, I think. It's all over Twitter and the rest."

"We're carrying that tomorrow," she reacted a little defensively. "You know anything about it?"

"Daryl? No way." He chuckled. "Him and me stopped trading Christmas cards years ago."

"But you were friends once."

Speaking outside the confines of any police station, with a pleasant young woman, the trauma of his violent bike ride mostly faded, Boris Ryder found himself in a better mood than while speaking with Kunkle—more inclined to reminisce and less self-protective. After all, with Daryl now dead, who was left from those times, aside from him?

"Yeah," he conceded genuinely. "We really were. I guess I am getting old, thinking that way, like everything's in the rearview mirror."

Rachel took a risk and asked, "I bet the police were interested in those stories."

In the same philosophical vein, he rested the back of his head against the wall behind him. "They were," he said. "I thought that was a little weird, if you wanna know the truth. Who cares?"

"What brought it all to an end?" Rachel asked.

Ryder looked at her. "What do you mean?"

"It sounded like your gang had a good deal going," she explained. "Why did it end?"

"This is like the conversation I had with that one-armed cop," he complained. "All this old crap."

"Everybody seems to think it's coming home to roost," Rachel guessed.

"Yeah?"

"Daryl's been killed, his handicapped son just died, his other son's missing. Something's shifting in the wind."

Ryder looked thoughtful. "Huh. Who knew? There's nothing that happened back then that rings any bells with me. That cop did keep asking about how Karen organized the jobs they pulled."

"Any one in particular?"

He smiled. "I did dick him around a bit. He was such an asshole, threatening me with jail time. I had to get a little dig in somewhere."

Rachel smiled indulgently. "That must've felt good."

"He had no clue."

"What did you do?"

"Not much. Gave him a taste, but then played dumb at the end. You don't wanna disappoint people if that's what they expect of you. And cops think they're such geniuses."

She rephrased her question. "What happened?"

"Oh, I was telling him how Karen ramped things up over time, from penny-ante stuff to bigger and better gigs. He was wondering how they moved out of Springfield, into a nice place like what they bought in Westminster, 'bout the same time she got pregnant again."

Rachel leaned forward, giving him some positive body language. "What did you tell him?"

"I sort of mentioned that maybe they hit a gold mine with something like a payroll robbery, but then I got forgetful. You know, 'Oh, it was so many years ago. Who can remember?' Stuff like that."

Knowing Kunkle as she did, Rachel was having a hard time believing he fell for something like this. "He went for it?" she asked.

"He didn't push for more," Ryder said. "That kinda surprised me. Like I said, I thought the whole damned thing was weird, chasing me down like they did, just to ask a bunch of stupid questions about people nobody cares about no more."

Rachel looked confused. "So, I don't get it. He just quit?"

"Pretty much, yeah. Course, I mighta oversold it, telling him I didn't know nuthin' about any details. He might've believed me. I was kind of bummed. I thought I had an ace, but he never really pushed for it. He looked happy enough when he left, but I still don't know what I said that floated his boat. He's a weird dude."

"You knew the details of the job she pulled?"

That brought him up short. "Not really. Maybe he figured that out, come to think of it. Still, I did know where she'd been sniffing around."

"Where was that?"

"She'd been hired by a company. I can't remember what they made, but it was big. Had government contracts, a lot of workers. A manufacturing outfit. I wasn't involved in any of it, and I suppose I'm mostly putting two and two together, saying that's where she got her payoff. For all I really know, that didn't pan out and she did rob an armored truck or something, like some people say."

"What was the name of the company?" Rachel asked.

He gave her another broad grin. "See? That's it. That's the question I was waiting to hear from him, that asshole cop. I thought it was like a perfect setup, you know?"

He scratched his head. "'Cept now, I'm startin' to wonder if it just didn't matter. If you wanna get technical, it probably doesn't. That company went outta business or got bought up, or something—years and years ago."

"As a result of what Karen did or did not do?" Rachel asked.

But he frowned. "Nah. That much I did tell him. Nothing happened after, which is maybe why I'm probably totally wrong. The company went under, or whatever, a few years later."

"What was it called?" Rachel asked, her pen poised above her pad to take note. It wasn't of great importance to her, but readers did like local references, and this big dope had dragged it out for so long, she thought the least she could do is collect the prize Willy had left without.

"Smith Wilkinson."

Their war room was on the second floor of the Caledonia County courthouse, on St. Johnsbury's elegant and historic Main Street, and across the street from the Athenæum art gallery and library, which, to the astonishment of many visitors, had an enormous Bierstadt painting of Yosemite hanging on one wall.

Like so many Vermont towns, St. J had once been a large, bustling, prominent junction of industry, culture, and commerce. Now, while alive and functioning, and a well-regarded Northeast Kingdom landmark for historic sites and architectural gems, it was mostly a throwback to more glorious times, its rail yard peaceful, its factory buildings thinly inhabited, and its appeal nostalgic. One by one, across the state, this had been the fate of dozens of urban clusters, from Bennington to Windsor to Barre and onward, where residents had claimed brief dominance as the biggest, busiest, most populated places on Vermont's expanding map of nineteenth-century progress. Almost all had slipped in importance and significance, as quarrying or lumber or train travel had or, in St. J's case, the Fairbanks company, maker of the world's first platform scale, which had also yielded to history's merciless march.

Nevertheless, the region's largest town remained the county seat, the home of VBI's northeast office, and, for the moment, the site of Joe Gunther's staff meeting.

He was seated on the broad second-floor windowsill overlooking the courthouse lawn and the street beyond, facing a group of eight agents, including Willy and Lester Spinney, and an assortment of state troopers and sheriff's deputies, all seated around two conjoined folding tables littered with coffee cups and doughnut boxes. Sammie Martens was back in Brattleboro, handling the office and coordinating with them remotely, connected to them now via speakerphone.

Joe held up his hand to quiet the general conversation, and began. "Thank you all for your help and hard work so far. What started as an unremarkable DUI has ballooned into something involving multiple murders, assaults, thefts, and who knows what else, going back decades. A few of our suspects are dead, others are MIA, and some may even be imaginary, for all I know. The discovery of Daryl Hicks's body outside Peacham, however, reveals that whatever the true narrative, it is alive and still taking a toll.

"Our job, here and now," he continued, "is to organize what we've found so far, and see if we can identify a pattern, a logic, and the person or people responsible for at least the more recent of all that mayhem."

"In other words," said a voice, "find Daryl's killer."

Joe addressed the point with emphasis. "Yes, but not only. Given the slim evidence we've got so far, we can't afford to dismiss any details in this convoluted series of events. I am not at all convinced that the forces behind Daryl's death are what we usually deal with, the you-pissed-me-off-so-now-I-kill-you school of homicide. That *may* be the case here, but there's much more that needs explaining. That's why, so far, we've been running down two parallel avenues. Besides the here and now, there's a very cold trail that seems to connect to when Daryl Hicks possibly shook the infant Peter Rust twenty-eight years ago, resulting in his recent death."

"Unless it doesn't," Willy commented dryly.

Joe responded enthusiastically, pointing at him. "*Exactly.* Unless it doesn't. That's why we're here."

He glanced at Lester, who rose to address the group.

"We've got a lot to cover, so please refer to the folders I handed out earlier for reference. From the top: Information is coming back from the lab about the items seized at Diane Wrinn's farm. We've got investigators digging in to an alleged knifing that occurred four years ago in Burlington, which possibly ties in to Daryl's death. We're getting intel locally about sightings made of unknown suspicious persons that were seen at roughly the same time Daryl made a run for it.

"Background's still missing about any company named Wilkins, whose photograph Daryl kept for some reason, but we're thinking they may have had something to do with Karen Taylor hitting her jackpot. Finally, there's John Rust, Karen's firstborn, who has fallen off the map. He's suspected of bearing an ancient grudge against Daryl, and might be one of the local sightings I mentioned a minute ago."

Joe slipped off his perch by the window and stood beside Lester. "I know that for some of you," he added, "most of this doesn't matter much. Your focus is on what happened to Daryl Hicks. So let's start there."

He held up his own copy of the distributed folder. "At the back of this are some photographs and computer printouts. There's a recent mug shot of John Rust, an older one of Daryl, along with as presentable a portrait as we could get from the ME's office. There are shots of Diane Wrinn's truck that Daryl was last seen driving, and a copy of its registration. You'll also see a print from a surveillance camera located here in town, showing a vehicle like the one belonging to John Rust, although you can't make out the plate. Finally, there's a copy of a complaint filed with the sheriff's office by a neighbor of Diane Wrinn's, about a vehicle with two men in it, parked late at night by the side of the road, as if positioned to keep an eye on her place. This is the same day Daryl beat feet for parts unknown. Sadly, it was gone by the time a deputy responded, and the neighbor didn't get a license plate, but she did describe it, and it fits neither Rust's car nor what Daryl was last driving. The nice thing is that the neighbor did clearly decipher two bumper stickers, one reading 'Take Back Vermont,' and the other, 'This Car Climbed Mt. Washington,' along with the vehicle's general color and make, which, as you can see, is an older model, rusty Toyota truck, probably dark blue."

"Any idea of its role in all this?" one of the troopers asked.

"Don't we wish," Joe replied. "At this point, we can only guess, and I think we've done enough of that so far."

"What about what was found under the floorboards?"

"I just got some feedback on that," Sam's disembodied voice announced from the speakerphone. "The lab did an expedited analysis of the blood on the knife and immediately got a hit off the state database. It belongs to Seamus Sweeney, of Burlington's Old North End. Mr. Sweeney was involved in a knifing four years ago that put him permanently in a wheelchair. We're still looking into that, but it's sounding like he's a minor gang boss of sorts and that Daryl Hicks might've been a member back then. However, the fingerprints lifted off the knife are not Hicks's—they belong to another Sweeney associate named Billy Belanger. Details to follow."

They could hear her riffling through some paperwork before she spoke again. "More prints were lifted from the gun found at Diane's. They do belong to Hicks and no matches have surfaced anywhere to a test bullet fired at the lab. We're still running the serial number through ATF. The cell phone's also been a dud, but something did come up concerning that photograph of the factory building—from a pretty unlikely source, no less."

"Okay," Joe said doubtfully.

"Rachel Reiling just filed a story on the *Reformer*'s website, prior to tomorrow's print edition, about the motorcycle chase up in Springfield. It's really an interview of Boris Ryder, and it mostly quotes him about how the whole thing was a misunderstanding, the cops overreacted, and blah, blah, blah. In the middle of it, though, he says how all we wanted was to ask him about the good old days. She quotes him as telling us how Karen had climbed the ladder in terms of opportunities, but how he never got the chance to tell us that her last job was at Smith Wilkinson."

"Oh, for Christ's sake," Willy said. "Smith Wilkinson. Not Wilkins. The picture cut that off."

"What did she do for them?" Joe asked.

"It doesn't go into detail. It's just a passing reference, but the context is that it was at the same time she and Daryl moved to Westminster, right before Pete was born."

Lester, Joe, and Willy exchanged glances. "I think," the last told his boss, "that somebody better have a talk with your kind-of-stepdaughter."

"And take a dive into the past activities and employees of Smith Wilkinson," Lester suggested.

CHAPTER SIXTEEN

The Forest for the Trees

"Where do we stand, locating John?" Scott Jezek asked his private investigator, loosening his tie and rolling up his sleeves. "The clock's ticking on his court appearance, and I heard through channels that the state's attorney is wondering if he might've done a runner, which I dismissed as nonsense, of course."

"Of course," Sally replied, keeping her voice neutral.

Jezek remained silent, watching her sitting in his office.

"Let me start with a question," she proposed.

"All right."

"Do you know for a fact that John didn't know Daryl made Pete the way he was?"

"No," the lawyer said without pause. "Why?"

"Possible motivation," she said, explaining, "As part of asking myself where John is, I've been wondering why he took off in the first place—if maybe hiring you had something to do with needing freedom to act, instead of fatalistically twiddling his thumbs in jail."

Jezek's naturally analytical mind fell in beside hers at the suggestion.

"Freedom to do what?" he asked. By now Daryl Hicks's death was common news, but Jezek didn't suggest the reasonable conclusion that John had done the killing.

"Given what we've learned so far," Sally said, doing it for him, "I'd say to avenge his little brother."

"He could have done that anytime," Jezek argued, probing her logic. "He had help with Pete's day-to-day needs. He could've cut loose to go after Daryl years ago, if you're right about his motivation. Why wait until Peter died?"

"That's been bugging me," she admitted. "'Cause you're right. There had to be more of a reason, unless the death was some sort of final tipping point—the last straw on the camel's back. Otherwise, yeah, why wait? For that matter, why all those years of dedication and sacrifice? And the empty bottles of booze do speak of sacrifice. I think it's because John was consumed by guilt."

That caught Jezek by surprise. "For what? He was twelve. What did he do?"

"I'm thinking it's what he didn't do," she explained. "I have nothing to go on here—John's the only living witness to what happened, after all—but let's say he saw Daryl shake Pete senseless and did nothing about it. Just stood there. Remember, this is the school of hard knocks. John's parents make money by stealing it. They live rough, act rough, don't follow the rules. It was a dog-eat-dog life, where you protect your own and are loyal to your tribe. What if John froze? Did nothing but watch as his baby brother was brutalized? Karen couldn't have been around, or you know she would've acted. So it was John, all alone. And he did nothing. See where I'm heading?"

Jezek had been nodding in agreement throughout, and now suggested, "And not only did he freeze when he felt he should've acted, but he must've gone along with Daryl's cover story when Karen got home, perhaps to avoid suffering a similar fate. A woman with her personality wouldn't have taken Daryl hurting Pete in stride. He had to cook up an explanation—perhaps an accidental fall or some other domestic mishap—and call on John to back him up, adding to John's guilt."

After a brief silence, Jezek asked, "So answer the earlier question, now that this is out in the open. True or not, why did John wait until Pete's death to go after Daryl, again assuming that's what he's done?"

Sally answered, "Because he's finally doing what he failed to do then. More than that, he took caring for his brother until death did them part to the nth degree. Call it an obsession in two parts, the first nurturing, the second bloodthirsty."

Jezek was thoughtful. "And this is all conjecture?"

"Pure. I have zero evidence to support it."

The lawyer nevertheless was on board. "It does sound plausible, though. His drunk driving charge is starting to look tame."

Across town at roughly the same time, Rachel was earning her pay fulfilling one of her less glamorous duties, in this case posing a basketball team around a banner and a trophy, with the high school gym in the background. She had been hired by the paper as a photographer only, and seen her mandate expand beyond that because of Stan Katz's appreciation of her talent and ambition. Yet he was as much a pragmatist as the paper was short of funds. Everyone—Stan included—had to regularly serve a broad number of different, occasionally menial, functions.

Rachel didn't mind. Having signed on fresh from college, she'd first embraced the prejudice against covering civic activities and club luncheons that were the bread and butter of most small-town newspapers.

Experience had quickly improved her attitude. She preferred the investigative and hard news work, but she truly enjoyed the pure unfiltered enthusiasm of softball teams and garden clubs.

She was therefore smiling as she returned to her car in the parking lot. Until she saw Sammie Martens lounging against her fender, waiting for her with arms crossed.

There was no doubt from the cop's expression that this was a professional visit.

Rachel liked Sam, respected her toughness and drive, and held her as a good exemplar of a female having succeeded on her own merits in a notoriously male-dominated occupation. That she had then given birth to a sweet, well-loved, highly personable little daughter only drove home Rachel's high opinion of the woman, even if the man who also benefited from that joy was someone Rachel had never warmed to.

It also didn't hurt that Rachel knew of Sam's devotion to Joe Gunther, for whom Rachel had the utmost respect.

This was all to the good, since Sam's identity was first and foremost a police officer, a societal ranking separate from bankers, plumbers, or carpenters, who were usually seen as simply having jobs. By contrast, Rachel had found that police officers were routinely wedded to their profession in the public eye. This wasn't unique—doctors and lawyers could complain of the same fate—but it often encouraged the lower-paid, routinely stressed cops to bunch together into clans, exacerbating their isolation.

And despite Rachel's grasp of this phenomenon, it still had its effect on her as she neared her friend. All she could see in Sam's expression was the cop.

"Hey, Sam," Rachel greeted her, unslinging her equipment bag and getting her key out to unlock the car.

"Hey, yourself," Sam replied with a smile. "It's been a while."

Rachel worked the lock and opened the door. "Well, two crazy schedules. Hard to find downtime. How's Emma?"

"She's good. You still enjoying the *Reformer*?"

Rachel paused as she dumped her bag on the seat, on top of a metal water bottle and an empty bag of chips, and cast her a glance. "You know something I don't?"

Sam raised her eyebrows. "Uh-oh. I hit a button?"

Rachel straightened. "*Ah*. This what they call verbal judo?"

That only broadened Sam's amusement. "Not hardly. I did want to pick your brain about something, before you start asking why I'm decorating your car hood."

"I was wondering."

"You wrote about Boris Ryder's midnight ride," Sam said.

Rachel was immediately intrigued. "Yeah. Seemed like an interesting angle, to interview the subject of a chase, instead of just those chasing him—especially since he wasn't in jail."

"It was a good piece," Sam complimented her. "I like reading your stuff."

"Thanks," Rachel said, not knowing what to add.

"There was one thing that came up," Sam helped her out. "He mentioned that Karen Taylor once worked at Smith Wilkinson. Was there anything else he said about that? He didn't mention it to us, and it might be good to know."

It was casually said, and Rachel appreciated the soft sell. She also gratefully acknowledged that, over the few years of their acquaintanceship, Sam had lent Rachel emotional support in several tough situations. The question, however, neatly represented the quandary of the traditional police-press divide. Echoing other shibboleths like patient-doctor confidentiality or a priest's protection of the confessional, a reporter's resistance to questions about his or her source material was an ingrained, time-honored reaction.

But that principle was harder-etched in urban areas than here. Both Gunther and Katz, separately, had preached to Rachel the value of a little cooperation, occasionally. She didn't see that this was any time to get hard-nosed.

Plus, she really had nothing to say.

"Nope," she replied.

Sam's eyes widened slightly. "That's it? 'Nope'? He had nothing to say, or you're not going to tell me?"

It was Rachel's turn to be amused. "No, no. The first. He told me how he was hoping to dazzle Willy with his cleverness, holding out that Karen had worked for Smith Wilkinson, but Willy never asked him for its name—that he suddenly seemed distracted by something else Ryder had said, and ended the interview. Ryder even seemed a little pissed off."

"Did he tell you what he'd been holding back?"

"Well, that was the joke. Aside from the company name, he conceded he actually didn't know if Karen had done anything illegal there. He told me Karen and Daryl seemed to have hit a gold mine at around the same time, but that, for all Ryder knew, they'd robbed a bank. Like I said, he really had nothing."

"No mention of anyone working there?" Sam persisted.

"Nope. Is it outside the rules for me to ask why you're so curious about Smith Wilkinson?"

Sam looked nonchalant, and waved a hand dismissively. "We're trying to figure out the source of their money. You already know that. Smith Wilkinson just seemed worth asking about." She shrugged. "Apparently not."

Sam began moving away toward her own car in the distance, saying, "Thanks anyway, though. I appreciate the help."

"Sure," Rachel said, suspicious of the offhand manner. She might not have been much interested in Smith Wilkinson when Ryder had told her of it. But she was now.

And planning to do some digging on her own.

Joe and Beverly were enjoying a little time together in Windsor. Her primary residence was an ostentatious pile of a building overlooking Lake Champlain, dating back to her marriage to Rachel's father and reflecting his need to show off his success.

The Windsor house by contrast was small, modest, and set next to a pond on the edge of downtown. In Joe's sentimental mind—to which he was prey more often than he let on—he saw this picturesque haven as a true love nest, reminiscent of the countryside dacha featured in *Doctor Zhivago*, where Lara and the doc repaired to canoodle in midwinter.

It was a romantically tangible symbol between them, an investment for two veterans of life, no longer interested in marriage but very keen on a physical, emotional, and intellectual companionship that continually enriched them.

Beverly's schedule was pretty reliable, Joe's less so, making this particular rendezvous on the late side, and celebrated first by huddling around a pizza on the screened porch overlooking the pond, side by side on the couch. The sun had set, leaving a rose-tinged blush across the lower sky. The night coolness was rising gently, on the heels of a pleasantly warm day, which meant they could better smell than see the first of nature's attempts to reverse winter's havoc.

"God, I was hungrier than I thought," she said between bites.

"I noticed," he chuckled, sipping from his glass.

She elbowed him. "You should talk. You've barely come up for air."

"I missed lunch," he admitted.

"This case has got you running," she said.

"I was up in Saint J," he explained, "trying to make sense of it with a mini–task force we have going up there, and I have to admit, it does feel like untangling the causes behind a ten-car pileup."

"Successfully, I hope?" she asked.

"Not sure I'd put it that way," he replied ruefully. "What with ancient history and current events mixing in together, it's still pretty much a head scratcher."

She looked at him sympathetically before laying a hand on his knee. "I hate to be the bearer of bad news, then," she said. "But two things I learned today are probably not going to help much. In fact, I hope you'll forgive me for waiting until now to tell you—I wanted to make sure you ate first."

"This doesn't sound good."

"No, it's fine," she reassured him. "I'm just being maternal. The first was sent to your office earlier, the autopsy results on Daryl Hicks."

"Let me guess," he suggested. "Blunt force trauma."

"That's the tricky part," she countered. "It was a myocardial infarction. I can't say the stress of being beaten didn't stimulate it, but he didn't die of his wounds."

Joe looked thoughtful. "Suggesting that whoever worked him over didn't get what they wanted—assuming they wanted more than to kill him."

"From my interpretation of the injuries," she said, "I'd say there was a definite escalation, implying either torture and/or what you're suggesting, an effort to extract information."

"That's curious, though," Joe mused. "If we're right about this four-year-old knifing in Burlington, and Hicks going underground as a result, what would he have that any of those guys would want? I guess that weights things toward the torture-for-revenge column."

They were silent for a beat, before he asked, "What was your other piece of bad news?"

"We heard back from the DNA results you'd requested on Peter Rust and Daryl Hicks."

"Right. Another father-son relationship from hell."

She only partially agreed. "Well, that's it. From hell, no doubt, but not father-son. They weren't related, Joe."

He straightened as he looked at her. "I'll be damned. Karen was stepping out on him. That had been floated as a possibility."

"Sadly," she followed up, "I can't take the next step and identify the father. That would truly be helpful."

He kissed her. "Don't worry about it," he said. "It still suggests a theory or two we didn't have front and center till now, especially if Daryl knew about his lack of paternal dibs."

She returned the kiss, responsive as always to his manner, his warmth, and a sensuality that—as a scientist—she'd only been able to identify as chemical. She slid her hand a little higher, saying, "You do have a way of soothing a girl's concern. And of planting an idea in her head."

His reaction was to reach for the top button of her shirt.

Lester looked questioningly at his Burlington host, Captain Mike McReady, surrounded by members of his black-clad special response team and a couple of the local VBI agents.

"We ready to roll?"

It was cramped in the windowless van, and uncomfortably warm. Fortunately, this group hadn't been here long. The surveillance of Seamus Sweeney's house—referred to by McReady as his "headquarters"—had started hours earlier, with outlying support troops put in position, including two snipers for good measure. In the van was the entry team, assigned to actually breach the building, and their quiet tension accounted more for the heat in the van than any vagaries of climate.

McReady in turn eyed his team leader, who gave him a thumbs-up.

"All right," the captain said. "Let's go."

Burlington's Old North End is populated with older buildings, many left over from a hundred years earlier. There are residential homes, here and there, and an overwhelming number of places cut up into apartments. It is not a tourist destination, local cops like to point out, but popular nevertheless, largely for calls for service.

According to the briefing Lester had received from McReady's intel folks, Seamus Sweeney and his gang had been a forceful presence in the neighborhood for decades—a small, rural version of the vicious variety Boston had been producing for over a century.

Large urban operations got FBI attention, front-page coverage, and even Jack Nicholson movies extolling their dubious achievements. Smaller ones like Sweeney's, because their national statistics approached the marginal, became headaches only for hometown cops. Victims of Sweeney's outfit—from protection, racketeering, prostitution, drugs, car thefts, and the rest—felt the pain, loss, and fear no less than big-city targets, but ironically were too often drowned out by the never-ending drumbeat of Vermont's Green Mountain, upbeat, public relations mantra.

The odd headline might tout someone's heartbreak now and then—if the circumstances or details were attractive enough to the assignment editor—but otherwise, the small, mostly unreported guerrilla war between crooks and victims in the blighted back streets of Burlington, Rutland, Bennington, and others across the state, continued apace with the regularity of an unhealthy heartbeat.

This was Seamus Sweeney's realm, and the world into which Lester and McReady's tactical team entered as they exited the van and spread out to surround and eventually access Sweeney's stronghold.

Gaining that access, however, was the rub. Unlike the flashy assaults featured on screen, where cops approach their objective like combatants breaching a Fallujah stronghold, police in Vermont are constrained by culture and the courts to use less belligerent techniques. Violence-prone, so-called no-knock warrants are only rarely issued, mostly against high-profile criminals who might escape or destroy evidence if warned. But they are hard to get, and Sweeney didn't qualify.

In fact, Lester's suspicions about Seamus's involvement in Daryl's murder were based solely on the items found under Daryl's bed and the fact that the truck spotted close by Diane Wrinn's farm—registered to Sweeney—matched the one now parked outside this house. The only reason Lester had been successful in lobbying for Mike McReady's help was because the BPD had other cases against the man, wanted to search his place and pick him up, and saw using Lester's interest as a good excuse to act now rather than later. Timing, Lester was hoping, had played in his favor.

Thus, appearances, adrenaline, and heavy armaments aside, the whole operation began gently. McReady himself—after waiting for everyone to get situated—pressed the front door bell and waited patiently for someone to respond.

This happened within a minute, when a large, bearded, tattooed man in jeans and a T-shirt opened the door. Only then did things ramp up. McReady shoved his paperwork into the man's hand, announced who he was and his reason for being there, and stepped aside for the entry team to rush by.

Most of this orchestration was probably unnecessary. Even with the prejudices separating good guys from bad, there was an almost professional regard between cops and crooks. Members of the former—even following an emotion-packed and physically demanding arrest—often engaged the latter in collegial banter afterward, on the way to jail. It wasn't a given. Drugs, drink, and residual anger could intervene. But it was certainly evident in the breaching of Seamus Sweeney's place of business.

The big man at the door shouted and swore, but didn't put up a fight.

Other people encountered throughout the building yelled out protests and struggled a little as they were corralled or handcuffed. But all in all—elevated heartbeats to one side—the operation was lacking in theatrical "gotchas." Something for which Lester was grateful, even with his past training for these actions and recollections of some near misses.

He'd been taught early on that his most powerful weapons were his mouth to speak and his pen to take notes. He could do the physical stuff—and had—but was perfectly happy with a peaceful outcome, every time.

That brought Lester, McReady, the entry team leader, and a couple of others to a dirty, cluttered, foul-smelling room on the second floor, confronting a skinny man wearing a Van Dyke and slicked-back hair, sitting in a shabby wheelchair, sneering at them.

"Seamus Sweeney?" McReady asked.

"Like we never met?"

"I have warrants here for your arrest and to search these premises. I will now read you your Miranda rights."

"Can't wait. I'll pretend I never heard 'em before."

McReady intoned the standard recitation and asked, first, if Sweeney understood them, and, second, if he was willing to talk anyway.

Unexpectedly, the man in the chair said, "Sure. What d'ya wanna know?"

McReady glanced at Lester. It was a telling reflection of the Burlington cop's character that he was allowing Lester first crack, and through him the VBI. This had been a BPD operation, planned and manned. Lester was here almost out of courtesy.

Lester wasn't going to quibble, however, and didn't hesitate addressing Sweeney.

"Why was your truck parked outside Diane Wrinn's farm three nights ago?"

"Because I wanted to rip Hicks's balls off and stuff 'em down his throat," Sweeney replied without hesitation.

The half-second of following dead silence spoke of the universal surprise.

"You admitting you killed him?" Lester asked.

Sweeney's face expressed wonder. "Wow, stupid and deaf, both. Is that what I said?"

Lester crouched down before the seated man, fixing him at eye level. "Seamus, he was tortured to death. That's what you just finished saying you had planned. It's not much of a leap."

"It is a leap, though," Sweeney came back stubbornly. "I got no clue why you all just kicked in my door, but if this is it, you're fucked. I had a beef against Hicks. And I been lookin' for him ever since I ended up in this fuckin' thing." He slapped his hand on the wheelchair's arm. "But hopin' for something and doin' it aren't the same. If Daryl ended up how he deserved, I'm a happy man, but I didn't have nuttin' to do with it, sorry to say."

"If that's true," Lester said, "how did you find out where he was living?"

Sweeney laughed. "Google, baby. Once I read those newspaper articles out of Brattleboro online, about some dead kid related to Hicks, I started connecting the dots. The more articles came out, the more I had to work with. Wasn't long before the forgotten sister in Peacham got picked up by one of those search engines. I only wish I'd reached the bastard first."

"Were you in the truck outside Wrinn's?"

"I'm not gonna waste my time on a stakeout. That was Jake and Billy. They were just supposed to keep an eye open, maybe tail the loser if they saw him go anywhere, and report back."

"*Did* they see anything?"

Seamus Sweeney grinned broadly. "Yeah. The lights go out at midnight."

"They must've done more than just sit in the truck."

"They looked around some," the older man admitted. "Only saw the sister through the window. I'm tellin' you. Daryl was a no-show. Probably dead already."

"You got connections," Lester pressed him. "You hear who might've done that?"

"Don't I wish. I'd buy the guy a steak dinner."

CHAPTER SEVENTEEN

An Alliance of Trust

Sally paused inside the lobby of the Proctor and Harris funeral home, impressed, as ever, by the aura such places exuded. Without exception in her admittedly limited experience, they were somber, solemn, and reminiscent of a long-dead grandmother's front parlor, complete with doilies on tables, furniture that discouraged use, and curtains heavy enough to challenge even Scarlett O'Hara's prowess as a seamstress.

"Are you Sally Kravitz?" came a soft, pleasant, suitably soothing voice from a side room.

Sally turned to see a middle-aged woman enter in a sensible dress and shoes. "Anne Proctor?" Sally asked.

The woman extended a hand in greeting. "Yes. You work for Mr. Jezek?"

"That's right," Sally confirmed. "Thanks so much for seeing me."

This visit was a true shot in the dark, born of a verbal jam session between Sally and her employer, where, as usual lately, the subject had been how to locate John Rust.

"It's entirely our pleasure," Proctor said formally. "I was told you were here to ask about Pete Rust's service. How might we help?"

Sally was starting to feel that the only thing missing was a body stretched out between them.

Instead, like something out of Monty Python, two gamboling, goofy, stumbling chocolate Lab puppies burst out of nowhere, made a mad dash toward the demure Ms. Proctor, whose mouth opened in muted protest, and knocked her backward into a thankfully placed chair by the door she'd just used. She collapsed in a heap, one shoe falling off, and began laughing hysterically.

The dogs showed no letting up, circling Sally like TV Comanches surrounding a wagon train, one of them with the shoe in its mouth.

"*Rob*," Anne Proctor called out, all decorum destroyed. "*Roy*. Stop it. *NO*."

It was utterly in vain, of course, and both women ended up on the floor with the puppies, ruffling their ears and trying not to be nipped.

"Don't tell me," Sally said. "You just got them."

"A week ago," Proctor replied. "If this ever happens during business hours, we're sunk. They belong to my son," she explained. "He's due back tomorrow, and it won't be a minute too soon." She fought off a sloppy kiss on the cheek, adding, "Not that I really mind, between you and me. It makes for a nice break from all this." She waved her hand at the décor. "Still, can you imagine if a service was going on right now?"

Sally thought that if the service were hers, she'd be charmed, but she kept that to herself.

"Well," Anne said, fighting off another friendly embrace, "I guess we might as well just get to it. Why did you want to see me? Mr. Jezek only said you'd explain."

"It's pretty random," Sally allowed. "That's probably why he didn't do it on the phone. What we're after is a list of everyone who attended the Peter Rust service."

Sally had wondered aloud earlier to Jezek whether one way to locate John might be through a friend or relative whom they'd missed so far.

What if such a contact had attended the funeral, he'd rhetorically countered, not only to lend John comfort, but possibly to supply him a haven afterward?

Anne rose awkwardly to her feet, answering, "Such a tragedy, what happened. Well, now, what we do is obviously not foolproof. It's a voluntary process. But we have a sign-in book. I can get you that. It usually goes to the family, of course, but John didn't want it. And we have our own tradition, which some people think is a little weird—so we always ask—but we offer to take a group picture, just in case anyone wants a remembrance. It's surprising how many want a copy, especially nowadays. I guess it's a reflection of the Facebook generation, or something. Anyway, we asked, and nobody said no, even though none of them asked for a copy afterward. Kind of odd."

She walked carefully to a desk against the far wall, trying not to step on any paws, and opened its top drawer, from which she extracted a ledger-sized bound book.

"I'm afraid you're not going to have much to work with. Maybe that's good news, since you're planning to contact everybody. There were only about five people here, and I think half of them worked for John, taking care of Peter. Still, it was nice of them to come, and it made it a little easier on John, I hope. It would have been tough on him to be the only person in attendance, don't you think?"

Sally agreed and laid the book down, open at the appropriate page, to take a picture with her smartphone.

In the meantime, Anne used a key and slid open another drawer, producing a color print on poor paper, of a small group of people standing in this very room, looking glum.

"I'm sorry about the quality," she said, handing it over. "It's just Xerox paper, for our own records."

"You used a digital camera?"

"Oh yes."

"Can you send me an email attachment of this?" Sally asked, brandishing the picture.

"Of course," Anne said brightly, pulling out her own phone and beginning the maneuver.

Sally gave her the proper address and, standing shoulder to shoulder, they double-checked that the transmission had gone through.

Anne spoke with wonder. "I'm still amazed by all that. Seems incredible to me, to be able to send things back and forth like magic."

Sally's pleasure at finding the picture overrode her inborn aversion to making small talk. She slipped her phone back into her pocket.

"Thanks."

"Was there anything else?" Anne Proctor asked, not noticing or caring. "You want a puppy, for instance? My son probably won't mind, especially after they do to his shoes what they did to his father's."

"Crap," Willy said. "You sure Sweeney didn't do in Hicks? A guy who knows a guy who owes him a favor, or something?"

Lester was shaking his head, but Joe was the one who spoke from his windowsill perch back in the Brattleboro office. "We checked alibis, did cross-interviews, McReady even offered to cut a deal on a few of the charges they have against him if he helped us out. Nothing. And the two guys Sweeney said were in the truck watching Diane's place confirmed his story.

"Not to mention," he added, "that the knife Daryl kept had a story of its own. Remember how it had Billy Belanger's prints on it? Turns out Billy stuck his boss in the back four years ago—thought he'd killed him—but then framed Daryl as the fall guy when Sweeney refused to die. Now Billy's under arrest, Seamus has to rethink his whole revenge motif, and we—more's the pity and more to the point—are dead in the water."

"Bummer," Lester chimed in philosophically.

"It also leaves John Rust on the hot seat again," Sam suggested.

"And us back to square one," Willy grumbled. "You're right."

"Not entirely," Joe argued. "What do we have on Smith Wilkinson, now that we know its real name?"

"It was a niche company," Sam reported. "Made electronic components for automotive drive shafts, among other things. Mostly assembling parts from all quarters, including overseas, into larger units that were then shipped down the line. It wasn't manufacturing, per se. More of a middleman thing. It fit Springfield to a T, though, since most of the town's empty old factories fit the bill.

"It was alive for about fifteen years," she continued, "and died less than two years after the time slot we're looking at—after the Rust family moved and Pete suffered his brain damage."

"Why?" Willy asked.

"Why did it die?" she asked. "Financial atrophy combined with a changing marketplace. That was the official line at first—baloney, as it turns out."

"You just wanted to say it," Willy challenged her.

She smiled. "True. In the end, it had everything to do with four of their top guys going away for long vacations, at government expense."

"Jail time?" Lester asked.

"Yup. They supposedly pulled so many fast ones—on the stockholders, the unions, the employees, and the board—that it took prosecutors over a year to sort out who to charge with what. Including manslaughter, since two of their outside investors committed suicide. And that's not counting the civil suits that followed."

"They all still inside?" Joe asked.

"Nope," she answered. "Out and wandering the world."

"And you're telling us this because it directly ties into Karen's big score and eventually Daryl's murder?" Willy asked, sitting back and placing his right hand on his stomach. "I ain't sayin' you're wrong, but it sounds awfully complicated for a girl who up till then was just a cut above ripping off gas stations."

"I grant you that," Sam agreed, adding, "So far, I've only been able to get news and industry reports on this. I will be going through the company records, once I find them. The feds grabbed everything when they shut the place down, hiding under that cover story about the changing marketplace so they could work in peace. The truth came out after charges were filed. So my digging has barely started. Keep your fingers crossed."

"Thanks, Sam," Joe said, moving on. "Did everyone get the ME's report about Daryl's COD?"

"Cardiac?" Lester asked.

"Right. Implying he died from the stress. *However*, let's keep in mind that his murderer, presumably John, might've been thwarted if this was about extracting information as much as pure revenge."

"I love it when you get complicated," Willy commented.

"What kind of information?" Lester asked more pointedly. "What did Daryl have to tell anybody, much less his own kid?"

"Could be nothing," Joe conceded. "But we have to ask. After all, *we* would have liked him to answer a few questions. Maybe we weren't the only ones."

Surprisingly, it was Willy, believed to have done things in and out of combat that none of them wanted to know about, who now spoke in support of Joe's thinking.

"I like it," he said. "There are types who torture for the fun of it. We know that. But they're rarer than we think. Usually, you're right. They're after something. Plus, from everything we've heard so far, John's more the caring, self-destructive type."

Joe pushed out his lower lip thoughtfully before asking, "With that in mind, what do we make of Daryl not being Pete's bio-dad?"

"The real question for me," Sam countered, "is did John know Pete was only his half brother?"

"Does it make any difference?" Willy asked. "He treated the kid like royalty for three decades."

"It might if it ties in to how and why Daryl was killed," Lester said.

"That's motive," Willy pushed back. "We don't care."

That was a gross overstatement, but as usual with Willy's blunt style, it had some basis in truth. On paper, cops follow evidence; prosecutors have to deal with motive—not that life ever follows what's been written down.

Joe decided to move on. "You all read the report about how they found Diane Wrinn's abandoned truck and had the crime lab go over it?"

No one in the room said otherwise.

Joe kept speaking, consulting the printout in his hand. "Unfortunately, it didn't yield much. Daryl's fingerprints were on the steering wheel, which fits. It was located in the parking lot of a down-at-the-heels motel not far from Barre, but there's no record that he tried to check in."

"He must've been grabbed there by whoever killed him later," Sam hypothesized.

"The easiest explanation," Willy contributed, "is that John used me and Les as a stalking horse, spotted the switch between Daryl and his sister, and followed him till he got where Daryl could be bushwhacked. Probably knocked him out, threw him in the back seat, and drove him somewhere nice and private to work him over. All before dumping him by the side of that road."

"The voice of experience?" Sam asked.

"Speaking of cars," Joe said, moving on, "Now that St. J team is on the alert for John's Subaru, it seems like that's the only car anyone drives up there."

"Has his actual reg been attached to any of them?" Lester asked.

"We're not that lucky," Joe confirmed. "It's been about twenty dead ends."

Willy argued against the whole idea. "If I was John Rust, hell-bent on righting a thirty-year wrong, and driving all over God's green acres to do it, I sure wouldn't be using my own car."

"I'm taking a wild guess here that none of our competitors-slash-allies has weighed in," Lester suggested, "meaning Jezek, Rachel, or Sally Kravitz."

That brought a pause to the proceedings. It wasn't often a cop admitted consulting with defense lawyers, journalists, or private eyes for intel.

But Joe, not surprisingly, smiled supportively. "I haven't heard from any of them," he said. "But setting up a meet might not be the worst idea. They all have a vested interest, especially Jezek, if he wants to keep his client out of jail, at least for the DUI."

"Or from being shot to death in some face-off with the cops," Sam said, half to herself.

As was almost routine by now, Rachel and Sally met over food. To call these events "meals" was an overstatement, even by an anorexic's standard. Both women had the eating habits of household pets, sitting down variously to canned soup, ice cream, half a box of shared Ritz crackers, and peanut butter. But the social function of such get-togethers still served, and the two of them looked forward to them to relax, exchange the latest news, and otherwise enjoy some time off the workplace treadmill.

This was a new development, for while different in temperament and style, each felt a yearning for a friend and trusted confidante whose honesty, integrity, and straightforwardness were reliable.

Until now, this had not been clearly available to either. And even more recently, upon their first few meetings, Sally had been aloof and ready to dismiss; Rachel more eager but uncertain, and prepared for rejection.

But something at once intangible and powerful, like a recognition of kinship, had quickly grown, overriding not just their own natures but the restrictions governing their jobs as well. This kind of open, instinctive, and unguarded friendship between a journalist and a private investigator had to be almost unique.

Of course, in part, that was true because of their regard for privacy. The irony of two people whose occupations defined inquisitiveness being deferential to each other's boundaries wasn't lost on either of them. But it did suggest a key ingredient of their bonding.

Tonight, however, there were no such restrictions. The subject, as it had been for days, was John Rust, and there they were happy and free to collaborate.

"You get anything new?" Sally asked, reaching for a bowl. Tonight's repast was a large can of fruit cocktail, which both agreed could be appreciated only under a towering cone of white, sweet, fluffy whipped cream.

"I did," Rachel said, spoon halfway to her mouth. "Courtesy of none other than Sammie Martens. She asked me what I might've left out of my article about Boris Ryder, and the subject of Smith Wilkinson came up. Her interest started me digging into it, and talk about a rat's nest. The whole business collapsed under a huge financial scandal, with four executives going to jail."

"And that was where Karen Taylor used to work," Sally said.

"Right. Curiouser and curiouser, no?"

"When was the collapse?"

"No more than two years after the Rusts moved to Westminster."

Rachel rose to fetch some paperwork and scrounged among several documents spread over a row of cardboard boxes doubling as a coffee table, returning with a selection.

She laid them out on the kitchenette counter.

"Supposedly, it was a scam from the beginning," she explained. "Four college friends with the work ethic of Bernie Madoff cooked up the idea of creating a company with the primary goal of making them rich. Something to do with electronic car parts. I'm a little vague on that. Good enough to get the job done, in any case, at least for a few years. Product quality wasn't a goal. They basically assembled big things from smaller ones and then called them their own. The heart of it was marketing, placement, pricing, and then cooking the books at the end to make it look legit. It was intricate, complicated, and arcane enough to glaze your eyes over, which I guess was partly the point."

"Therefore the need for more than one guy dipping his hand into the till," Sally surmised.

"Exactly," Rachel replied. "With each of them running a part of the company where their sleight of hand would dovetail into what the other three were doing. It was the perfect solution to the old checks-and-balances challenge. If your own people are doing all the checking and balancing, you're good to go."

"Until you're not," Sally said.

"Right," Rachel agreed. "I guess their system was off by just enough to get them caught. Still, if they had any brains, at least a couple of them must've set up a rainy-day fund for when they got out of prison." She followed that with a sigh before saying, "But I suppose that's not really in the nature of guys like this."

Sally agreed. "No argument from me." She reached out and picked up four mug shots from among Rachel's paperwork. "These them?" she asked.

"Yup. Names on the back of each."

Sally flipped over the pictures to see. Unsurprisingly, none of the names rang a bell with her. "You gonna chase 'em down?" she asked. "I'm guessing they're all out by now."

"I'd like to try, if it doesn't get too complicated. I can't justify spending a ton of time on it, since I don't really know what I'm chasing."

"It ties in to the whole Rust case, though, doesn't it?" Sally asked. "Did you find out if Karen worked for Smith Wilkinson?"

"That's what I was told. I'm hoping the actual company records will give me more, if I can figure out where to find them, but I have to watch out that Katz doesn't start asking me what the hell I'm doing that isn't producing column inches."

Sally smiled. "Always the crunch, ain't it?"

"What did you find out?" Rachel asked her. "Any closer to finding John?"

"Working on it," Sally said, adding more whipped cream to her bowl. "I went to the same funeral home that called you and talked with Anne Proctor. I started thinking they might have a sign-in book for Pete's service that might help me out. Turned out they had, and that Anne took a group picture, too."

She exchanged the can of whipped cream for her ever-present smartphone and showed Rachel the photograph she'd copied.

Rachel studied it, blowing it up and scanning the close-ups of each person's face. "What did you learn?" she asked, returning the phone.

"That you and I are a little in the same boat. I know a few of the people there—John, Martha Jones, the Munroes from next door. But there's a woman in the back, too, who looks uncomfortable being there. Anne had no idea who she is, and there was no entry in the guest book that matched."

Rachel picked up the phone and looked again. "Huh. I see what you mean," she said. "Looks like she didn't expect to be posing for a photograph. What're you going to do?"

"Show that around. See if anyone knows her. There must be some reason she came, along with why she didn't want to identify herself. It's a long shot, but I need whatever I can get to jump-start things." She pointed at Rachel's research. "Like whatever that's all about, for example."

Rachel straightened and looked at her friend thoughtfully. "This may run against some PI rule or something, or maybe one of Scott Jezek's. But what if we join forces? We both want to find John, and sure as hell Smith Wilkinson has got to have something to do with what's lurking in the background here. Do you see any conflict with us collaborating?"

Sally mulled it over. Certainly, she had employed fellow investigators in the past to chase down details that were too distant to justify billing the client for her own travel expenses. Here, there wouldn't be any outlay at all. Rachel was offering free labor in exchange for her own noncompeting benefit.

"Match made in heaven," she finally declared, reaching across the counter for a handshake. "You got a deal, and I have a suggestion."

Rachel was pleased, especially since, despite their equal footing, she couldn't help feeling a bit like the Robin to Sally's Batman—a holdover, she thought, from growing up under an utterly confident and high-achieving set of parents, not to mention a bossy sister, now a lawyer herself in Colorado. "Sure. What?"

Sally held up her phone. "That we start with the mystery woman. Unlike everything else we're looking at, we know she was alive and well a few days ago, and presumably is still in the neighborhood. If we're lucky, she might end up being the church key that opens up this whole can of worms."

Rachel made a face. "Yuck, but you're on."

CHAPTER EIGHTEEN

Assembling the Pieces

Sammie studied the man who'd invited her to lunch, thinking how easily he could have doubled as an elderly spokesman on late-night TV, mouthing euphemisms like "late term" or "final expense" while selling funeral insurance, or Geritol, or access to an impressively expensive assisted-living residence. He was tanned, with dazzling white hair, a row of strong teeth that looked like his own, and a relatively lean, athletic build.

Ironically, they were at such a facility right now, south of Burlington, where John Laware was living. He was a widower, had all his marbles, and was considered a prize catch, judging by the admiring looks he received from several passing female residents.

For Sam's purposes, he had other qualifications. Prior to a multiyear stint as a highly compensated security advisor for one of the area's largest banks, Laware had been a criminal investigator for the US Attorney's office in Vermont.

"How big a deal was the Smith Wilkinson case?" she asked him along those latter lines. "You headed it up, didn't you?"

He finished a mouthful of Caesar salad, wiped his lips, and said with a sunny smile, "I did, and it was a pip. Twenty-five years ago, more or less. We burned a lot of hours putting that to bed. I had a bunch of people assigned to it. You know the details?"

"Only the headlines," she said, leaving her soup untouched. They'd landed a corner table in an enormous, high-ceiling dining hall, near the end of the lunch period, and so mostly had the place to themselves. It was peaceful, and filled with sunlight pouring in through a bank of towering windows.

"What I'm missing is the insider stuff—about the major players, what happened to them, where they are now, what tipped your office off in the first place. Stuff like that."

He nodded. "Right, right. Larry, Harry, Chuck, and Paul. That's what we called them, like they were the Beatles or part of the Seven Dwarfs. It became a mnemonic, so much so that it was hard to say one without the others. You should've seen us in court, trying not to do that."

"I heard they were fraternity brothers," Sam said. "Was one of them the alpha dog?"

"Not strictly speaking. Paul was definitely a follower. He was the accountant—the book-cooker, as we labeled him. Really smart, really nerdy, and, I always thought, in dire need of better friends. But the other three were pretty much cut from the same cloth. Harry Murchison, the president and CEO, was the flashiest, but I thought the dumbest, too. And a mean bastard. Beat his wife, treated his kids terribly. A good front man, though—smooth talker and an old-school public backslapper."

Laware paused to reflect. "They did a decent job thinking this scam out, I'll give them that. Murchison could've filled one of the other slots, but he was a natural for president."

"And the others?" Sam asked.

"Larry Gage was finance VP, Chuck Dietz was purchasing."

"Paul's last name was Legasse, wasn't it?"

"Yeah, sorry. Poor bastard. You probably know he hanged himself in prison."

Sam looked up from the file she'd placed beside her, as reference. "No, I didn't. Don't know how I missed that."

Laware raised his hand dismissively. "Ancient history. It kind of fits that Paul would get lost in the final shuffle. Bad karma from the start."

"Is everyone else alive?" Sam asked, now concerned about her research.

"Oh yeah, as far as I know," Laware replied, adding, "Not like we keep in touch. Larry's in Hawaii, last I heard, Harry, of course, landed back in jail on a state rap, this time in Florida. Chuck, I have no idea. I always wondered if he did a Ted Kaczynski and built a cabin in the woods, or wound up running a local Salvation Army office. He could've gone either way, in my opinion. He may be the toughest one to find, if that's what you're looking to do."

"Couldn't he be skiing in Aspen?" Sam asked. "The whole point was for them to get rich. Or did you empty their bank accounts when you rounded them up?"

"As best we could. But I know a Brink's-truck's-worth went missing. These were college boys, after all; they knew about offshore banking. And maybe you're right about Chuck. He just never struck me as the type to settle down in front of a view and commit to ruining his liver. He always seemed too . . . I don't know . . . crazy, I guess. Maybe 'restless' is more PC."

"How 'bout the scam they had running?" she asked. "Why did it go under? You made it sound a whole lot better run than some of the Marx Brothers imitations we see in the news. It should've lasted longer, no?"

Laware chuckled. "Too true, too true. They really did have it worked out. Each was responsible for exactly the part of the business where the other three would need an ally to keep the game going. But despite that, to answer your question, we got an anonymous tip."

"A whistleblower?"

"I wouldn't call it that. Whistleblowers in my experience want money or revenge or maybe credit for sticking their necks out. I'm not saying that wasn't in play, but nobody surfaced to take a bow at the end. A letter was mailed to our office—no prints, no return address—stating in detail how the four were doctoring the accounts."

"Did you ever think it might've been one of them?" Sam asked. "Someone like Paul, who'd been treated poorly?"

"We looked at everything and everybody," Laware replied. "But when it was all said and done, it was clear that leak had come from outside. The odd thing was, none of us could find where the four had ever spilled their guts to anyone else. Wives, kids, friends, girlfriends, you name it, we interviewed 'em all. Nothing."

"You talk with a woman named Karen Taylor?"

Laware looked at her blankly. "Taylor? Don't think so. Not that it means much," he hastened to add. "I'm actually impressed I remember what I do. She could've been a player somewhere—you know, a secretary or something. The name just doesn't mean anything to me right now."

She sensed it was futile, but Sam followed with, "How 'bout Daryl Hicks?"

"Uh-uh."

"Boris Ryder?"

"Nope. Sorry."

"Okay. I'll stop. Does your office still have the records?"

He laughed. "Do they? Well, sure, of course—in a warehouse somewhere—unless there's been a fire I didn't hear about. I'll make a phone call and get somebody to bird-dog it for you."

"Thanks, John. Could you also get them to earmark the transcripts or tapes or whatever they've got of any and all interviews conducted of—" Sam hesitated to think. "—I don't know . . . the most valuable sources you used to build your case?"

"Inside or outside the company?" he quickly asked.

She considered that. "What're we talking about?"

"A lot. Like I said, this took us a long time, and most of it involved reconstructing contracts and professional relationships from the outside in. Remember, these guys ran a tight ship, and it was designed to be confusing. There was no leakage of information from inside the company. That's what made the tip—presumably from an insider—so surprising in retrospect."

"Okay," Sammie said. "I got it. Let's start there, then. If you could get me the insider list, I'd really appreciate it. As to exactly what I'm asking for, I'll leave that to you. You know the ins and outs better than I ever could. But we're stuck right now, and at this point, the more information we can get, the better. We need to find that one gold nugget."

Laware was cataloging in his head, searching through the years for guidance. "All right," he finally said. "I'll ask them to isolate interviews of the four guys, the people who worked directly for them, any relevant friends or relatives, and any summations that might be helpful to you in drawing a road map of what happened when, and who was responsible—assuming," he added ruefully, "that they'll even answer my call. I am retired, after all. I'll just be asking for a favor."

He hesitated thoughtfully and threw in a footnote. "I hope you're not doing this on your own. I'm not sure you realize the amount of work you're asking for."

Peggy Munroe looked understandably surprised as she recognized Sally Kravitz at her door—and a little uncomfortable. Not to mention that Sally had another woman with her this time.

"Hi, Peggy," Sally said cheerily. "Sorry to bug you again. This is my friend Rachel. We're working together. I was just hoping I could ask you one more short question about your neighbor."

Peggy compressed her lips in reaction, saying, "Your timing's a little bad. Sorry." She remained standing in the entrance, her hand firmly holding the door's edge.

Sally ignored the body language. "Oh, not to worry. In and out in two secs." She pulled out her cell phone as she spoke. "You told me you'd attended Pete's service at Proctor and Harris. Do you remember seeing this woman there?"

She brandished the group shot she'd been given by Anne Proctor. Reluctantly, and without moving her feet, Munroe bent at the waist and peered at the photo. "Yes."

"Did you happen to get her name?"

"No."

There was a motion behind her, and a man widened the door—tall, an athlete slightly gone to seed, a pleasant expression.

"Hey, hon. What's up?"

"This is the woman I told you about, who was asking about John Rust the other day."

"Oh, sure." The man pushed by his wife and shook hands. "Brad Munroe. Peggy told me you'd visited. Sorry we weren't too useful. We hardly knew them."

"It was nice of you to go to the funeral home, though," Sally said soothingly, noting that Peggy's expression had softened slightly with her husband's appearance.

Sally's phone was still in her left hand. She repeated her earlier gesture, saying, "I was just showing Peggy the group shot Anne Proctor took that day. I was hoping you knew the woman in the back."

"I told her we didn't," Peggy said under her breath.

"That's right," Brad seconded. "She never said a word to anyone. Have no clue who she was. And she didn't stay long. Course, we didn't, either."

Sally repocketed her phone as Rachel asked, "Did you see where she went afterward?"

Peggy was doubtful, but Brad spoke up. "Kind of. We pretty much left at the same time. We were a little behind her, since we said goodbye to John. I'm not sure he knew who we were, but he was nice about it."

"What did you see?" Sally asked.

Brad hitched a shoulder. "She got into a car and drove off. Not very helpful, I'm afraid."

"What kind of car?"

"A dark SUV—one of those small ones. Japanese, I guess."

Seemingly snapping into consciousness, Peggy abruptly said, "Smiley."

"I'm sorry?" Sally replied.

"I just saw it in my head, like a memory flash," Peggy said.

"You do that all the time, hon," her husband said, bumping her hip with his own.

Rachel cut in. "What did you mean, 'smiley'?"

"That was the license plate. I don't know why I remembered it. Maybe because she was the last person I ever would've connected to it. She didn't smile once."

"Neat," Sally said.

Emma could not have been more pleased. She was back from preschool early, both her parents were home. One of her favorites among their friends, Joe, was here, too, and he had just finished making her a lunch of Velveeta, mayonnaise, and jam, which he'd made her swear not to divulge to her mother. Life, to this small, bright, energetic tot, was right now unimprovable.

The reason for this windfall, however, was less penetrable. Piled on top of most of the dining and living room furniture and floors of her home were more cardboard boxes and stacks of papers than she'd ever seen. And the three adults had been slowly and diligently working through them all, sometimes exchanging their discoveries and chatting, otherwise just working from box to box, like Emma did when she inventoried her toys, in search of that one missing Lego piece.

Shielding her sandwich from her mother's casual eye, she retreated to a corner of the living room they'd set apart just for her, complete with blocks, books, crayons, and paper, and settled down happily surrounded by a fort built of boxes.

From his own spot by the room's coffee table, amid a semicircle of piled folders, affidavits, summaries, and photographs, Joe glanced fondly at the child, the product of what only he in the early days had seen as a quirkily well-matched union. As a man predisposed to see people in a good light, while accepting their propensity toward error and even evil, Joe had nurtured, protected, and encouraged Willy and Sam from their first days as members of his Brattleboro detective squad. Now here they all were, members of an elite unit, Sam and Willy blessed by a precocious and happy daughter, still working together, even through times of adversity and heartbreak.

In point of fact, they'd convened at the couple's house, rather than the office, not just for the extra space but also to combine work with a little family time, which Joe knew his two subordinates didn't get enough of.

John Laware hadn't lied. The US Attorney's office had cooperated with their request for the case files concerning Smith Wilkinson, to the tune of almost fifty containers of documents, which they'd divided equally into three islands around the house. The challenge was that while Laware's squad had been triggered by a tip to pursue the company's management team, Joe and his people were more at sea. They were looking for whether, how, and with whom Karen Taylor might or might not have extracted money from the firm. Additionally, they didn't know whether any of her actions—real or imagined—had anything to do with Larry, Harry, Chuck, and Paul's shenanigans.

On one point, however, they'd been rewarded. Eventually Willy, working from the kitchen, and within sight of both the dining and living rooms, let out a shout of triumph, "*She lives*, goddamn it."

"What's that supposed to mean?" Sam challenged him.

They could each see him brandishing a sheet of paper as he said, "Employee pay record. Karen Taylor."

"Thank God for small favors," Joe said, mostly to himself. Nevertheless, the discovery served to stimulate them with a renewed sense of purpose.

"You know what I wish?" Sam said eventually from her corner of operations.

"You're not gonna give us an option, are you?" Willy countered.

"Very funny," she shot back good-naturedly. "Imagine how easy this would've been if all this crap had been digitized. What've we got? Two thousand pages of interoffice memos alone? Nowadays they'd be emails. Type 'Karen Taylor' into a search engine, and bingo."

It went without saying that Sam had wound up with most of the boxes containing those memos.

Several hours later, the four of them were enjoying a light supper in the backyard, where each took a turn entertaining Emma on the swing set. The air was still cool, but the novelty of having daylight this late in the afternoon was more than any of them could resist.

The men sat drinking lemonades, watching Sam crawling around after her daughter in an energetic game of catch-me-if-you-can.

"You holding up?" Joe asked generally. "Or you think we're wasting our time?"

"Nah," Willy replied without pause. "This is a variation on walking into a whorehouse and hoping you'll get lucky. It'll happen. We just have to pay for it."

Joe was grateful he hadn't been swallowing something or drinking when he heard that. "That's one way of putting it, I guess."

"Hey," Willy said. "She was crooked, so were they. Her popping up as an employee, like we were told, isn't just dumb luck. It's confirmation. All we have to do is separate whatever scam she was pulling from the woodwork."

"So you're voting on her knowing that Huey, Dewey, and Louie were crooked," Joe suggested.

"Better than even odds," Willy agreed.

Joe cradled his glass on his stomach, his eyes absentmindedly on mother and daughter in the distance. "If you're right, that suggests Karen might've tumbled onto them before she signed up."

"It eliminates pure chance," Willy agreed.

"It does bring it down to a manageable size," Joe mused.

"What's that mean?"

"Not liking coincidence doesn't mean it never happens. We shouldn't entirely cut it out of our thinking. But you're right. Karen hiring on to one of the biggest frauds in the area's history—by dumb luck alone—is a stretch."

Willy finished the thought for him. "On the other hand, her bumping into one of the key players beforehand, and then hiring on, might make sense."

"I think so," Joe said, before taking another sip of his drink.

"You saying there's a missing player?"

Joe cast him a glance. "There *might* be. Just because we've been told those guys were closemouthed doesn't mean some pillow talk didn't take place, especially if one of the parties was very persuasive."

Later that night, after Emma had been put to bed, Willy entered the living room from the kitchen, gesturing to Sam to join him there. They sat on the couch, on either side of Joe.

Willy was holding a large color photograph, which he laid down on the coffee table, atop Joe's piles of papers.

"Company picnic," he explained in a low voice. "Back when such things were supposed to disguise the wage gap, lousy benefits, and life-threatening work conditions."

"Thank God I never suggested one," Joe muttered, squinting at a large semicircle of faces staring up at a camera presumably in the hands of someone perched on a ladder. The setting was a warehouse, with palleted goods in the background and a scattering of food-heavy tables up close. There were perhaps 250 people assembled, including kids and family members.

Willy silently tapped a finger in one corner of the shot.

"There's Karen," Sammie said. "I'll be damned."

"With a young Daryl Hicks by her side," Joe added. "Lot skinnier then. I'll give him that."

"Yeah," Willy agreed. "Doesn't make the two of them as grotesque a couple as when we had his older version in our heads."

"He did not age gracefully," Joe seconded, still studying the picture. "There are our four ringleaders," he added, pointing. "Fitting right in with the other managers with their wide ties and cheesy white shirts."

"Even their kids and wives look uncomfortable, if that's who they are."

Joe sat back, remembering his earlier conversation with Willy over supper. "We need more people working on this," he mused.

"Don't have the manpower," Sam reminded him. "Even with the Daryl killing, no one's making enough noise about this to let us steal more bodies from our own ranks. Plus, we already got some state police, a couple of deputies, three or four pilfered agents."

"How 'bout Nancy Drew and your not-quite stepdaughter?" Willy asked. "Two informed, motivated outsiders with fresh perspectives."

Joe stared at him. "What?"

"Come on," Willy pressed him. "We've been stumbling over them from the start. Rachel and her articles, Sally and her boss coming to you about Peter Rust being a homicide victim. Hell, they're already acting like a ghost squad, working from the fringes. Why not sit 'em down and find out what they got?"

Joe barely gave it a thought. "Okay. Let's do it."

CHAPTER NINETEEN

An Alliance of Necessity

"You two good and uncomfortable?" Willy asked with a raised eyebrow.

"Sure," Sally said neutrally, sitting with her back against the wall of the VBI office.

"The first or the second?" Willy persisted.

Sally remained deadpan. "The second."

"Fair enough," Joe said from across the room. "We appreciate your coming in."

"It does feel like I'm about to see the integrity and independence of a free press violated," Rachel commented, sitting beside her friend.

Lester looked surprised. "Wow. Dramatic. You don't even know why we asked you here. And the fact that you accepted proves you're having your own problems cracking this nut. You can't be *that* opposed to the idea."

Both young women kept silent, as did the last member of the meeting, Sammie, who for now was waiting to see what evolved.

Joe propped a foot against his desk. "Let me start with a proposal. We'll put what we've got on the table first. You can ask questions, within reason, poke holes if you want, or make any suggestions. In exchange, what we're hoping is that you'll eventually feel comfortable enough to pay us back in kind, showing us what you might've dug up. If at any time, you truly do become ill at ease, for any reason, you can leave."

"And it's all on the record?" Rachel asked pointedly.

"No," Joe said after a split second. "Not this time. At least not right now. This is new territory for all of us. Let's see how we get along for starters."

"Just so you know," Lester explained. "We're not all that happy about this, either. We're not supposed to play with folks from outside the clubhouse."

Sally was untroubled by this back-and-forth. Despite her show of reserve, she actually had little to lose. Her job, after all, was pretty straightforward. She may have preferred working alone, but she'd already hitched her efforts to a journalist's; how far a reach was it to tack on a few cops? In a paraphrase of the famous musical refrain, she just had to get John to the court on time.

"Speaking for myself," she therefore said, hoping to move things forward. "It sounds almost risk-free." She looked at Rachel, speaking to her directly, "Once everything's been laid out, we can make our choice then. We can't be accused of aiding and abetting the enemy if we leave before saying a word."

After a telling pause from everyone, Joe resumed cautiously. He, too, after all, had to watch his step. Sally and Rachel weren't the only ones with strict rules of integrity to observe. A misstep on his part could be breaking the law, or imperiling his case. "I'd like to begin by emphasizing common knowledge and courtesy. I don't want to jeopardize our efforts by saying too much, nor do I want it said later that I somehow coerced the press into cooperating against its will.

"That being said, is it fair to assume that both of you have no secrets between yourselves concerning this? Because, if you do that'll make things even more complicated."

"You've been exchanging what you've collected with each other, right?" Lester reinterpreted.

"Yes," Sally spoke for the two of them.

"Okay," Joe resumed. "Then, since it was Scott Jezek who came to me about Peter Rust's death possibly being related to an abusive event, it's safe to say we're probably dealing with a homicide. A homicide originating from inside the Rust household—at the moment by a party or parties unknown."

"Jesus," Willy said from his corner of the room. "Thank God we have the whole day ahead of us."

"Hold it," Sally interjected, ignoring Willy. "Are you saying you really don't know who did it?"

"Right now, it's John versus his mother versus Daryl," Sam answered.

"We can't answer with an absolute," Joe added. "When you put the parts together, they work best with Hicks as the bad guy, John the witness, and Karen missing until after the fact."

"And subsequently taking a nosedive into depression," Willy added.

"But with two out of three dead and one missing, you don't know," Sally proposed.

"Correct," Joe said.

"What if Hicks killed Karen and made it look like an overdose?" Rachel asked.

"For the mysterious cash that Karen supposedly delivered?" Willy suggested.

"Right."

Joe addressed Sally, holding back their discovery that Hicks wasn't Peter's father, and how that, too, could have been a motive for murder. "You're working for Jezek. Skipping where the money came from, how was it set up to work? A trust for Pete? Working capital for John when he turned eighteen? Did Hicks have a trustee role at all?"

Sally shrugged, also guarding her cards, in her case her theorizing with her father earlier about this very topic. "Wrong lawyer. We're thinking Karen set up something, but it had nothing to do with Scott. And unless or until John is proved dead and/or legally incapacitated, I doubt any unknown attorney of his is going to appear from nowhere volunteering to spill the beans about his client, even lawyer-to-lawyer. That'll probably have to wait till probate court, if ever."

"All right," Joe said. "Let's look at where the cash came from to start with."

Rachel spoke up. "You don't want to talk about who killed Daryl? He's like the elephant in the room, isn't he?"

The cops exchanged glances, protective of their lack of progress in finding a suspect.

"No," Willy said bluntly.

"Let's stick with the money for now," Joe suggested. "Since we're on the subject."

Sally smiled. "Nice punt," she said.

"Okay," Rachel said, "you read my opinion in the paper. I think it came from Smith Wilkinson."

"How?" Willy asked.

"We're working on that," Sally said quickly, in case Rachel was forming a more generous response.

Lester clapped his hands together with pleasure. "Cool. And here we are at last, at the O.K. Corral, guns drawn. This is the crux of this get-together. Who's gonna shoot first?"

"You guys," Sally answered him evenly, pointing to Joe. "Those were your rules. We might only be here to listen."

"Not if you have something that'll give us a jump start," Joe clarified. This was where his version of pulling a rabbit from his hat had to be muted and discreet, so as not to scare away his guests. Withholding evidence could be seen as a crime under the right circumstances, and Sally had just cracked open that door.

But only just. As Lester had suggested, now everyone in the room was alert, focused on the value of what each might know for a fact.

"Let's define our positions," Sam said diplomatically. "Sally needs to find John Rust before the state's attorney nails him for not showing up at his court appearance. You, Rachel, want to maintain the momentum with your series of articles, or you're gonna look like the marathon runner who got lost on her way to the finish line. And, as the two of you can plainly tell, we're sitting on an ocean's worth of research and data, but we need to create a single hole in the dike to get everything flowing."

"Data that may or may not tell you about both the money and who killed Daryl," Sally said.

"Yes," Joe agreed.

"Maybe this'll help," Sally offered. "We all know how Smith Wilkinson was a huge con job, organized by four of its executives. That was headline news at the time, for months, so nobody needs to be coy about it."

"Have you connected Karen's windfall with that?" Willy asked, trying to read between the lines.

Sally remained evasive. "They were something like two years apart, weren't they?"

"Spare me," Willy grunted, tired of the gamesmanship.

"Conceptually, we have made a connection," Sally therefore conceded, respecting his point if not his manner. "It's too big a coincidence otherwise."

"We may be getting somewhere, then," Joe commented hopefully. He slid off the windowsill and reached for a file folder on his desk. Removing four photographs, he crossed to the whiteboard beside the wall-mounted computer monitor and stuck them up with magnets.

"These four look familiar?"

Rachel rattled off their names in response, "Gage, Murchison, Dietz, and Legasse."

Willy laughed. "The AG started calling them the Beatles."

"As in Larry, Harry, Chuck, and Paul," Lester explained.

Sally smiled. "I like it."

"I take it," Rachel continued, staying on point, "that when you said you were hoping for a hole in the dike, you meant you've got nothing on any of them, at least in the here and now."

"Paul's dead," Willy said, "if you can stand the irony."

Joe wondered if either of their two young visitors understood the Beatlemania-era joke.

Apparently not. Sally asked, "Who killed him?"

"Suicide."

Sam took over, happy to have moved beyond the momentary tension. Not unlike Willy, her tolerance for negotiation was limited. She preferred dealing in facts. "Larry's in Hawaii, from what we were told; Harry's back in jail, for something else—we've confirmed that; and Chuck's nowhere to be found."

"Are you thinking Larry or Chuck killed Daryl?" Rachel asked.

"Daryl again," Willy added. "Dog with a bone."

"As if you weren't," she shot back, turning to Joe. "Are you?"

"They're under consideration," he answered carefully, "as are others."

"Like John," she stated flatly.

Joe held up a hand. "I'd still like to stick with Smith Wilkinson. I know a homicide's sexier, but my hope is that following the money will be the good advice it usually is. Also, from what I'm hearing, that company not only brought all these people together, it's also the one place where you and we have made some inroads."

"Meaning you've connected Karen Taylor to Smith Wilkinson, too," Rachel immediately said, "like Boris Ryder told me."

In silent response, Joe pulled out another photograph—this one of the company picnic—and stuck it under the four head shots.

"Toward the back, left side," Willy directed.

Rachel and Sally left their chairs to study the picture. Their heads together, they could be heard murmuring to each other, pointing out various people as they spoke.

"Do you know what she did for them?" Sally eventually asked.

"Shipping," was Willy's terse reply. "And before you ask, Hicks wasn't an employee. I'm even wondering if one of the rug rats you can see way in the back might not be John as a kid. He would've been the right age."

"Who's this?" Rachel asked, her photographer's eye caught by a slim blond woman standing among the management group.

At that, all the detectives except Willy rose and gathered around to look.

"Somebody's better half?" Lester ventured.

Willy laughed from behind his desk. "That's sticking your neck out."

But Joe addressed Rachel directly. "What made you single her out?"

Rachel instead looked at Sally, who shrugged and said, "Why not? Nothing to gain by not telling them."

Rachel returned to her chair, reached into her bag, and produced her own photograph of the awkward group shot taken at the Proctor and Harris funeral home.

She stuck it up beside the one Joe had placed on the board. "This woman appeared at Peter Rust's service the other day. Nobody knew who she was, but she was seen getting into a car with the license plate SMILEY."

Lester hastily retreated to his desk and his computer as the others stayed put, still comparing both pictures.

"I can definitely see it," Sammie said.

"Me, too," Joe agreed. "She doesn't even look that different. Nice job."

"Registered to Norman Smiley," Lester announced from across the room.

"Is there a Mrs. Smiley?" Joe asked him.

It was Willy who answered. He, too, unnoticed by the rest of them, had been working his computer. "Laura."

They turned as one toward him.

"And you'll love this," he added, sitting back. "It's pure soap opera. Laura Smiley's middle name—probably from an earlier marriage—is Gage, as in Larry."

CHAPTER TWENTY

Revisiting the Old Days

One of the selling points of the Windsor house for Beverly—especially this time of year—was the screened-in porch facing the pond. Her South Burlington mini-mansion, as Joe called it, fronted Lake Champlain, but with an open patio, allowing swarms of dusk-triggered mosquitoes to make the view an indoors-only enjoyment.

She was therefore setting the evening table on the porch, for the first time in months, looking forward to soaking up the region's brief window for such activities—a summer season some native Vermonters referred to as "three months of damn poor sledding."

She had set three places for tonight, as Rachel had announced she was joining them. This was not unheard of, and Beverly was always happy to see her, but the girl's tone—if such could be inferred from a text message—had felt almost curt, as if she had something more businesslike in mind than merely partaking of her mom's cooking.

It turned out Beverly was right. From their almost simultaneous arrival at the house, by separate vehicles, Joe and Rachel were transparently watchful of each other as they helped carry the dishes and drinks outside—slightly more polite than necessary, distinctly less spontaneous, and even physically a little distant.

For most people in a similar situation, one impulse might have been to probe the problem and seek a reconciliation. But Beverly was not most people. A scientist, a stickler for process and careful methodology, she was attracted by the notion of watching whatever developed around the table tonight. As the partner to one party and the mother of the other, she stood naturally ready to render comfort if called for. But until then, she was much more interested in seeing how things might unfold.

Rachel, befitting her youthful impatience, was the first to address what lay between them, even as all three had barely placed their napkins in their laps.

"You know you wouldn't have Laura Gage's name without us."

"Very true," Joe said equitably, dishing out helpings of shepherd's pie. "And you wouldn't have photographic proof of the connection between Smith Wilkinson and Karen Taylor."

He then glanced at Beverly to explain, "Sorry. Shoptalk."

"No, no," Beverly protested, pouring wine for herself and Rachel, knowing Joe didn't drink it. "Carry on. I'm the happy onlooker here."

Rachel took her cue—or was ignoring social graces anyhow. "But it's not fair that you get to go ahead on what we gave you, while you basically gave us a gag order at the end of that meeting. I'm not even sure that's legal, by the way. I'm press."

"Who opted to stay put after the rules were agreed to," he replied. "Also, not to split hairs, but I merely reminded you of that fact at the end. No gag order came into it. I also said you'd be the first person I'd call if anything broke, and that if you independently picked up some of what you'd learned at the meeting, from another source, you were free to run with it. That's hardly a gag order, which can only come from the bench, anyhow."

"Okay," she countered. "Maybe. But it's hardly the same. Showing me Karen Taylor in a thirty-year-old group photo gives me nothing. I *knew* she worked there."

"You only knew what Ryder told you," Joe corrected her. "Which you put in quotes in your article, in case it wasn't true." He added quickly as she opened her mouth to protest, "It was a good story, carefully reported. You didn't claim something as a fact when you didn't have corroboration. You toed the line, and now you have corroboration."

"Which I can't use."

He tried comforting her. "Not yet, but it's another brick in the wall you're building. Back when I chased smash-'n'-grabs on patrol, how do you think I went about catching who did it?"

"How?" she asked reluctantly, pushing her food around on her plate.

"I waited. Life is not static. People talk. Key elements change all the time. It's not in the nature of a journalist to bide her time, but sometimes, that's what it takes. You helped in that process today, at the office. We were stalled—what Sam said about needing a hole in the dike. My gut tells me we'll now get somewhere with what you gave us. And where we gain yardage, so will you. I'll see to it."

Rachel tried a bite of her food, but they could tell she was still upset. Unfortunately, Joe knew he'd only begun to stoke that disappointment. He had more coming.

"This is delicious," Joe complimented Beverly.

"Thank you," she replied, casting her glance toward Rachel to let him know her gratitude extended to his handling of her daughter.

"So who killed Daryl?" Rachel asked after swallowing and taking a sip of wine. "Since I know I can't write about that, either."

Joe ignored the melodrama and tried to answer as best he could without further eroding his professional probity, which had already taken a beating today. "I wish I knew. You know yourself that John's well positioned for it, but I can't deny that it conflicts with my reading of the man's character. You spend decades devoted to a brother who'll never get better, only to torture/kill the guy you think's responsible? That's like Jekyll and Hyde to me."

"I heard rumors you'd focused on people unrelated to the ancient history stuff," she said.

"It didn't pan out," he told her vaguely. "I was hopeful, but it went nowhere. All the more reason why Laura Smiley's become such a person of interest."

Rachel gave a disappointed grimace at the reminder, which stimulated Joe to deliver his bad news now, in large part to get it over with.

"Which brings up something else you're probably not going to like," he therefore continued. "I personally would appreciate if we could have first swing at her, before either you or Sally. I'm hoping you can understand my reasoning."

"That I'm just a cub reporter for a Podunk paper while you're saving the world from terrorists and murderers?"

"Ouch," Beverly said with a slight and telling edge to her voice.

To Rachel's credit, she acknowledged her misstep. "Sorry. It's just so frustrating. Makes me feel like a twelve-year-old."

"And act like one?" Beverly asked gently.

Rachel, thankfully, took that as she'd been brought up to, and smiled. "Ouch to you, too, Mom. But, yeah, a little like a jerk." She smiled at Joe and said further, "Sorry. My bad. You know that feeling when you think you're the only kid at the table?"

"Sure," he said. "Don't expect that to ever disappear, by the way, not until it's too late to do you any good."

"Well, I got a double dose of that at the meeting, I think," she allowed. "I really like Sally. She's the best friend I ever had. But she's pretty tough, and I have a hard time competing with the life she's led and the way she turned out. So to be there with her and the rest of you guys, I felt about that high." She held her thumb and forefinger up, half an inch apart.

"I know what you mean," Joe commented. "I thought you held your own just fine, though. You're still finding your sea legs." He pointed at her for emphasis and referred to some of the close calls she'd had since he'd first known her. "You've kept your head better than most, you know. People killed right in front of you, getting into scrapes, wrestling with bad guys. Don't sell yourself short. Sally may have a tough-guy presence, but you have a different style. You're tenacious and dogged. If you want my honest opinion, I think that as a reporter, you have the makings of becoming a perfect pain in the ass."

Rachel laughed in mid-drink and spilled some of her wine onto her plate, adding to her reaction. She put down her glass, dabbed her chin with her napkin, and told him, "Okay, I'll leave Laura Gage to you, but I'm still gonna nip at your heels."

Joe looked at Beverly and tilted his head to one side. "See? Putty in my hands."

"That'll be the day."

One of the pleasures Joe enjoyed was catering to the individual strengths of his team. Each member had distinct styles—some, like Willy's, spanned quite a reach—but they all offered Joe a choice of advantages when it came to fitting personalities to a given situation. The end results rarely disappointed.

A perfect case in point was the mysterious woman who'd appeared at the funeral service of a child kept cloistered for twenty-eight years, and who also happened to be the ex-wife of a larcenous mastermind, long gone from public memory.

For that tricky interview, on which so much depended, Joe chose Sam and Lester, his instincts telling him their sensitivity and often lighter touch would serve better than Willy's less predictable manner. He was also hopeful that a female investigator would be better received than a battle-hardened, tough-looking, handicapped man—even one who could, when pressed, turn on the charm with startling conviction.

Laura Gage Smiley lived in Chester, Vermont, a town of three thousand people, named after the eldest son of "mad" King George III, under whose watch the empire lost the American colonies. It is an appealing place, dotted with gingerbread-accented architecture and picturesque rows of shops, and old enough for two of its districts to merit listings in the National Register of Historic Places. It is also safely distant from I-91—some eight miles—and thus spared most of the tackier appendages common to interstate corridors. Indeed, for Sammie at least, Chester remained a refreshing and pleasant opportunity every time she went there, if only, perhaps, because she so rarely did so.

The address Sam was given belonged to a trim, small, neatly maintained house down a short dead-end street off the town's main drag. It had newly freshened flower beds on each side of the front walkway, obviously the labor of someone with a green thumb and a trained eye for New England's short growing season.

The woman who answered the doorbell was slim, with shoulder-length gray hair and a worn expression displaying neither pleasure nor alarm, but rather the look of someone for whom life had run out of surprises.

"Laura Smiley?" Sam asked.

"Yes," was the neutral reply.

"Laura Gage Smiley?"

Nothing moved among her features, but somehow they hardened in unison.

"Yes."

"I'm Special Agent Samantha Martens. This is Special Agent Spinney. We're from the Vermont Bureau of Investigation. We were hoping you'd allow us a few minutes of your time, if you have a minute."

Laura Smiley paused, either weighing her options or brought up short by the request. Whichever it was, she stepped back and swung the door open wide.

"I guess I have to," she said, and walked into the darkness behind her.

The two cops eyed each other.

"Not exactly an invitation," Lester said.

Sam placed her foot on the threshold. "Not a rejection, either."

They found Smiley in her kitchen, just off the hallway. Like the house itself, it was squared away and clean. Sam noticed that the artifacts and pictures on the wall and stuck to the fridge reminded her of the generic backdrops of many TV shows—representative of everyday humanity, but devoid of personality, whether this woman's or someone else's entirely.

"You want coffee?" their hostess asked without enthusiasm.

"I'm okay," Lester answered quickly, unsure of what she might add to the brew.

"I'll pass, too, thanks," Sammie replied.

Smiley leaned one hip against the edge of the sink, a cup cradled in both hands. "What do you want?"

As before, her tone was strictly midline, as if she'd learned that the more leeway on either side, the better.

"Is there a Mr. Smiley?" Sam asked.

Laura raised one eyebrow, an ability Sam had always envied. "You're a little late, if he's who you're interested in. He died seven years ago of cancer."

"I'm sorry."

She sounded bored. "You get used to it. It's history."

"And before that?" Sam asked.

Laura studied her, took a sip of her coffee before placing the mug on the counter, and said, "Ah. Here it comes."

Lester was about to say, *Really?* but Sammie beat him to it with, "The past catching up?"

"Doesn't it always?"

Sam suspected Laura meant Larry Gage, so she went for something off-script. "Pete Rust?"

The indirect reference to Smiley's attendance at the funeral service created a rewarding reaction. The stillness of Laura's face—not to mention her almost hostile manner—faded into a sad smile of acknowledgment as she suggested, "Why don't we move to the living room?"

It was one door down, carefully furnished and decorated along the house's overall theme. Smiley chose an armchair while the two cops sat on the facing couch.

"Who was Pete to you, Laura?" Sam asked, adding, "Is calling you Laura okay?"

Smiley waved the second question aside without comment as she answered, "A friend's child. I actually never knew him. It just seemed right to be there."

"How did you hear about it? It was a tiny event."

She shrugged. "Small world. Word gets around. There might've been something in the paper. I don't recall."

Sam let it go, asking instead, "Twenty-eight years later? You and Karen Taylor must've been tight."

"Tight?" The incredulity ran at odds to Sam's almost casual referral to Karen.

Sammie persisted. "If not that, then what?"

Smiley looked away, fidgeted, before settling back like a briefly disturbed bird. "Call it closing a chapter."

Sammie took a calculated step into the unknown. "A chapter involving Larry?"

Laura allowed a weary half smile. "All roads lead to Larry."

Lester pushed back gently. "Not really. We're actually more interested in Karen."

"How did you know her?" Sam followed up.

"We bumped into each other," Laura said vaguely, adding softly, "Or she bumped into me."

Sam guessed again. "I take it not by accident?"

"Not much happened by accident with Karen," Laura said. She paused to correct that with, "Not everything, anyway."

Lester was struck by a notion. "Did Karen use you to get her job at Smith Wilkinson?"

Sam looked at him, taken by surprise.

"Among other things."

"She couldn't just apply?"

"Didn't want to leave it to chance. Plus, I don't know if she knew about the company when we met."

Sammie used that to roll things back a bit. "Laura, help me out. Can you take us to the beginning? How you and Karen met, what happened? How that led to Smith Wilkinson?"

Laura began to fidget again. "Why?" she asked. "Why dredge that up again?" She slapped her knee in frustration. "I *knew* I shouldn't have gone to that service."

"The why is that we're not reinvestigating Larry," Sam explained. "Or the Smith Wilkinson case, or any of that. We're treating Peter Rust's death as a homicide, Laura."

"And we're trying to find whoever murdered Karen's husband a few days ago," Lester contributed.

"We see the two as connected," Sam explained.

"Murdered?" Laura echoed, her face slack with shock.

"That's why this matters," Sam stressed. "It's no longer ancient history or licking old wounds. There's something going on, here and now, and it's costing lives. We need to know where it's coming from, 'cause we're pretty sure its roots go back to those days."

Smiley was visibly struggling again, causing Lester to worry that her regrets about attending Pete's service might prompt her to throw them out.

"Will you do that for us, Laura?" he asked softly, hoping to evoke her sympathy. "We know it costs you, but we need help."

Whether it was that or some other stimulus, she sank back into her seat and said dully, "All right. What do you need to know?"

"What I said before," Sam repeated. "Pretty much everything. You said you bumped into Karen when you met by chance. Let's start with how that happened, especially since you implied she might have really planned it."

"It was at a community food shelf. I was doing volunteer work, trying to help out." Laura paused and then conceded, "Probably helping myself more than anyone else, finding something to do."

"You didn't have a job?" Lester asked.

"Later on I did, at a bank, after the divorce. But back then, I was pretty blind to everything, including being under Larry's thumb. He didn't like me working—said he wanted me available at all times."

Neither cop responded, but Laura addressed Sam in particular to say, "I know it sounds lame, but a lot of women did that. In my defense, I knew even then it wasn't the healthiest relationship. They say you sometimes marry your father. I guess that would be me."

"Larry was a control freak?"

"You could say that, among other things."

Sam tried being supportive, also not having been the best judge of men in her youth. "Hey, you did get rid of him, Laura. Take some credit."

"Was Karen a customer at the food bank?" Lester asked, bringing them back on topic.

"No," Laura said. "She was a volunteer, too. Not a very convincing one."

"What's that mean?"

"She seemed more interested in me than doing the work."

"A little creepy?" Sam asked.

But Laura's face opened briefly in protest. "No, not at all. Not to me, at least. Not then. It was flattering. I didn't have any friends. We'd moved from western New York State to create the company—or Larry and his buddies had. They dived right in and I was left to fend for myself. That's not something I did very well."

"The other founders of Smith Wilkinson were from New York State?" Lester asked, having thought otherwise from their research.

"No. Sorry. We were. They were from all over. It was a college thing, the four of them. That's how Smith Wilkinson was hatched—in a dorm room. Right up there with some pals getting drunk and planning a bank robbery, except, like Larry used to say, it was a gift that kept on giving—*Groundhog Day* with a never-ending payoff . . . Until it did end."

Sam didn't want them to get ahead of themselves. "Can we go back to you meeting Karen?" she asked. "How did that develop? You said before you didn't think she even knew about Larry."

"I never figured that out," Laura admitted, brushing her fingertips against her forehead. "Things moved so quickly, and everything went off the rails so completely, I lost track of that. I wondered about it. Did they know each other earlier? Did she target him through me? How did she know what kind of man he was? How could she be so sure he wouldn't turn her in afterward?"

Sam held up a hand to stop her, embarrassed at having committed the rookie's error of asking two questions at once. "I'm sorry, Karen. Let's hold off on that for a sec. Just tell us about the start of the friendship. How it got warmed up."

Laura startled them by laughing, displaying a split-second glimpse of a younger, happier woman, untouched by regret and loss. "Warmed up?" she repeated. "That's saying more than you know."

"How so?" Lester asked.

"We became lovers," Laura said.

"You and Karen?" Sam asked.

The woman's earlier mirth was wiped away by disappointment. "I know, right? Who saw that coming?"

Sammie remembered Willy quoting Boris Ryder about how even women ate out of Karen's hand. "We heard she could be very persuasive."

"I was in love," Laura said simply. "It felt like for the first time."

"I'm sorry," Sam responded.

Laura flipped her hand in a halfhearted gesture. "Oh, hell. It was a moment in time, feeling happy and a little dangerous. It was like rolling down the car window for a few seconds in the middle of winter. A blast of fresh air that can't last—bracing, exciting, almost breathtaking. It ended badly, but I remember the happiness."

"Did you know she was married and had a son?" Lester asked.

Laura was guileless. "I didn't care. If anything, it added to the attraction. She told me she'd gotten married only because she got pregnant. That seemed like the kind of old-fashioned thing I'd done by marrying Larry and not working. It was part of our common bond."

Sam filled in the inevitable conclusion. "Until things turned out otherwise."

"Yes," Laura said wistfully.

"How did the segue to Larry and Smith Wilkinson take place?" Lester wanted to know.

"Karen needed a job," Laura told him. "I knew the company was hiring."

"And then she met Larry," Lester concluded.

"That's what I thought," Laura confirmed. "I don't know anymore."

"So, what happened next?" Sam asked, adding, "If it's not too painful."

She sighed. "She dumped me, in a nutshell."

"For Larry?"

"Larry, the job, money, a better life. It was hard to compete with all that, and Karen was a woman who knew what she wanted."

"Do you know the details about the money?" Lester asked. "How she got access? How much it came to? Was Larry duped or complicit?"

But Laura was shaking her head. "I've pieced together what made sense to me, but it's not like either one of them took me into their confidence."

She suddenly got up and crossed to the woodstove in the room's corner, now adorned with a houseplant, in homage to the warmer weather. She fussed with a couple of the perfect plant's leaves before quickly abandoning the effort and turning back to face them.

"I didn't handle any of this well," she explained. "I fell into a hole after Karen left me—became a drunk. What she and Larry may or may not have done together was of no interest to me. And then, afterward, when the company went under and everyone got arrested, well . . . None of it mattered. I had to decide whether to die or rebuild a life."

"Nevertheless," Lester persisted, ignoring a natural urge to show sympathy, "you wondered a few minutes ago if she'd targeted him using you, and if she knew what kind of man he was. And how she could be so sure he wouldn't turn her in afterward. All of those questions imply you knew—or at least sensed—*something* was going on."

Laura looked a little lost at first, as if stumped by a complex puzzle. "I'm sorry," she finally said. "This should be burned into my memory, I know. But instead, what with the strain of losing Karen, my falling apart, and then Larry being arrested, the company closing, our money disappearing, it's all become a jumble—not to mention that it was almost thirty years ago. Now I can see things as they probably were, but is that because of hindsight? I don't know."

Sam explained, "We've been working on the premise that somehow, she absconded with a lot of cash when she left Smith Wilkinson—enough to set her family up, pretty much for life. You even referenced something like that. Do you have any specific memory of Larry mentioning what Karen did to him financially?"

"I do," she replied. "He didn't go into detail. He was angry, drunk, and on the phone at home, speaking to one of the others. He didn't know I was listening. That's how I put most of this together, at least I think it is. It's a little like remembering a dream, if that doesn't sound too crazy."

"If he was so angry about it," Lester asked, "why did you think he wouldn't sic the police on her? Was it because he was so crooked himself that he didn't want the attention? That he'd just absorb the loss?"

Sammie was suddenly smiling from her corner of the sofa as she suggested, as if out of thin air, "Peter Rust. *That's* why you attended the service, wasn't it?"

The other two stared at her, Lester quizzically, but Laura with a sad and knowing expression.

"In his convoluted, inside-out way, Larry was a sentimental man," she said. "Pete was the child he and I could never conceive. And he was Karen's ace in the hole."

CHAPTER TWENTY-ONE

Weighing Options; Cutting Deals

"Tell me this is getting us somewhere," Willy said aloud in the darkness.

"It is," Sam replied without hesitation, lying in bed beside him.

Neither one had been asleep, although each had been faking it for the other's sake. The digital clock's bright red numerals proclaimed 2:34 A.M., which, for them, didn't mean much. What with Willy's eccentric, paranoia-fueled nocturnal habits and the often disruptive hours demanded by their jobs, they didn't give the same weight to the middle of the night as most people.

Willy didn't move, still addressing the invisible ceiling. "And why's that? All we've done is unpack a bunch of old, forgotten trunks from the attic, filled with long-gone corporate crooks; heartbroken, jilted lesbian lovers; illegitimate children made dead by jealous husbands; and a conniving, manipulative, obsessive, drug and sex addict in the middle of it all, who finally did herself in. Where's that leave us in the killing of Daryl Hicks, who probably deserved what he got anyhow?"

"Huh," Sammie grunted.

He turned his head toward her. "That's it? 'Huh'?"

"I was just thinking," she said. "Why did Karen overdose?"

"Like I care."

"It's funny, though," Sam persisted. "It doesn't really fit, especially the way you just pictured her."

"Her kid had been brain damaged," Willy replied, thinking that, were the same to happen to him, it would be the end of his life as he knew it. Losing Emma would guarantee his death.

But Sam was thinking logically. "That had happened a couple of years earlier, and I know it sounds hard, but if we're right about why she got pregnant by Larry Gage—for leverage—it doesn't sound like she was too invested in Pete to begin with."

For Willy, this was all too close to home. "Having a baby takes you over," he said. "It may be mostly planning and logistics at first. Call it managed panic. But the little suckers grow on you."

Sam realized what she'd uncorked, and reached out to lay a hand on his chest. "They're not the only ones who do that."

He took her hand and kissed it. Not a gesture usually associated with him.

He then asked her, "Why's this bothering you?"

"Because of Daryl," she said without hesitation. "He died of a heart attack while being beaten. That could've been old-fashioned sadism or revenge, which best points to John Rust. Or it might've been torture, by somebody trying to extract information."

"And that connects to Karen's overdose how?"

"I don't know. That's what bugs me. You said all we'd done is unpack a bunch of old trunks. I'm thinking maybe the ancient history isn't just a distraction. We got sidetracked by the Seamus Sweeney angle, 'cause here-and-now cases are what we do. And we responded to it as usual. But it didn't pan out."

She raised herself up on one elbow and rolled toward him, in the process pressing her bare breast against his chest. He could simultaneously feel her warmth and growing excitement. "I think we need to change how we're looking at Daryl's death."

He reached out and brushed the backs of his fingers across her exposed skin, feeling her respond. "John Rust is still our best suspect, now that Sweeney's off the table," he said. "Isn't that what you're talking about? John's from the past, and he's not some ghost with no name and no motive."

She slid her leg across his, almost straddling him. "Yeah, but there's something missing. Call it a ghost if you like. It's like we still need to reach the bottom of that trunk."

"Yeah," he agreed, kissing her and moving his hand from her breast down her body. "Maybe we do."

It was Beverly on the phone. "Joe?"

He smiled. "Right the first time. Uncanny."

"Very funny."

"I've been told I'm hysterical."

"Of all the many very nice things I could say about you, that is not one of them."

"I am crushed," he replied. "I'm also curious. You don't often call me in the middle of the day. Am I intuiting something professional? Like that word, by the way? I've been practicing."

"Hysterical," she commented dryly. "Yes, this is professional, relating to the late Mr. Hicks."

That brought him on track. "Do tell. We're getting dizzy running around in circles down here."

"You recall my findings that were consistent with torture?" she asked.

"Like I could forget. Yes."

"I took fingernail clippings, as per protocol," she relayed, "but I also went a little further, almost on a whim."

"Aha," he said happily. "Here it comes."

He could almost feel her pleasure. "Well, yes. I suppose it does. Of the various injuries inflicted, one was strangulation."

"I remember."

"The interesting aspect to that was that it appeared to have been administered manually."

"Okay," he said slowly.

"My shot in the dark," she continued, "was based on the very remote possibility that there might be trace residual DNA left behind by the strangler."

He anticipated her next line. "And there was."

"Indeed. Not only, but it matched additional material found under Mr. Hicks's fingernails."

"Who's it belong to?" he asked.

She was enjoying her own form of torture, evidently. "That's the usual rub, is it not? DNA by itself is useless. You need a match."

"Thank you, Professor."

"You don't know the half of it. That match belongs in part to young Peter Rust."

She'd done well. Joe was suitably floored. "What?"

"The paternal alleles of the samples I collected are the same as those found in Peter Rust."

"Hang on. We were thinking John was looking good for killing his dad. That's not what you're saying, is it?"

"You know it's not. You would need to collect a sample directly from the source to be absolutely sure, but from what you were told by Laura Smiley, those alleles have to belong to Larry Gage."

"Damn, Beverly. You have no idea what you've just done."

She laughed. "I actually think I might."

• • •

Joe liked what he saw in the faces of his squad. After so much frustration bordering on resignation, it was nice to see some enthusiasm.

But they had a ways to go.

As Willy put it, "So where the fuck is Larry Gage? He sure as hell ain't on a beach anymore."

"We double-checked that," Joe confirmed. "I put out a call to his Hawaii parole officer—a guy named Perkins. Their contract ran its course some time ago, but I was hoping he knew of any friends or contacts Gage might've made out there. Perkins not only had that but he offered to make a few calls, to save me time, and sure enough, Gage is gone, last overheard saying he was heading back to the States on urgent business."

"I would qualify torturing someone to death as that," Willy agreed.

"He also told me," Joe added, "that Gage had hit bottom—skid row, living on handouts. Perkins had no idea how he could've afforded to fly off the island, much less travel way over here."

"How 'bout connections local to Vermont?" Sammie asked. "He might've been staked the cash."

"Exactly what I was thinking," Joe agreed. "Suggestions?"

"The ex?" Lester asked. "It's pretty crazy sometimes how deep those old love affairs run. If he'd approached her just the right way, she might've given him money and a roof."

"More likely there're ex–Smith Wilkinson employees still living in the area," Sam suggested, her expression doubtful. "People who just worked there, even as management, and never got caught or were clueless about the stealing. We could data-crunch the records we got and see who's around and might still be pals with their old boss."

"Here's the catch, though," Willy argued. "Assuming we decide to put all our money on the wife or whatever colleagues we can find, then we have to decide whether to sit on them and wait, or interview them to open more leads. We can't do both, or we'll spook 'em and Gage'll run—assuming he is hanging out with any of them."

"I vote on sitting and watching," Sam said. "If nothing happens, then we can move on to interviews."

"Attagirl," Willy said happily.

"Hard to argue with that," Joe agreed. He sat at his desk and pulled over his computer, adding, "Time to rally some serious backup from other squads. Pulling all those old Smith Wilkinson names together fast is gonna take manpower again."

The phone call, when it came, reminded Joe of the twelve o'clock train in *High Noon*—unavoidable and bearing bad news. Except it came on a cell phone, and the caller was Rachel Reiling. Worse than a hammy gunslinger, she was someone to whom he owed a debt.

"Hey, Rachel," he answered.

She didn't mince words. "You talk to her yet?"

"Laura Smiley?" he replied.

"Come on, Joe," she complained. "You promised."

He had, and now that they were virtually in hot pursuit, he was wrestling with that decision. He glanced around the empty office. "Where are you right now?"

"Downtown Bratt."

"My office," he said.

"Cool."

Police work is designed to go by the numbers. There are statutes, ordinances, protocols, procedures, algorithms, ladders of escalating response, and more. A Maine game warden Joe knew had once complained that the entire back seat of his four-door truck cab was packed with reference books of laws and guidelines, just so he could keep up.

By contrast, the job is also gut-driven, reactive to any and all spontaneous situations, and heavily dependent on officer discretion. In the final analysis, prosecutors know to keep their fingers crossed, hoping that beneath whatever casework they receive every day is the submitting cop's reliable, time-tested, bulletproof integrity. They also know that to screw things up is human nature, and that no police officer is immune.

But are all mistakes fatal to a case? Are they even noticed, if they're incidental enough? Will they matter if a plea bargain is agreed to by all parties, as it usually is? Police sometimes use subterfuge to achieve results, they let a suspect's imagination and paranoia do the heavy lifting. They even lie on occasion when such a ploy can be justified.

That's the murky realm where Joe's conversation with Rachel and Sally Kravitz had taken place, because of the perceived necessity at the time. But looking back, might every cop in that room have behaved otherwise, now that they knew what they did? Probably.

Except that they hadn't known where things were about to head.

Officer discretion, Joe pondered. You do what has to be done to get what you need. Call it exigent circumstances at the time. Or a screwup later on.

Who was to know?

There was a light knock at the door and Rachel stepped into the room, her equipment bag as usual hanging from her shoulder.

"Hey," she greeted him.

He gave her a welcoming wave. "You know that sooner or later, you're going to have to put a chiropractor on retainer because of that bag."

She settled into Lester's desk chair, facing Joe, and slipped the offending object onto the floor with a soft thud. "Tell me about it."

"So," he began, "Laura Smiley."

"Yeah," she replied. "What did you find out?"

"You good with some rules first?"

Rachel hesitated before answering, "I'm good with you proposing them, sure. I don't guess I can stop you anyhow."

"True," he conceded with a half smile. "All right, then. First and foremost, what follows is on deep background only. This conversation, here and now, is between you and me, and never to appear in quotes. Nor is it to be attributed to me or some anonymous law enforcement source."

"Deep Throat?" she queried.

"If you'd like."

Rachel barely considered her options. From her perspective, she didn't have a choice. Joe had her where he wanted her, despite his obvious discomfort with the entire conversation.

She did, on the other hand, give him high marks. Against his training, instincts, and better judgment, he was honoring his pledge to her, when he could have shut her off and prohibited her interviewing Laura Smiley, perhaps even by physically making the woman unavailable, for all she knew.

Additionally, in Rachel's mind, by exhibiting such fairness, Joe was almost forcing her to match it in kind.

"I agree," she therefore replied, won over. After all, without divulging a thing so far, he'd already essentially admitted that the tip about Laura's existence she and Sally had delivered was what they'd hoped it would be.

"Thank you," he said before pondering which cards to lay out and how.

"I've got a problem," he told her candidly. "If things work out as we hope, I'm on the verge of launching an operation that'll land me the fish I've been after since this case began. But everything hinges on discretion and surprise—"

"—which'll be blown if I expose Laura in the paper," Rachel interrupted.

"Exactly."

"And you went and promised to spill the beans to me."

"Right again."

It was her turn to ponder before saying, "I suspected as much when you asked me up here. What you're talking about is a matter of timing, right? This thing is about to happen, isn't it?"

"Yes."

"Win or lose, it'll be over pretty fast?"

Joe considered the chances of picking up Larry Gage's trail, either through surveillance or close questioning of his ex-wife and past associates.

"A week at most," he ventured, wondering where she was going with her questions. "The person we're targeting is in motion, as well, so I'm thinking *something* is going to happen on one side of this equation or the other."

She considered and responded, "Then I guess it's up to me to cut you some slack and let you have a few days."

He looked at her, astonished by the unexpected generosity. Trained as he'd been in his younger days by Stan Katz's ruthless style, Joe wasn't prepared for such consideration.

"There is a catch, though," Rachel added, in small part regretting her generosity.

Her surprise tactic worked. He was brought up short.

"I want the exclusive when you're ready. Not just to be first in line, but the only one you call. No press release, no private chat with Katz or some other news buddy from the old days. Just me."

He was relieved. "Hell, I don't care about that. You got it."

Rachel wrestled with the deal she'd struck as she headed back downstairs. She'd chosen a higher road over a traditional reporter's righteous indignation, which made her feel good. But in an anomaly she chose not to face full-on, that emotion was tainted by resentment. Recalling her admission to Joe and Beverly over dinner about her conflicting feelings of insecurity and affection for Sally, she remembered Joe's generous and thoughtful countering that she could hold her own without a doubt.

This latest encounter, however, had really rankled, reviving Rachel's agitation. The feeling was similar to having won in a contest that was itself belittled or disparaged, like a sporting event where the rules had been suspended for the lesser players.

All her life, she'd been the good girl, the nice one. Well mannered, respectful, the one seeking accommodation over conflict or confrontation. It had been fine for years, indeed an asset through her teens, when her elders were so transparently appreciative as a result.

But that time was past. Now she envied the Sallys of the world, or the Beverlys before her, who could not only hold their ground but what's more, were expected to do so by those around them.

She knew that her youth and natural impatience were to blame for this hunger and frustration—jealousy, even—for what she perceived as the natural and enviable stature of such women.

She also recognized, in an apparent contradiction, that she liked the appreciation she received from the likes of Joe and her mother, just as she herself preferred dealing with people who were inclined toward compromise.

This inner debate, of course, was heightened by the growing conviction that she was teetering on the edge of a story that might grant her renown.

How to honor the deal, therefore, get the story, and retain Joe's high regard?

She let escape an exasperated sigh. Did Woodward and Bernstein ever go through such growing pains?

CHAPTER TWENTY-TWO

Returning to the Scene of the Crime

The basement of Brattleboro's municipal building housed an emergency ops center designed for any crisis exceeding the normal capacities of the town's fire and police dispatchers, as when, years before, Tropical Storm Irene had put much of Vermont underwater. The room was windowless, not enormous, and fully equipped with phones, computers, fax machines, copiers, and its own independent radio system.

This was where Joe was allowed by the local emergency management chief to set up a team of agents borrowed from across the state. Covering three rows of tables were the by-now familiar boxes of old Smith Wilkinson files, and facing them was a full complement of investigators, all variously reading, phoning, typing into computers, or collating, according to the list of priorities that Joe's squad had distributed.

Such saturation research efforts had occurred in the past, but rarely where the sense of a deadline was so immediate. The combination of John Rust's ongoing absence, Larry Gage's possibly lethal but evasive reappearance, and the lack of knowledge about what was motivating whom, all lent an urgency to this effort that a more generic massive push often lacked.

There was a strong, overarching suspicion in the room that if they didn't find something that led them to Gage, Daryl Hicks might not be the only body found by a roadside.

"This reminds me of what John said on video when he was being processed at the barracks," Sally recalled.

"What was that?" Rachel asked, whipping up a batch of scrambled eggs late at night.

"He talked about a bug called the deathwatch beetle," Sally said. She stretched out on the secondhand sofa they'd both lugged into the apartment earlier, part of Rachel's efforts to make the place more livable. "He started out because some ticking water pipe reminded him of it, but it stuck in my head for another reason."

Rachel added a little milk and cheese to her concoction, which was haute cuisine by her standards—one of the things she and Joe had in common. "How so? Weird name."

"A long time ago, supposedly, people associated the beetle's tap, tap, tapping with the fact that it was mostly heard during the quiet of nighttime death vigils. I think it was just a random comment Rust made because he was drunk at the time, but I was reminded of it now because the bug was also a borer that got into a house's wood beams and ate them from the inside out. It's like a metaphor for this whole case."

Rachel stopped long enough to turn away from the stove and suggest, "Larry Gage and company cannibalizing Smith Wilkinson."

Sally grunted. "Not only—Pete's forever twilight state, John's decades of sacrifice, Daryl being killed for something buried in history. All a countdown for self-destruction. Makes me wonder if somehow John knew more than he was letting on when he brought up the beetle in the first place."

Rachel thought back to her talk with Joe earlier, and the negotiated next stage they'd reached in their awkward alliance concerning Laura Smiley.

The image of the beetle gnawing away, unseen and unnoticed, reminded her once more of her own ongoing agitation about that agreement.

"Mr. Gunther? I think I found something."

Joe looked up from his own pile of folders, locating who'd just spoken among the VBI agents before him. He found a fresh-faced young man with his hand in the air, newly recruited from the Burlington police, and clearly intimidated and unsure how to address his legendary superior.

Amused, the Legend rose and crossed over to the man, stopping beside his chair to see what he was holding. "What've you got, Josh?"

"It's an interoffice memo from the AG's team of investigators, discussing how to refer to one of their intel sources."

"You mean a code name?" Joe asked.

"Yeah. Somebody who absolutely didn't want to get pulled into the limelight. Made a big deal out of it, to the point of saying she wouldn't spill what she had unless she was guaranteed anonymity."

"Immunity from prosecution?"

"Wasn't that kind of informant. What she had was purely informational. She wasn't involved in anything illegal."

"What did she have?"

Josh looked into Joe's face. "The whole shebang, as my dad used to say. She was the one who alerted them that Gage and his pals were up to no good."

Joe could feel his cheeks flush. John Laware had clearly told Sammie that the key to this whole puzzle for the AG had been an anonymous letter, telling of Smith Wilkinson's dark doings. Now it seemed that

Laware's harboring of his informant—for whatever reasons—had not ended with the case's successful prosecution.

The irony was that Joe didn't suspect any subterfuge or malfeasance. He'd been in Laware's shoes. The commitment to an informant's confidentiality can become second nature, where even the passage of decades can't loosen your grip on it.

"That's how they tumbled to this? An inside snitch?" he asked, choosing to move along.

"Yes and no. She worked there only briefly, and when she dropped the dime on them, it was almost two years later and she'd left. The point is, she did get lost in the wake—getting granted anonymity—just like she wanted. The AG—once they were on target—built their whole case without her. She was like the hand grenade a ski patrol uses to start an avalanche."

"Okay," Joe replied, ignoring the number of metaphors. "So give me the bottom line. What's her real name?"

Josh smiled broadly as he delivered his own explosive answer. "Karen Taylor. One of the names on our watch list. She blew the whistle on her own kid's father."

Joe resisted hugging the kid and pulled out his phone to spread the news to his squad.

Scott Jezek liked working at night in his office. The usual reasons of no phone calls or drop-bys applied, but he preferred it, too, for how the ambience of the surrounding town changed with the extending darkness. Traffic lessened outside, sounds of doors opening or closing in the building, footsteps on the stairs—everything faded to virtual nonexistence. He felt encased and snug, and heightened the mood by using only a single lamp on his desk, eschewing the large overhead frosted globe.

He was therefore disappointed and surprised when he more heard than clearly saw the office door open and a dark figure enter the room.

"Sally?" he asked, knowing of her nocturnal habits. "That you?"

But as the words left his mouth, he knew it wasn't. The shape and movements of this person were wrong, which was confirmed when an older man with short white hair settled into Scott's guest chair and became fully revealed by the lamp's cone of light.

As was the large semiautomatic pistol he was holding in his lap.

"May I help you?" Scott asked, his brain in overdrive, trying to place the man without success. The gun should have helped, he thought, but instead, it only added to the confusion.

He forced himself into lawyer mode, as if in court, anticipating all arguments and proposals, and formulating ahead of time any possible responses that might play to his advantage.

"Do we know each other?"

"We will," the man answered.

Scott chose to approach from the outside in, hoping to gauge the man's intentions. "That your Mike Hammer best?" he asked, crossing his legs.

"Who?"

That was a surprise. "Tough guy from books and movies. I guess you're not a fiction lover."

The man seemed nonplussed by Scott's reaction to him. "What the fuck're you talking about?"

Scott was pleased by that. He took a second to study his guest, from the hard face, short hair, cheap clothes, and worn shoes to the fact that he'd made an effort to look professional. He was wearing a tie, for example, although not completely closed at the throat. The look reminded Jezek of Humphrey Bogart somewhat, when he played down-and-out—and fresh from jail.

The notion struck Scott as possibly relevant.

"What did you want to see me about?" he asked in as neutral a tone as he could muster, despite his stomach being at war with what he hoped was his face's calm and businesslike expression.

A furrow appeared between the man's eyebrows, telling Scott that things weren't proceeding as anticipated. A good sign, he hoped. "John Rust," his guest said. "I need to find him."

"And I'm supposed to know Mr. Rust?" Scott asked.

That was a mistake. The furrow yielded to a scowl. "Don't do that, lawyer. You were in the paper as representing him. You try to get slippery, I'll cut both your eyes out, one at a time."

It was a disturbing if revealing escalation, Scott thought. This person's use of English, while profane, was also educated and thought out. "You know how we are," he said. "I had to try."

"Is it worth your eyesight? Answer the question."

"What do I call you?" Scott asked instead.

Instead of responding, the man rose, circled the desk, and towered over Jezek, simultaneously reaching into his pocket. Defeating his own efforts to appear calm, Scott pushed back his chair, trying to escape. The man shoved him against the wall behind, pinning his neck there with his left hand as his right reappeared with a switchblade that snapped open with a loud and ominous click.

Almost sitting on the lawyer's lap, the intruder held the knife's point just below Scott's right eye.

Scott moaned slightly, blinking furiously and not daring to move.

"Who's Sally?" the man asked in a tight voice, his face inches away. He smelled of sour laundry, poor hygiene, and despair.

"My colleague."

"Another lawyer?"

"No. Private investigator."

"What does she do?"

Scott was caught off guard. "She . . . I don't know . . . She investigates."

"John Rust?"

The knife tip was stinging, and Scott was pretty sure he could feel blood trickling down his cheek, although by now, he imagined it might have been tears.

But the question put him in a dilemma beyond his own peril. Conjuring up a chess move of his own, the man with the knife had abruptly maneuvered Scott into a corner. If Jezek said yes, he was endangering Sally; if no, he opened the door to this maniac using that blade.

Scott swallowed hard and said, "I refuse to answer that."

The man pulled away, amused, pocketing the knife. "You just did, asshole. I hope you're a better lawyer than you are a crisis negotiator."

Scott touched under his eye with his fingertips as the man collected the gun he'd left on the desk. He found a smear of blood on his index. "Why do you want John Rust?" he asked, volunteering, "You should know, by the way, that he's pulled a vanishing act. *Nobody* knows where he is. I've been looking, Sally has, the police, the state's attorney's office, you name it. He's disappeared."

"That's all right," the man replied. "I'll talk to Sally about that. Amazing what people in her profession hold back from their employers."

Scott flushed with anger and he stood up, his legs trembling. "You leave her alone. You can think what you want about lawyers, but she's good people and knows no more about where Rust is than I do. I have no idea who you are or what your beef is, but leave her out of it."

In response, the man circled back again as Scott stepped back and raised his hands to protect his face. The intruder grabbed him by the shirtfront and half dragged him toward the door.

"What're you doing?" Scott demanded, stumbling, embarrassed at being handled so easily.

"Locking the back door," the man said. "I don't want you squealing to your girlfriend or the cops after I leave. You got a wife?"

"Fuck you."

"Whatever. Hands behind your back."

After cinching Scott's wrists together with a zip tie, he pushed his gun hard into his prisoner's back and pushed him out into the darkened hallway. "Outside, to the right," he ordered, heading for the building's exit. "You make a noise, you try to draw attention to us, you die."

They almost dance-stepped into the parking lot, like a two-person conga line, where the man steered Scott toward a nondescript sedan, remotely triggered its trunk, and without pause, toppled the lawyer into its yawning void. Scott had barely time to brace against the impact before he felt the lid close behind him and found himself twisted up and in pain, in utter darkness.

Moments later, the front door slammed, the engine caught, and the car began gaining speed.

It was a short drive. Scott did his best to emulate what he'd seen in the movies, where the victim concentrates on right and left turns, the sounds of railroad tracks being crossed, and the like. But he quickly made a muddle of it, having to lump the effort next to his singular lack of heroics earlier.

This was not becoming a day he would remember with great self-respect.

The blast of cool night air came as a relief ten minutes later when the trunk sprang open again and Scott blinked up at his tormentor's silhouette.

"Get out," the man ordered.

Laboriously, he did so, whereupon he was seized by the collar and pushed toward a compact row of metal storage containers. He recognized the spot, a rental business on the edge of town, catering to pack-rats or people between housing.

"This is crazy," he protested. "You can't put me in one of those. How's that going to help you find John?"

"Watch me," the man replied, ignoring him. He chose a small unit, opened its already unlocked door, and escorted Scott inside.

All the way down to having left the lock open, Scott realized, this man had planned things through. Indeed, as soon as the door was swung to behind them, a flashlight came on and Scott saw a mattress against the far wall, complete with a set of handcuffs already dangling from a metal crosspiece.

The man pushed him to his knees onto the bedding, roughly cut the zip tie and attached him to the wall, and said in the dim half light, "Your new home. Bottles to keep you hydrated, a pot to piss in, as they say—so don't knock it over—and a nice comfortable place to sleep."

"People will miss me within hours," Scott tried explaining. "What does this gain you? Kidnapping and unlawful restraint? Even in Vermont, that spells trouble. And what if I have a heart attack and die? That's murder. Think about this, for Christ's sake."

The man laughed. "Right. 'Cause this is all so spur-of-the-moment. You really are an idiot. Open your mouth."

"What? No way. Why the hell're you doing this? What's John ever done to you?"

The response sounded almost mystified, giving Jezek the tiniest flicker of hope. "Done to me?" His tone was incredulous. "Nothing. He's irrelevant. He's the key to the cash. That's all."

"What cash?"

"The cash, moron. *My* cash. I read about it online, in that article. The only money I have left after all these years, which that little bloodsucking son of a bitch is gonna hand over. I don't even care if it's down to ten bucks. *She* stole it, *he's* got it, and *I* want it. Open your fucking mouth or I'll cut your lips off."

Scott heard the sharp click of the knife reopening. He did as he was told, again, his brain teeming with what he'd just been told, and felt a hard rubber ball inserted between his teeth, along with an attached band of some sort slipped behind his head to keep it in place.

"That'll shut you up," the man said with satisfaction. "I'm liking the benefit already."

He stepped back and played the light around to admire his handiwork. "I customized your gag so you can't take it off without removing your head, which I wouldn't recommend. You probably think you can't drink from those bottles now, but you're wrong. It'll make a mess, but you can get enough around that ball. I hope it doesn't get too hot in here, or you may not need a heart attack to kill you. You better pray your friends are persistent."

He crossed over to the storage locker's entrance, paused, and added with a laugh, "Try not to move around too much—it'll only kill you faster," before locking the door behind him.

CHAPTER TWENTY-THREE

Willy Unleashed

Joe stepped outside the emergency ops center, into the dimly lit basement corridor, and punched in Willy Kunkle's speed dial number.

"What?"

"Got one right up your alley," Joe answered him.

"Hard, dirty, and probably without purpose?"

"Complete with a cross you can climb up onto afterward," his boss replied without apology.

"What is it?"

"It's a 'who,'" Joe explained. "I'm in the ops center. The new guy, Josh, from the St. J office, just dug up something else, on top of Karen having squealed on Gage. As the AG's people were building a case, they went hunting for CIs, I'm guessing in hopes that Karen would be one among many."

"We can all dream," Willy commented. "Why did Karen turn in Gage and company? You didn't say in your text. And why two years after she left?"

"We'll probably never know," Joe replied. "But given what happened to Pete and how Karen ended up the same year Gage was brought down, it doesn't sound like life was working out as hoped.

"Anyhow," he resumed, "the AG found a couple of willing minor players, and put them to use, but what Josh dug up was just the opposite, and might be worth chasing down. There was a woman doing clerical work in the admin area of Smith Wilkinson who copped a notable attitude about cooperating with investigators, specifically on the subject of Chuck Dietz, who oversaw Purchasing."

"He was particularly good pals with Gage," Willy interjected. "I remember reading that."

"Right," Joe agreed, continuing. "What Josh discovered was a report concerning this woman—Holly Thorpe—in which the AG investigator posited that she, Dietz, and Gage were possibly a clandestine item."

Willy burst out laughing. "A trio? No kidding. What a place that must've been. And Gage got around."

"Well," Joe equivocated quickly, "maybe, maybe not. It was just one man's opinion, and it went nowhere because Thorpe was in no mood to play ball."

"And they probably had nothing to hold over her."

"Correct," Joe said.

"So why're you telling me this?" Willy asked.

"She's still in the area," Joe revealed. "Lives in Putney."

"And maybe still carrying a torch for old Larry," Willy finished for him.

"Not only," Joe said. "You remember that Dietz was the one we couldn't find of the four of them? The one John Laware joked could've become either a Unabomber wannabe or a do-gooder for the Salvation Army?"

Willy paused before saying, "You think Gage and Dietz have hooked up again? Why? To kill Hicks?"

"I don't know," Joe told him. "That's why I want you to stake out Holly Thorpe's place and see what you can find."

Joe could almost visualize his old sniper colleague nodding in agreement, eager to start.

"You got it, boss."

Joe gave him Thorpe's address, satisfied he'd assigned the right man to the task.

"There's no wiggle room?" Sally asked her.

Reading criticism in the question, Rachel again rued her agreement with Joe. "Not in spirit."

Sally's response, however, was purely pragmatic. "Which means there is. It's not that you can't *meet* Laura Smiley, and even get down what she says. You just can't publish it. What's the harm in introducing yourself, at least, before the shit hits the fan? That way, you'll have a relationship you can use later. Right now, she doesn't know you from the man in the moon."

Rachel considered the idea. Sally's logic was appealing, and if she handled things right, Joe might not even discover her sleight of hand. "I could enlist her as an ally," she ventured. "Pitch whatever story I'm planning as a collaboration of sorts."

She reflected as Sally ordered a chocolate-and-vanilla softie from the girl behind the counter. They were in West Brattleboro, celebrating the spring opening of the Chelsea Royal Diner's ice cream stand, located beside the actual restaurant. Spring in Vermont was remarkable for how it brought people outdoors, all of a sudden, virtually blinking in the sunshine like survivors of an arctic blackout.

"The only hitch I can see," Rachel continued, licking her own pistachio offering, "is that I don't know what he has planned for her. I don't want to step into the middle of some juggling act he's got going. If he has her under surveillance, for instance, or staked out like a sacrificial goat, it could end up being both dangerous and stupid to go blundering in, not to mention a betrayal he wouldn't likely forget."

Sally collected her change and pocketed it in her jeans. "That's true," she said agreeably. "It's dicey. If you want, we could drop by Laura's house together, scope it out, see how it feels. If she's just living there, like normal, then chances are she's not at the center of anything covert, but more like a pawn Gunther doesn't want disturbed with a lot of publicity, which is not what you're planning."

Rachel took a second taste of her ice cream before asking, "You wouldn't mind?"

Sally smiled broadly. "You kidding? My general caseload's under control, and it sure beats waiting around for John to show up, or, for that matter," she held up her phone for emphasis, "for goddamned Scott Jezek to answer his messages."

Willy was back in his element. Given the VBI's presently stretched resources, and the uncertainty of his target's legitimacy, he was operating by himself—as he preferred.

In the dark woods on the edge of Putney village, however, outside Holly Thorpe's house, he was neither military sniper nor urban cop. His only weapons were his service pistol, a backup gun he never admitted having, and two knives discreetly tucked away. And he had no sniper-associated ghillie suit to help him blend into the background. He was just a man among the trees, by that measure. But a man impossible to hear and hard to spot, even from five feet away.

This version of himself was at once ghost and predator, as focused on his task as a jungle cat or snake, attuned to the slightest breeze, the vegetation underfoot, and the subtlety of the moonlight infiltrating the tree limbs. In contrast to the man people saw at work in the streets, this variant was silent, lethal, and patient—an unimaginable contrast to the Willy so many believed to be incapable of sitting still.

So much for perceptions.

In the years between working for Smith Wilkinson and now, it appeared that Holly Thorpe had done all right for herself. The house, just outside the village, along Fred Houghton Road, wasn't ostentatious, but well kept, expensively tended with elaborate landscaping and stone walls, and as freshly painted and attended to as a house primped up for sale.

This was at once good and bad for Willy. The cleared woods and lawns made navigation easy; the outside lighting challenged staying covert.

Lights were on inside as well, two cars were parked on the gravel drive, and he could glimpse the odd human form passing before a window.

The trick was going to be getting close enough to see more, and identifying all the occupants—a task Willy was eagerly anticipating.

In Chester, farther north, Sally was using her more urban-honed skills to assess Laura Smiley's neighborhood, driving slowly as if in search of an address, while in fact taking note of cars, people, and potential hiding places for observers she didn't want to alarm.

"How's this work?" Rachel asked beside her, the reporter in her alert to new insight.

"I call it looking for normal/abnormal," Sally replied, her eyes roving as they went. "There are no absolutes, unless you're dealing with real amateurs, which is most of the time. Those jokers will smoke in their cars and drop butts out the window, leaving a pile where you can see they've been parked for hours. Or they'll loiter, completely out of context with their surroundings, standing out like sore thumbs—in downtown Brattleboro, for example, staring into a single store window until you want to yell at them, 'I see you.'

"Around here, in a village, you drive the circuit once, taking mental notes, then you break for a meal or get some gas, and then return to see what's changed. It's not a science, but it's usually enough to spot most people who have no reason to be there."

"What're you seeing now?" Rachel asked.

She was relieved when Sally answered, "Nuthin'. Not a thing."

Nevertheless, she followed her own procedure, stopping for sandwiches with Rachel at the local market before returning to Smiley's street to run a second inventory.

Finally satisfied, she pulled over, positioning her car for a rapid getaway if necessary, and led the way down the sidewalk a couple of hundred feet to Smiley's almost self-effacing home. Lights were on behind two of the windows.

The slender woman who opened the door to their knock was wearing a sweatshirt, jeans, no shoes, and had her hair back. Rachel and Sally instantly recognized Laura Smiley.

"Yes?" the older woman asked.

Rachel got straight to the point—make or break—having convinced herself that she was on the edge only of her contract with Joe, while repressing the obvious fact that he would interpret things otherwise. "We hate to intrude, Mrs. Smiley, but I was hoping you'd be willing to speak to us about Larry Gage and Smith Wilkinson."

Smiley stiffened and frowned. "Who are you?"

"I'm Rachel Reiling, from the *Brattleboro Reformer.* This is my colleague, Sally Kravitz."

Smiley began slowly closing the door as she said, "I don't think so. I have nothing to say."

"We know you attended the funeral service for Peter Rust," Rachel said quickly. "The last thing I want is to get anything wrong, or cause you trouble just because we didn't get to talk."

Their quarry shook her head. "I'm sorry."

Sally used a less pointed approach. "Ms. Smiley. We're only looking for background right now. Whatever article that might follow is still in the making. We just want everything to be accurate."

The woman hesitated, allowing Rachel to add, "You call the shots. You don't want to talk about the funeral, that's fine. Maybe we could start with some basic historical stuff."

"None of it's news," Smiley complained. "Nobody cares about this anymore. It's been done with for decades."

Sally challenged her. "It hasn't, Ms. Smiley. You know it. Others have talked to you about this recently."

The woman dropped her chin in resignation and let out a sigh, apparently defeated by the sheer weight of inevitability. "This'll never go away," she said, barely audibly, before stepping back and widening the doorway.

Rachel and Sally filed past her, Rachel restating, "I promise, it won't be as bad as you think. I just need some background."

Smiley didn't respond, leading the way instead into her bland living room. She sat down without inviting them to do the same, reducing them to work that out for themselves, which they did by choosing the sofa opposite her.

Rachel began by pulling out her notepad. "What do you prefer I call you? Ms. Smiley? Laura?"

"Laura's fine." Her tone was flat, disengaged.

Rachel steered away from what seemed to be touchy ground. "Okay. So, given how long ago this was, could you refresh our memories with some basic history? What Smith Wilkinson was all about, what made them choose Springfield, Vermont, of all places, to set up shop? Things like that."

Sally fine-tuned the question to make it more personal to Laura. "We know what was written at the time, but the scandal stole the show. What got missed was the genesis. I think it's been forgotten that people were employed there, and that it probably benefited the community, at least for a while, right?"

Laura's expression softened. "It did. You're right. That was the part I knew about. I had no clue Larry and the other three had cooked up their scheme. I just heard the dreams and saw the beginnings of it become reality. There was a time when it was a good thing—right place at the right time, and for all the right reasons."

"Did you even know the three men Larry worked with?" Rachel asked.

"I got to know them, but not really. Not at first. We were all at college together, but separate. There was Larry and me on one side, and Larry and those three on the other. I knew about them, but without the details—certainly without knowing what they were planning. That was just business to me, and not interesting."

"Larry was a pretty seductive guy?" Rachel asked.

"I thought so," Laura conceded. "Later, I realized how corny most of it was, and how gullible I was to fall for it. I was something to add to his trophy case, and flattered by the attention."

"Not a woman of the world," Sally suggested.

Laura laughed without humor. "Hardly. Larry was the second man I'd ever had sex with, and the first was some messy fumbling in a back seat that embarrassed us both. I actually felt sorry for the boy. Compared to him, Larry was a movie star. He had the kind of self-confidence you hear all movers and shakers have. It was just part of his character."

"Why Vermont, for Smith Wilkinson?" Rachel asked, sensing that a rapport with this woman was in fact gaining strength.

Laura shrugged. "I don't know. Not really. Like I said, I wasn't included in that part of his life. I do remember how excited they were at a party we attended, when they got the news that Springfield had offered them a tax break and an old factory building. I imagined that was the deciding factor right there. They'd sent out feelers, looking for a town that would offer them a sweetheart deal. I actually wasn't that thrilled with Springfield, if you want to know the truth. Larry and his friends had something to do. I was just stuck there."

Like Lester before her, Rachel unknowingly asked, "You didn't get a job?"

Laura wasn't falling into that trap again, revealing her inner feelings and her affair with Karen. "Larry didn't want me to," she answered instead. "So I busied myself in other ways."

Naturally ignorant of what lay hidden in that answer, Rachel veered back toward what she could see. It was a reflection of how conversations with the same people often yield different results, sometimes hinging on dumb luck.

"Returning to Larry's three friends and the business," she therefore said, "I'm guessing that with time, you did get to know them."

"I did," Laura admitted, frowning. "Not that it left me very impressed. I ended up liking Paul Legasse. He ran Accounting—definitely the odd man out. He seemed very sweet, but I always thought he was like the beach ball being batted around by a bunch of bullies. They made fun of him and talked behind his back. It was cruel, and he never did anything to deserve it." She stared sorrowfully at the rug before concluding, "He killed himself in prison. If he'd had better friends, he'd probably be playing bad golf at some retirement home today."

"But he was right in the middle of it, being the accountant," Sally gently protested.

Laura defended him. "He was doing what Larry told him to. Larry was CFO. He called the shots. Paul's only crime was that he wanted to be liked by the cool kids."

"What about Dietz and Murchison?" Rachel asked.

"Murchison made my skin crawl," Laura said, instinctively hugging herself. "All bright teeth and fast hands and loud laughter. I could never understand what people saw in the man. But according to Larry, he could charm birds out of the trees. The perfect front man, Larry called him. I just remember the awful clothes he wore—reminded me of a used car salesman."

"And Dietz?"

Laura paused, thinking back. "He was Purchasing," she started neutrally. "I didn't know what that meant at the time, but I learned later it was a crucial part of their operation. He would arrange for whatever equipment and materials came into the plant, but would work closely with Paul to make sure all the pricing and contracts would be slanted to the advantage of the four founders. He was the one I liked the least—even over Murchison. He was bad to women, rude to me, dismissive of the workers. I sometimes did volunteer work at the plant, setting up day care and outreach to workers' families and things like that. Chuck Dietz always made a point of saying insulting things about it. He was a user, as far as I could tell."

"How do you mean, he was bad to women?" Sally asked.

"You were fair game if you wore a skirt," Laura said. "And we didn't live in the Me Too era. If you spoke out, you were fired. That was it. Finished. Chuck took full advantage of that."

"Sounds pretty risky," Sally pursued. "Given the game they were playing, you'd think he would've been more cautious. Didn't your husband tell him to cut it out?"

Laura looked at her pityingly. "You think any of them cared about a scorned woman? You *are* a youngster. That was part of the appeal of all this—the company and the money and the power that went with it. These four men—my husband included—saw themselves as boys in a candy store, and the women were part of it. Maybe that's why I liked Paul. As far as I know, he was the only one who didn't fool around."

"Larry, too?" Rachel asked.

"Sure, Larry, too," Laura replied, her earlier pallor flushed with anger. "He had several affairs, if you want to call them that."

"That must've hurt."

Laura stopped and glanced at her hands in her lap. Her body language exuded a reluctance to continue.

"It did," she said shortly.

"Did you know any of the women?" Sally asked.

Laura sighed deeply. "Karen Taylor, of course. I assume she's why you're here. She had Larry's child. Peter."

Sally swallowed her surprise, maintaining her line of questioning. "And the other women?"

Laura answered indirectly, distancing herself from her own visible discomfort. "I knew one of them carried on with Larry and Chuck at the same time."

"Damn," Rachel said. "You knew that then?"

"She's the one who told me," Laura replied sadly. "Looking back, which I hoped I never would, those years at the end of Smith Wilkinson were a nightmare. Everything that could go wrong, did. I went into that time newly married, fresh out of college, with an ambitious, upwardly mobile husband, and ended up betrayed, broke, suspected of collusion by the police, and almost suicidal."

"You were clearly brave enough to have saved yourself," Sally commented, looking around.

"I guess," Laura conceded halfheartedly. "Meeting my second husband was a blessing, although I was through the worst of it by then. But he was a good, decent man. Not like Larry. He was stable, unimaginative, not the life of any party, and completely, utterly reliable. Larry would've hated him."

"Why didn't you move?" Rachel asked, as if out of the blue. "You're not native to here. Staying must've exposed you to memories all the time."

"I don't know," Laura answered her. "Maybe it was just too much. I don't have family I care about, didn't have kids I could live near. I guess it didn't really matter that much."

Her eyes widened at the thought. "Come to think of it, I do see things—or people—that go back to then. Even the woman I was talking about, who dated Chuck and Larry at the same time. She lives in Putney. I see her once in a blue moon, usually shopping or something in Brattleboro, and it doesn't do anything to me. No more than seeing a rat go by. It just is."

"Really?" Sally asked, her investigator's interest piqued. "What's her name?"

"Holly Thorpe," was the answer. "Her and Karen, I'll never forget."

CHAPTER TWENTY-FOUR

Showdown

"Is this Joe Gunther?"

Joe looked at the name on his office phone's screen—W. MATTHEWS. It meant nothing to him.

"Yes," he said. "Who's this?"

Her voice was tremulous, almost tearful. "We've never met. My name's Wendy. I'm Scott Jezek's wife."

"Oh," he said, making the connection. "Sure. What's up?"

"Well, that's just it. I'm not sure. Scott's not home, he's not at his office, and he's not answering his phone. I'm really scared something's wrong. It's been hours now."

Joe frowned. "Did you call the local police? I'll do everything I can, but they have a lot more people available than I do."

"Scott gave me your number if something like this happened."

"He did?" Joe asked. "Why?"

"He's working on a case he told you about, I think. At least, that's what he said to me. He stressed it was no big deal, but it might be getting bigger than he thought. I could tell he was trying not to worry me, but he still gave me your number. I sensed it was his way of sending out an SOS if something went wrong. Well, I think something has."

Gunther did, too. While gathering details from Wendy, he began entering a text on his phone for those he had out in the field.

By necessity, the dynamics of Willy's assignment had to be fluid, which put him at a disadvantage. People with his training prefer to stay put, blending into their surroundings, waiting until their target presents itself. But he was alone, had a whole house under scrutiny, and his target or targets were both unknown in number and inside the residence. He could have hunkered down and kept watching for movements through a single chosen window, but that option had such low potential yield that he'd dismissed it out of hand.

That limited him to staying on the move, in the dark, circling the house without drawing attention, and keeping close enough that he could actually see through the windows at a wide enough angle to study most of the interior.

It was, to his experience, the best scenario for error and exposure, shy of simply walking through the front door and announcing himself.

Of course, unsurprisingly, it also heightened his enjoyment.

His pleasure was restricted to the challenges only, however. He was less than thrilled with his results. Holly Thorpe, he'd identified and tracked throughout the house, but he knew from her body language and seeing her speak, albeit inaudibly, that she was not alone. But therein lay the catch. Whoever else was with her had a well-honed and instinctive ability for staying out of view. Willy didn't go so far as to think he'd been spotted and that the building's occupants were actively ducking him. It was more feral than that. In his opinion, he could almost sense the wariness of whomever Thorpe was hosting. It was as if they knew something he didn't, perhaps beyond these walls. Whatever it was, he felt its influence driving the final act of this decades-old drama that had trapped these people with their ambitions, greed, hatreds, and thirst for revenge.

It was then, as if on cue, that a pair of headlights slowly wobbled up the dirt driveway.

Willy, who by now had circled the house enough times to single out the best bolt-holes and observation points, moved to where he could see the front door and, through one of the home's windows, observe what was going on just inside that door.

It wasn't comforting, any more than the text message he received from Joe simultaneously, telling him of Jezek's disappearance—a jarring note enhanced by seeing Sally and Rachel emerge from the car and approach the house.

"Jesus," he said to himself. "This just keeps getting better."

Through the window, he saw Holly Thorpe approach the front door upon hearing the bell, but not open it. Instead, she waited, her hand on the knob.

The explanation appeared as an older but recognizable Larry Gage slipped by Thorpe and took up position behind the door.

"Naturally," Willy muttered, quickly communicating his discovery in a return text to Joe, recommending that any and all nearby police be asked to respond silently to the scene for backup.

Only now did Thorpe open the door, smiling, and begin speaking with the two visitors.

Willy decided to change modes, from observation to possible intervention. It was time to enter the building while everyone's focus was on the entrance.

• • •

In the car, Rachel and Sally had been discussing what they'd learned from Laura Smiley about Holly Thorpe, before leaving her and driving directly to Thorpe's house.

To Rachel's increasingly myopic way of thinking, this fell outside her agreement with Joe, which had concerned only Laura. Thorpe was an entirely new lead, and probably as peripheral as Laura had described her. She'd once worked for the company, had known at least two of the four major players intimately, and was well placed now to be at least an outstanding background source, not to mention an important next step in Rachel's progression toward completing her story.

That was all.

"What do we know about Chuck Dietz?" Sally asked, changing subject slightly. "That he's unaccounted for?"

"The invisible man," Rachel confirmed, ignoring the slightly ominous implication behind Sally's question. The revelation of Pete's true paternity had made meeting Thorpe a necessity. It closed the circle on Rachel's initial assignment, which was to write about two brothers caught in a unique situation, while providing a tremendous human interest bonus that was virtually guaranteed to catapult the story onto the front page.

"Laura was clearly clueless about his whereabouts," she added, as if convincing herself. "Could be he went to Hawaii to reconnect with Gage, since they were chummy in the old days. If he were still hanging out with Thorpe, Laura would've seen them both around town."

Sally grunted as the car bumped slowly up Thorpe's driveway. "I'd say you were right if it weren't for Hicks getting killed. I know we think John did that, and God knows, he had his reasons, but I'm still smelling something rotten going on."

Rachel killed the engine in front of the house. "Well," she said, smiling, happy for once to be the driving force in one of their joint outings, "with fingers crossed, you'll have nothing to worry about. Thorpe'll end up being the source of newspaper lore, wise and all-knowing."

"Leaving us only to find John Rust," Sally said dourly, reminded of the task she'd been given so long ago. "Alive or dead."

Rachel stared at her, slamming the car door, almost regretting how good she felt by contrast. "Damn, you're cheery. I'm surprised you don't like Kunkle more. You two should be drinking buddies."

"Neither of us drinks."

Rachel led the way to the front door, choosing to move on. "My point exactly."

The door opened a half minute after Rachel's thumb left the buzzer.

Before them stood a stocky woman wearing too much makeup and a skunklike row of white hair roots startlingly at odds with her otherwise dark tresses.

"Hi," she greeted them, her smile glued in place, her eyes narrow and watchful.

Sally didn't like the energy she was feeling, but her friend forged ahead, her voice holding an unusually assertive edge, in Sally's estimation. "Hi," Rachel said, introducing herself. "Are you Holly Thorpe?"

The smile didn't flicker. "Depends."

Rachel paid that no attention. "Right. I've been doing a series of articles about some people I'm sure you don't know, but who have a common history with yours dating back to when you worked for Smith Wilkinson. It's really just historical research, as far as you're concerned, but we're having a hard time finding people still living in the area who worked there."

"I bet," the woman replied, not inviting them in.

Rachel hesitated, leaving a gap for Sally to suggest, "Maybe this isn't a good time."

That's all that was needed. The door opened wider, to show a paunchy man with unnaturally white teeth, displayed too readily as he spoke, as if he was forcing himself to be pleasant.

"Hi there, pretty ladies," he said, gesturing to them to enter. "Come on in. We didn't mean to be rude. Of course, we'd be happy to tell you what we can. You know old people, right? Always ready to reminisce, especially with girls like you."

"It is getting late," Sally said, holding back as she recognized Charles Dietz. "We should've called first."

Dietz reached out and touched Sally's elbow, urging her along. It was as if he recognized her as the warier of the two. "No, no, no. Please. It's no problem at all. As it turns out, I worked for the old outfit myself, so I might be able to help."

Slowly, the party shuffled into the foyer, where the door was finally closed.

Revealing a second man standing behind it.

Both Rachel and Sally froze, recalling him from their briefing with the VBI.

"You got lucky," this one said, barely smiling. "I worked there, too. Larry Gage."

"Oh," Rachel blurted out, struggling to transition from meeting Laura's rival to finding herself face-to-face with two of the primary players in this saga.

In the proverbial bat of an eye, her self-serving expectations had abruptly collided with reality, and dropped her right into the center of something immediate, relevant, and more than faintly ominous.

And adrenalizing. She suddenly felt like the kid in class, pining to lead but too shy to admit it, being shoved to the front and expected to deliver.

"Wow. This is a surprise."

"I'm Chuck Dietz," the fat man confirmed, shaking hands, unlike Gage, seemingly not wanting his erstwhile partner to get exclusive attention.

Holly finally got her hostess bearings, saying without visible pleasure, "Why don't we go into the living room and get comfortable? Anybody want something to drink?"

They ignored her, but traveled the short hallway into a cathedral-ceilinged room, complete with oversized fireplace—none of it self-confidently monumental, but more reflective of a middle-class budget being stretched to its limits, as evidenced by inexpensive carpets and worn-out furniture.

"Sit," Gage told them, pointing Sally and Rachel toward the couch.

The two of them sat, neither one leaning back. Sally, for her part, hadn't ruled out having to leap into action at a moment's notice.

Rachel, by contrast, had been seized by a subtler, if parallel, emotion. As if caught in a still photograph, she saw herself poised not for self-protection, but for pursuit. She felt on the edge of a diving board, or balanced atop a sprinter's starting blocks, ready to cast aside self-doubt in favor of an unaccustomed boldness.

It was at once exhilarating and scary.

"Gosh," she began slowly, struggling to keep both responses to herself. "How often do you three get together? Have you been here all along?"

"After prison, you mean?" Gage asked easily, sitting in an armchair and crossing his legs. "No point being coy, is there?"

"No, no," Rachel agreed, interpreting the response as a good sign.

"I live in Hawaii," Gage answered her. "I'm just here on a visit."

"What brought you back?" she asked, using his frankness as a way forward. "Couldn't have been the old memories."

But Gage had been only faking it. Abruptly serious, he demanded, "What do you want, Ms. Reiling?"

"Okay," Rachel replied, spurred by an unexpected jolt of anger about the harm this man had caused. "To business, then." She pulled out her ubiquitous pad and flipped to a fresh page. "Since you broached the subject, and it is a matter of public knowledge, can we get to the heart of all this and talk about Smith Wilkinson?"

In response, Holly Thorpe, who alone hadn't taken a seat, walked to a distant door and announced, "I'm getting a drink. Not my kind of conversation."

No one objected, least of all her two male companions.

"What do you want to know?" Gage asked carefully. Dietz, despite his peacock display at the door and brief flurry of social niceties, had lapsed into silence. As had Sally, not that Rachel noticed, too zealous by now to heed any such tension.

"Like I suggested," she began, "your financial troubles are well enough known, along with the legal fallout afterward. The articles I've been writing don't have much to do with that, at least not directly. Without boring you with details, I've been focusing on the family members of one of your old employees. She's long dead by now. But they seem to have mysteriously benefited from her association with Smith Wilkinson."

"Who're you talking about?" Gage asked, not revealing his online awareness of Rachel's string of articles.

"Karen Taylor. We believe you knew her. Personally."

"Really," Gage stated, not as a question. "Where did you get that idea?"

"Your ex-wife," Rachel replied shortly, unable to control her heartbeat, or the flushing of her cheeks she could feel accompanying it. Returning to one of the two images she'd imagined earlier, she'd left the diving board and was now either twisting in acrobatic grace or plummeting in free fall.

Gage studied them in silence for a few seconds, calculating what to say. He settled for casual insouciance.

"Ah, right," he said. "A lot of water over that dam. I do recall Karen."

"I can imagine. She had your baby."

Willy hadn't restrained himself after the door had closed on Rachel and Sally. Convinced that exigent circumstances ruled, he retreated from his post and circled around to a basement bulkhead he'd tested earlier and found unlocked.

Holding a small flashlight between his teeth, his fingers brushing the wall for steadiness, he stealthily descended the narrow wooden steps to find himself in a cellar as dirty, messy, and jammed with junk as the upstairs was not. Like a man filing through a crowded bus, he threaded a passage toward a second staircase on the opposite wall, barely visible in the gloom and among the towering boxes, shelf units, piles of newspapers, and old furnishings that lay in his way.

Over the earpiece he'd attached to his phone earlier—which in turn, he'd dialed in to a conference line being used by his colleagues—he could hear responding units getting closer, now all aware of the primary suspect in Daryl Hicks's murder being in residence. Given Vermont's rural nature, this would be no official TAC team of black-clad warriors, as on TV—such a unit would have taken at best ninety minutes to organize and put in place. But any available responders—from whatever agencies—would supply well-armed backup nevertheless.

With that in mind, when he finally reached the foot of the second set of stairs, Willy entered a text to let everyone know there was an officer not just on the premises, as before, but inside.

He and Gunther—and no doubt the state's attorney—could hash out the legal details later.

He started up.

Sally was alarmed by Rachel's apparent recklessness, if not also a little impressed. Her admittedly inquisitive friend's style could be notably self-effacing, sometimes to Sally's exasperation, who tended to be the more aggressive of the two.

But Rachel was on fire this time. Certainly, throwing Gage's paternity of Peter Rust at him hadn't suffered from any delicacy. There was always the question of time and place in these situations, however, which was where Sally was having concerns.

As if on cue, Gage uncrossed his legs, his attitude mirroring a glowering expression. "My personal life from thirty years ago is none of your goddamned business."

"The police would argue with that."

He blinked once. "What's that mean?"

"I'm just the reporter here," Rachel stressed, hoping to redirect some of his anger. "You have to know what's been going on. Pete Rust finally dying. Daryl Hicks being found murdered. The whole story being looked at all over again. It's only reasonable that the police would be interested in how both Karen Taylor and your child Pete ended up."

"That woman died of an overdose," he stated angrily, "after giving me the screwing of a lifetime. And I'm not talking sex. She was a user, up and down. Ask around. You'll find a lot of people who'll say the same. And as for the kid, who the fuck knows? Not my problem, and sure as hell not my fault."

Rachel pressed him, overriding caution even more to chase her opportunity. The midair feeling she'd been experiencing was tilting more toward purpose than simply tumbling. "Is this your way of saying that she did extract money from you?"

He paused, perhaps considering the wisdom of this conversation. His reply reflected the hesitation. "Any statute of limitations has kicked in by now," he began, "and she's long dead, anyhow. All right, I'll tell you. Maybe I did commit an indiscretion. It happens. Laura and I had nothing in common anymore. But that bitch, Karen, used what she wheedled out of me to hold me up just as if she'd stuck a gun to my head."

He slid forward in his seat, passion animating his face. "The company was doing well, money was pouring in. And she was smart. She didn't ask for enough to cripple me—just enough to make it hurt like hell, and set her up for life. But she blackmailed me, all the same, and then sealed the deal by having the brat, just for good measure."

Rachel pressed her self-perceived advantage, feeling slightly giddy. "Meaning you had good reason to kill her later, and make it look like an overdose."

Sally gently shifted her footing, getting ready to spring up if necessary. But the comment actually seemed to settle him down.

"I had no reason to do that," Gage explained. "The money was already gone. Plus," he added ironically, "I had other things to worry about. You forget—the cops were all over me by then. Karen was the least of my problems."

Rachel was committed. "Maybe then, she was," she said. "But what about now? I don't buy for a second that you're here on vacation. It's too much of a coincidence, what with everything else going on."

She took a wild guess, as if finally addressing the upcoming pool's smooth, inviting surface, and threw in, "Not to mention that, as if out of left field, Daryl Hicks shows up, tortured to death. How is it, Mr. Gage, that you and he suddenly appear at the same place and time, like two meteors that've been flying through space for thirty years? What was your connection to him?"

Propelled by the thought, Rachel completed her acrobatic metaphor and sliced cleanly into the water, concluding, "We have proof you knew the guy, after all, back when you were having an affair with his wife. We've seen a photograph of you in the same room together."

Gage leaped to his feet, prompting Sally to drop into a crouch. "What Kool-Aid have you been drinking?" he yelled at Rachel, his features contorted. "You're throwing shit together like it's a perfect jigsaw puzzle. Don't you get it? *That* asshole killed his wife, not me—he fed her a hot shot. Chuck and me and the others may've skimmed some off the top, but Karen and Daryl were like rats in a dump. There was *noth-*

ing they wouldn't do. Hicks assaulted that kid and then murdered Karen for *my* money. The stupid fucker didn't even know she'd locked it up in a trust." He seemed slightly dazed, before admitting, "I didn't either, more's the pity, or I wouldn't have come back to this fucking woodchuck state."

He pointed at Dietz accusingly, "That asshole paid my plane fare here, so I could collect a little of what was mine after fucking *years* on skid row."

"I felt bad, Larry," Dietz complained. "I had it good, living the quiet life with Holly. I wanted to do you a favor after we all read the newspaper articles—figured the money was just lying around."

The silence following that exchange allowed Rachel to ask the obvious question, "Mr. Gage, how could you know about the trust, unless you extracted it from Daryl just before he died?"

Willy eased the door open from the basement, and found himself in the kitchen, adjacent to where the conversation was escalating in volume. Not liking the tone or language, he began stealing toward the living room door.

Unbeknownst to him, Holly Thorpe returned from down the hall in her stockinged feet, saw him crossing the floor away from her, and in one fluid movement, ran at him—collecting a meat tenderizer as she went. Willy turned, his instincts alive to something threatening behind him, but too late to avert upsetting her plans. She gave him a glancing blow on the side of the head, sending him crashing against the open door and into the next room.

Larry Gage had just finished springing up in rage, ignited by Rachel's pointed questions.

The explosion from Willy's sprawling semiconscious onto the floor, and Holly now falling over him, her momentum unchecked, was enough to at once stimulate Gage to pull a gun from under his sweater, and Sally to spring up and hit him broadside with a tackle that sent them tumbling toward the fireplace.

Rachel and the virtually forgotten Chuck Dietz sat frozen in place as the gun went off harmlessly, the front door blew back on its hinges, and a medley of eight shotgun-, rifle-, and/or handgun-equipped troopers, deputies, and VBI agents entered the building, yelling for nobody to move.

Nobody did.

EPILOGUE

The Missing Piece

Scott Jezek's wife had urged him to stay home longer, but he was getting antsy. After the police had removed him from the rental unit—following Gage's arrest and his admission of Jezek's whereabouts—Scott had been dehydrated, bruised, and shaken, all of which had been cured by a single night's sleep.

As he'd put it to her simply, it was time to get back to work.

And it felt surprisingly good to return to where the kidnapping had occurred, surrounded by his diplomas and pictures, files full of past cases, and old Christmas cards—as corny as his friends found them to be.

He'd wondered about feeling traumatized, but it hadn't come about. Joe Gunther had dropped by to pay his respects, and over coffee, they waxed philosophical about the often tangled merits and costs of pain and suffering, greed and self-advancement. Sally visited to update him and collect some money, and a new client had appeared to lay out an admittedly minor legal woe.

Life, with the exception of the still-unaccounted-for John Rust, had resumed much of its old familiarity. Even Sally, despite her frustration about Rust, had been upbeat, given her friend Rachel's success in both writing and becoming front-page news—not to mention that the homicides of Peter Rust and Daryl Hicks had been cleared up. Daryl had indeed died of a heart attack, while Gage was trying to extract information about the remnants of Karen's blackmail money—something over which Hicks, of course, had never had control. A mad and desperate effort, Jezek thought, born of Gage's threadbare financial state and his discovery in Hawaii about Peter's death.

It was yet another example, he was convinced, of how often people reorganized reality to perfectly fit their own lunacy.

Contrasting with that, however, was Scott's crowning achievement of the day so far, and the paramount reason he was in such good spirits. Despite his meditation concerning Larry Gage's mental state, Scott had also just balanced the books with his sparring partner, the state's attorney. An hour earlier, in a very civil conversation, the latter had agreed to drop all charges against John Rust.

While the SA had cited as his reasoning the previously unknown circumstances stimulating John's inebriation that night, along with the now revealed background of the Rust family's turbulent history, Scott was keenly aware of how Rachel's sympathetic and evocative articles had—to a politician's eye—essentially made John untouchable. Nevertheless, Scott had displayed only his best manners, showing pleasure and gratitude, if nothing else, for the prosecutor's broadmindedness.

The only thing missing now was the recipient of this good news.

John Rust, for his part, sat silently in the back of the church basement, where the AA meeting had just concluded, gazing across the skeletal assemblage of empty folding chairs to a few people clearing away the last of the coffee and doughnuts along the far wall.

He couldn't remember having felt so whole—his spirit rested, his thoughts free of immediate concerns—especially about the source of so much anxiety over so many years.

He still missed Pete. What others had coined a "blessing in disguise," or glossed over with, "He's in a better place now," John had felt as the death of his best friend and steadiest companion. As he'd joked more than once with Martha Jones, while they'd worked together on Pete's behalf, "How can you knock a brother who never tells you how bad your jokes are?"

In fact, their fraternal bond had transcended such banalities. Pete had been fully aware of John's efforts, showing his appreciation via an invariably easy comportment and the tiniest of gestures, like the hint of a smile or a loving glance. This, all through awkwardly physical and sometimes painful procedures like bathing and the treatment of bedsores. Throughout, John knew Pete had sensed his older brother's guilt for having allowed a baby boy to suffer the frustrated wrath of Daryl Hicks.

There had been only the two of them, after all, within that family of four. When not in jail, Daryl had behaved as an unfeeling brute. Karen, whip-smart, blindly ambitious, instinctively sensuous, had been trickier to gauge. More mercurial than her simpleminded husband, she was possessed of varied and inconsistent impulses driven solely by her hunger—for love, control, money, and whatever she hadn't had right then. What others termed playful, seductive, and impulsive, John had come to recognize as carnivorous neediness.

When a youth, in his mother's embrace, John had been transported as by an elixir. By his teens, that had turned toxic, replaced by an older mother's scorn for an older child's lack of compliance. She had even accused him once—no doubt on an occasion when she'd especially needed Daryl's help—of being the one who'd damaged Pete—a charge he'd feared might be shared by the one true innocent among them.

In the end, he had watched her like a spectator retreating from the circus tent in which she'd worked so hard to be the center of attention. Until she'd died.

John thought back to when he'd been pulled over by Tyler Brennan. That night had begun the journey leading John to this basement hall. From an initial sense of lassitude and inevitability at being stopped for drunk driving—again—he had slowly realized, perhaps as a consequence of the young trooper's care and thoughtfulness, that a major chapter had ended at last. He was no longer teetering daily between despair and responsibility. He was either on the cusp of following an endless spiral down, or of being reborn on his own, healthier terms.

He quietly rose, waved silently to the people at the far end of the room, and left the church for the sidewalk outside, a few hundred yards from his final destination, Scott Jezek's office.

Whatever happened from now on, John was convinced, guilt would no longer play a part. During the stretch of days between that last DUI and today, he had entered a retreat upstate. It had been a virtually spontaneous gesture. He hadn't told anyone, and had abandoned all phones, computers, and credit cards, and opened himself to the luxury of uninterrupted reflection—along with help from AA.

It wasn't a guarantee. He'd been told as much repeatedly, and known it in his heart. But it was a start. He still had to confront the legal charges against him—and was mentally prepared to continue his treatment in prison if it came to that. But an actual jail cell struck him as little different from the one he'd built for himself decades ago.

With the one crucial and comforting expectation that whatever prison sentence he may be facing would be a lot shorter.